In the Long Dark

IN THE
LONG DARK

Brian Carter

Illustrated by the author

Best Wishes,
Brian Carter

Torbay Books
7 Torquay Road   Paignton   Devon TQ3 3DU

By the same author

Yesterday's Harvest
South Devon Inn Outings

A Black Fox Running
Lundy's War
The Moon in the Weir
Jack
Nightworld
Where the Dream Begins
Walking in the Wild
Carter Country

First published 1989 Century Hutchinson Ltd.
Republished 2007 Torbay Books
Copyright © 2007 Text and illustrations: Brian Carter

Torbay Books
7 Torquay Road, Paignton, Devon TQ3 3DU

Printed and bound by CPI Antony Rowe, Eastbourne

*To my neighbours and my home town – Paignton,
South Devon*

The Monastery
Lions' Club
Skeets
Car Park
Shadow's
Berry Drive
Huccaby
Fairview
Torview Gardens
Monastery Road
Monastery Gardens
Coffey End Park
Clifton Road
Ivy Lodge
Maylands
Winner Hill Road
Orchard Patch
No.1. Vines
Dan y Graig
Building Site
Golden Lily
Garage
Book Shop
Winner Street
Chip Shop
Torbay Labour Club
Slaughter House Lane
Silver's Patch
Crown and Anchor Way
the Coach House Inn
Well Street
Church Street
Victoria Hotel
Paignton, S. Devon
(Not to scale)
Church Path
Parish Church
..... Ben's Hunting and Scrounge Trail
Dolly
Brian Carter

Contents

1	Ben and Lucy	1
2	Mooncrooning	8
3	Shadows Have Hooks	15
4	Another Black Stranger	24
5	Dancer	29
6	Catmint High	37
7	First Blood	43
8	Storm Warnings	49
9	Skeets	55
10	Like Dogs	59
11	Lull	67
12	The Battle of Maylands	70
13	Lucy Alone	82
14	Exodus	88
15	With the Sea Mist	101
16	Games	110
17	In Cloud Country (i)	116
18	In Cloud Country (ii)	121
19	Thoughts on Life and Death	126
20	Whispering Grass	133
21	To Hay Tor	140
22	Peace Council?	145
23	Night Roads	150
24	Lights in the Chip Shop	156
25	Dreams	164
26	Stalking	171
27	A Little Street Fighting (i)	177
28	A Little Street Fighting (ii)	182
29	The Cricket's Song	188
30	Games in the Rain	197
31	Goodbye to the Seasons	204
32	Welcome to my Dream	212
33	Nightwatch	219

34 The Fight   226
35 Teddy   232
36 The Good Place   240

1
Ben and Lucy

Ben came out of the catnap, flattened his ears to his head, yawned and licked his lips. The she, whose name was Lucy, smiled at him and he yawned again. He was a chunky tom with a black head and ears and a black 'bandit mask' on a white face. He had golden eyes, a black back, flanks and tail, and white underparts, throat and legs.

The cats were ferals, born of different gone-wild mothers but raised as orphans by the same foster-she. They were alert and hungry. Sitting together on the little concrete terrace outside Torbay Labour Club, they stared through the iron railings at the lighted plate glass window of the Central Fish Bar and breathed the aroma of frying fish and chips.

Between them and the chip shop a triangular flower bed divided Church Street where it joined Winner Street. In front of the shops next to the Central Fish Bar were two more flower beds full of forget-me-nots and red tulips. It was late spring and a blackbird was singing from an evening of fading sunlight. Traffic swished by then a cat dashed down the Winner Street bottleneck and vanished beneath a parked van. He was a large black tom, a stranger to Ben and Lucy. Lifting their muzzles they ransacked the evening for scents.

Lucy's hazel eyes were watchful. They flickered over the buildings and the street, settling briefly on the pigeons as they landed in the flower beds then straying upwards to locate and hold the sparrows under the guttering. Ben laid his tongue on her shoulder and delivered three long, slow licks which had her wobbling. She was a small, short-haired tabby, blotched and barred with dark brown and sienna markings.

1

After accepting Ben's tokens of affection she raised a back leg and scratched an ear and said, 'Ebony answered Scarnose's call last night.'

'Ebony wears a collar,' Ben said, as if he were addressing himself.

The tabby crinkled her nose to sift through smells heightened by dewfall. What was happening in the chip shop could not entirely overwhelm the faint stink of cigarette ends lifting off the pavement or the reek of dog muck in the gutter. The delicate yet thrilling scent of the pigeons mingled with the smell of exhaust fumes.

'Ebony was a stray before he got the collar,' Lucy went on.

'Did he fight well?'

'There was a lot of fuss and noise.'

Ben smiled and unsheathed his claws and examined them before withdrawing them into his paws.

'I'm glad Scarnose didn't hurt him,' he said.

His ears were pricked and his whiskers relaxed. He was at ease despite the Spring Rut which brought toms and shes together for the mating. But Lucy was his almost constant companion due to the bond formed in their kittenhood, and he loved her as he loved no other creature.

The tip of her tongue showed between her teeth. She was purring gently and letting her mind wander.

The buildings opposite climbed in façades of weather-beaten stucco to a sky of deepening blue. Above the rooftops swifts screamed. People and cars passed and the door of the Labour Club opened and closed again. A shoe kicked a dandelion growing between the paving slabs below the terrace and a handful of white seeds sailed away. Ben swung a forepaw at them as an ambulance raced up Winner Street.

Threading through the railings, they dropped onto the pavement and darted across the road to come down Church Street past the Animal Magic pet shop and the butcher's into Crown and Anchor Way. A Volvo cornered and roared through the archway of what had once been the entrance to an old coaching inn. Ben and Lucy ran ahead of the car and flung themselves into the lane on the right. The long archway magnified traffic noise but the pigeons in their roosting holes behind the bakers didn't seem to mind.

The ferals walked up Slaughter House Lane at the rear of Church Street, between old sandstone walls, ignoring the dustbins and black plastic bags bulging with garbage. From behind green double gates the chatter of the pet shop birds in their aviaries intrigued the cats and they paused to decode the smells.

The lane was a narrow cul-de-sac ending at a high red gate, but Ben and Lucy never went beyond the backyard of the Central Fish Bar. They came and sat in the grass gazing expectantly at the gate, and before long it was opened and they heard the fish scraps being placed on the up-ended teachest. Then a human voice called them and they trotted into the yard as the back door of the chip shop closed. Once they were certain all was well they leapt onto the teachest and bolted the pieces of cod and haddock. But they didn't clean themselves until they were in the lane once more. Then they slid their tongues over their lips with something close to exaggerated satisfaction. And presently a forepaw was raised and wiped over cheeks and ears, again and again. Finally, Ben stood on his hind-legs and dug his claws into the gate to drag them down in scratches, half a dozen times.

Beneath his scruffiness the muscle was toned to perfection but physical well-being could not cancel out a feeling of unease. Something was wrong. It was a sensation like the one he experienced when his body reacted to an approaching storm.

'We've got company,' Lucy said.

The black tom they had seen near the Labour Club was crouching among the weeds by the pet shop gate and Ben's whole demeanour changed. He was as ready for action as a cocked pistol.

'OK,' he whispered.'So you're there. OK. OK.'

The stranger grinned, turned and ran alongside the wall into Crown and Anchor Way, halting defiantly to lift his tail and spray the wild flowers. By now Ben was more curious than angry. He trotted to the mark and sniffed it. The stink told him the stranger was young and fit, but it also contained the essence of a self-confidence that puzzled him. Local cats left clues to their identity and condition wherever they could spray but there was something odd about this mark.

He ran his nose over it, jaws slightly parted and hind feet raking the mud. Lucy was less concerned and rolled before him, pawing the air.

Stepping over her Ben said, 'Who was that? Who is he?'

He glanced up. Above the roofs of the bakery and the Coach House Inn the illuminated clock face on the church tower shone like the moon. The small dark shapes of swifts passed across it. Dusk was in the air and bats were on the wing.

Ben licked his lips and swallowed.

They ran up Church Street and crossed over Winner Street to the pavement in front of The Pocket Book Shop.

'He's nothing,' Lucy said.

Ben shook his head and led her past Dell's Antiques and the empty shop into the bottleneck, which was just wide enough for big lorries and vans to squeeze through. Lucy could see the black tom had disturbed him.

The bottleneck was quiet and the ferals lolloped through it to make the abrupt left turn into Winner Hill Road. The stranger had sprayed the hoarding at the bottom of the hill so Ben had to poke about on the building site, walking stiffly around the piles of breeze blocks, the rubble and weeds because it was part of his territory.

'He's nothing,' Lucy repeated gently. 'Lots of cats come and go. Forget it. He's just a tom on the loose.'

The piercing, long drawn-out top note of a starling set her teeth chattering over little strangled cries of frustration. But Ben would not leave until he had satisfied himself and laid his own scent under sandstone walls which were falling apart, running wide of the doors of Winner Hill Garage and on beneath the telegraph pole

4

and the blackbird's song. The tarmac was covered in Kentucky Fried Chicken cartons, cigarette packets, crisp bags and empty drink cans. Gulls and crows had gleaned the best of the pickings but the ferals still meandered hopefully from empty carton to paper ball. A sudden gush of bath water escaping into a drain made them jump but they were approaching their home ground and Ben was beginning to relax.

In Monastery Road their pace slackened. It was good, Ben thought – the evening, the street smells, Lucy. He ran his eyes over her blotched autumn shades. Her tail was upright now and curled forward at the tip. She stopped and sniffed the valerian hanging over the gutter. Light gleamed on the empty Pepsi Cola cans at the wayside.

They walked shoulder to shoulder on their toes as cats do. The old farm hedge was to the left facing a high wall. The hedge was all that remained of the countryside lost to building development decades ago. It was one of the boundaries of Maylands, where the ferals and strays of Silver's gang had their home patch. Bramble, elderberry, ivy and nettles sprouted from the hedgebank of red soil; and the stumps of elms killed by the Dutch disease stood among hazel, ash and hawthorn. Towering above everything were three firs about eighty feet high, and in one of them a pair of carrion crows had nested.

Any of three cat runs in the hedge would have brought Ben and Lucy into Maylands' garden, which had been allowed to return to nature by the elderly recluse who hardly ever ventured off her property. But the ferals chose to go through gaps in the bottom of the heavy wrought iron gates which were painted silver.

They often slept in the summerhouse on the far side of the garden beyond a lawn no one had cut for years. The grounds of Maylands were a jungle of overgrown shrubberies, flower beds and rockeries. The southern end was bounded by a hedge of old Lawson's cypresses. Eastward ran a thicker hedge of hawthorn high above a containing wall and Winner Hill Road. It met the northern limits at

5

a fenced-up gateway and the hedge of dead elms with Monastery Road behind it.

Maylands house stood large and off-white in the west of this private wilderness. To the right of the silver gates was a gone-over flower bed and a walnut tree. The twin wooden garages set further back were close to collapse but the strays used them as sleeping quarters. Behind them was a vegetable garden lost to weeds and brambles. A gravel drive ran from the silver gates past a pond to another entrance that had been fenced-up. At each end of the pond were stands of bamboo.

The lawn grass was tall enough to conceal a cat but not high enough to hide the stone birdbath and a sundial which displayed the legend – *Horas Non Numero Nisi Serenas* – in green copper letters almost unrecognisable under the snail trails. The shrubbery of hydrangeas, buddleia, flowers and weeds against the hawthorn hedge was beginning to creep out over the lawn, and had partly hidden the stone plinth supporting the copper bust of Sir Francis Drake.

Numerous cat runs penetrated the shrubberies and cut across the lawn to the wooden summerhouse. A muddy stain, pitted and scarred with clawmarks on the side of this building, advertised the coming and going of ferals through the broken window. A hole in the bottom of the door was also used. Behind the summerhouse, a horse chestnut grew among hawthorns and ash.

Maylands was the sort of home patch ferals dream about. The lady loved cats and most mornings and evenings she put out food bowls on the terrace with its sea views and called the tribe. Then she sat and smiled and chatted to them as they fed. Sometimes, though, she forgot what she was doing and they went hungry.

The summerhouse provided shelter for the ferals under the leadership of the white tom, Silver, who had strayed to the garden as an abandoned youngster just out of kittenhood. Ben and the short-haired black tom, Sam, shared the summerhouse with the she cats, Lucy, Belle, Lucky, Louise and old Jessie. Occasionally they were joined by the stray shes Rainbow, Pepper, Rita and Maria, and the gone-wild toms Scarnose, Ginger, Button, Scrumpy and Parson. These weren't members of the kin group and they lacked Silver's sagacity and charisma. They were accepted but were not, as Jessie put it, 'family'.

When Ben and Lucy were halfway across the lawn she said, 'You're still thinking about the stranger, aren't you?'

'Yes,' Ben admitted. 'I dunno why. There have been other newcomers. But this one – '

He drew a deep breath and his pupils dilated. Lucy bunted his chin with her head and rubbed against the length of his body.

'This one,' Ben continued, 'is a sick feeling in my gut.'

'Forget him,' she crooned.

Inside the summerhouse they groomed each other and joined Belle and Jessie in a loose tangle of warmth on the settee, which the lady had covered with an eiderdown. Lucy was pregnant but it would be a month or so before Ben's kittens were born.

2
Mooncrooning

A day passed and Ben and Lucy spent most of it sleeping, although they went their separate ways in the morning. It was sundown when they were reunited in Maylands.

'Did you see Blacky?' Ben enquired, giving her a sideways glance.

'Don't bother about him,' she said.

'I can't get rid of the gut feeling – the bad feeling.'

She leaned against him, taking in his body scent and looking up into his face to read his mood. The forward bristling of his whiskers told her he was upset but the birds were singing and the evening was calm and still.

They trotted down the drive to the first stand of bamboo and Ben's nostrils twitched.

'Scarnose,' he said. The name emerged in a bell-like tone.

The ginger tom sat by the pond staring at his reflection.

'After the fish?' Lucy asked mischievously.

They joined the big, grubby stray at the water's edge. In the centre of the pond, which was oval and about the size of a double bed, lay an island of reeds and rushes surrounded by lily pads.

Scarnose cocked a tawny eye in their direction. 'I was thinking of other times,' he said. 'The man hated me.'

'But why did he give you food and shelter?' Lucy said.

'Because the woman liked me. When she wasn't around the man gave me a bad time.'

He had deserted his home to fight for a place in the Maylands gang. An awful temper and talent with the hooks – feral jargon for claws – had earned him a reputation. Any tom of his size commanded respect.

'Ach! So what!' he said from the beginning of a stretch.

8

'Being sworn at and booted was bad news but a lot of good animals have surrendered their cathood for the food bowl and the fireside.'

He drew back his top lip in a mirthless grin and Ben looked at the sky. Bamboo leaves and the darker foliage of the firs were printed on the sunset glow, and the crows that lived in the treetop nest returned to their fledgelings. Scarnose's teeth chattered and suddenly Ben was depressed. He gazed at Scarnose and the ginger tom turned away to brood once more on his reflection. Every so often he perceived depths in Ben which even Silver lacked. Dropping a paw in the water he splashed at his image.

Catching the fish had proved impossible but the three cats crouched side by side watching the dance of the golden carp while blueness swamped the shadows. Before long the Jack Russell in the house behind Maylands started to bark until a human voice silenced him. A door banged and they turned to see the light on in the lady's bedroom.

Ben and Scarnose strolled around the bamboo and under the hydrangeas, knocking the dew off the columbines and crumbling the soil between their toes. Lucy followed them onto the dew-soaked lawn. The swifts were so high above the roofs their cries were barely audible. A breath of wind shook the bamboos.

The toms paced uncomfortably through the grass to the rockery and sprayed with shivering, upright tails and ears tight to the skull. Lucy watched, the excitement of approaching night churning in her stomach; but the gulls wailing from the chimney pots distressed her. They went on and on in a manic duet as the cats climbed the rockery, halting every now and then to test their reflexes on fleeing woodmice. Scarnose had been bitten on the nose by a rat during a similar expedition shortly after his arrival at Maylands, so he was wary. The scar was shaped like a dark brown clover leaf.

Up on the terrace they sat facing the sea. Clusters and strings of lights marked the streets and houses of the

Three Towns spread around Tor Bay. Brixham was to the south, Paignton in the middle and Torquay lay northwards. A continuous blaze of lights traced the horseshoe of land from Hope's Nose in the north to Berry Head in the south. Out to sea the lights of ships were dimmer but their steady progress fascinated the cats.

Slowly the moon came up until it hung full and yellow between Hope's Nose and Thatcher Rock. Right on cue a tom loosed his yarool of mating passion from the bottom of Winner Hill Road and Ben and Scarnose answered him. The screeching reduced Lucy to a squirming heap but the toms did not respond to her play.

Their war cries were punctuated with moans and growls.

'If that sprauntsy mouth-on-legs wants trouble then I can supply it,' Scarnose smiled, but his voice lacked malice. He did a little shadow boxing and moonlight sparked on his hooks.

'OK, let's go,' he said, and they ran hard for the silver gates and bounded down to the building site.

A couple of strays sat by the breeze blocks and Scarnose took in Mellow's smell and snorted it out again. The grey and white patched tom had been scratching the soil and spraying the foot of the hoarding. His ears were erect and folded back at the tips. His eyes were vertical slits.

'So, is this what you're after? Is it? Is it? Issssssss it?' Scarnose hissed, his own ears pricked and his tail swishing. He was riding an adrenalin overload and the yaraowl that seethed in his bowels threatened to take off his head on release.

Mellow slowly laid his ears tight to his head and his eyes rounded. 'You, you,' he said, staring at Scarnose. 'You . . . you . . . you . . . you . . .'

'OK, I'm a you-you,' Scarnose said. 'So c'mon, come and get me.'

The words flew out of him in growls but Mellow's heart was bucking and the other toms knew it.

'C'mon, All-Mouth,' Scarnose crooned. Extending his

neck he forced Mellow into the eyeballing. 'C'mon – do the thing. Do it.'

Mellow licked his lips and retreated, body close to the ground, unwilling to meet Scarnose's glare.

'Scarnose,' he managed. 'I ain't fit to lick your hooks.'

'Well, then, may the blowflies never nest in your brains,' Scarnose said cheerfully and both toms grinned, although Mellow's laid-back whiskers betrayed his nervousness. He had wanted a fight but not with a celebrated crazy like Scarnose whose flailing tail was a warning only an idiot would ignore.

'May you never get bitten by a rat,' Mellow said.

'Too late, I have been,' Scarnose chuckled. 'But may you father a thousand kittens.'

'And may all the kittens you father be toms.'

'OK,' Scarnose said. 'That's the May-Yous out the way. So what about your brother?'

He nodded at the lean grey tom behind Mellow who was licking the matted fur close to the base of his spine. He had a skin condition called Stud Tail and the irritation was driving him mad. But Scarnose did not know this and thought it a gesture of contempt.

'You want a double set of hooks in your face, friend?' he cried from an ear-splitting screech. 'You want it, hey? C'mon – do you? Tell me. Tell me.'

'No,' the grey gulped.

Several cats had gathered on top of the wall overlooking the building site. Ben recognised the toms Sam, Ginger and Parson, and the shes Pepper, Maria, Rita, Belle and Lucky. He joined Scarnose in a swagger around the site, tail erect, halting to aim his hindquarters at a clump of plantain or a breeze block.

Lucy lolled in the grass at the top of the vacant lot and Belle, who was a beautifully marked tortoiseshell, nodded approvingly. Lucy's generous nature endeared her to the colony shes. Ben caught her eye and smiled. He remembered how he had made her laugh by jumping up to catch blue-bottles and hold them in his mouth, so that they buzzed against his clenched teeth.

11

Lucy harvested the individual and highly attractive smells of the toms while their voices provided the discord the gang admired. The mooncrooning intensified and toms outside Silver's patch added their cries from gardens as far off as the council estate on the hill.

Eventually Ben retired to a corner, managing to retain his cool from a slow motion strut. Violence prickled his fur and Parson became so agitated, he nipped through the moonlight to spray Ben's head. It was a bit of bravado the onlookers appreciated but Ben wasn't amused and sank his teeth in Parson's rump. The skirmish that followed caused Parson considerable embarrassment. He was a skinny black stray with a white ring of fur on his neck that looked like a collar, a little white round his left eye and white hindfeet.

'When it comes to fighting,' old Sam observed, 'Parson is about as useful as a cat with no teeth in an ass-biting contest.'

But in the end the mouth music won and the chorus of yarools made the shes restless. Sensing their availability Scarnose returned to the rectangle of moonlight and his taunting of Mellow.

'Hooks,' he hissed. 'Show me your hooksss.'

He shot his own claws and beckoned Mellow.

'These have maimed dogs – scratch!'

The claws swung and caught the moonlight again and again – four quicksilver bursts in rapid succession. And Mellow's cowardice was eclipsed by rage. He approached crabwise and the toms stood face to face for an electric display of eyeballing. But the onlookers weren't fooled. They knew Mellow was a sham and Ben was joining in the laughter when Lucy appeared at his side.

'Up there,' she nodded.

Sitting on the highest part of the wall above the building site was the black stranger, and coldness closed on Ben's heart.

'Will he fight?' Lucy asked.

'Maybe.'

Scarnose joined them. 'What's so interesting?'

'Up there,' Ben said, but the stranger had gone.

'A newcomer?' Receiving no reply Scarnose added: 'Is he troubling you?'

'Yeah.'

'But you could take him?'

'There's something else and he's part of it.'

'Part of what?'

'Something different.'

Scarnose nodded, unconvinced. One tom was just like another. You showed him your hooks and took your chance. Lucy walked between them and Ben turned to her. When he licked her muzzle she began to purr.

Scarnose dabbed at an ear and grinned. It was difficult to dislike the pair. Inclining his head he permitted Lucky to trail her tongue over his face. Then he blinked.

'No Silver,' Ben said. 'That's unusual.'

Lucy arched her back and he absently licked one of her ears. The night grew darker and the moon brighter. A couple of people plodded through the Winner Street bottleneck eating fish and chips.

'I'm starving,' Lucky groaned.

Ben and the two shes stretched but Scarnose curled up with his chin on his hindlegs and tail.

'Let him be,' Lucy said. 'Mellow and his brother won't do anything.'

The shes trailed behind Ben up Winner Hill Road and as Scarnose drowsed the smell of a tom he could not identify filled his nostrils. Raising his head he saw the large black stranger on the wall.

'Hey, you're real,' Scarnose murmured. 'OK, you're on my patch. D'you wanna come down and flash your hooks?'

'One night, maybe,' the stranger chuckled. 'Then you'll discover just how hard you aren't. One night I'll show you aggravation so black you'll think you've been hit by a car.'

'What about now?' Scarnose grated, getting to his feet. 'What about it, All-Mouth?'

'One night. Don't worry, one night it'll happen. I promise.'

'Yeah yeah, OK.' Scarnose raced across the rubble and leapt onto the wall. 'Let's make it happen now.'

But the stranger was clawing up the sandstone into the maze of gardens behind Colley End Park and Scarnose soon abandoned the chase.

3

Shadows Have Hooks

The church clock struck the hour and light flashed on the ivy leaves near Ben's nose. Inside and all around the shattered cold frame nettles grew. The morning was sharp-edged and clear with the promise of rain, but for the moment the sun was touching the rooftops of Paignton and the sparkle beneath the freshening breeze made stalking enjoyable. Swifts were flying low and the gardens were loud with birdsong.

Ben yawned, opening wide his little bucket mouth and looking stupid and sleep-starved. The she cats were hunting elsewhere. They sat beside the pigeon loft in one of Winner Hill Road's back gardens waiting for the mice to get over-confident.

When Ben yawned his breath smelt strong like the breath of all healthy carnivores. He was glad to be hunting by sight, running then clapping down and creeping forward in the hope of hitting the prey at the end of a charge and a pounce. There was enough light now for him to spot mice and voles on the move. His ears were part of an early warning system and his nose provided insurance against dangers which fog and darkness might conceal, but movement was the thing he really responded to. A flutter, a scurry, a flick of a tiny tail and he was instantly primed.

The scrounging at Maylands and around the back doors of shops and takeaways was easy and rewarding but stalking was essential to his cathood. Yet, for all his stealth, the thrush hammering open a snail shell on a building brick lifted easily out of reach and he missed strikes at two chaffinches, a blue tit and a jackdaw. It wasn't his morning and out of sheer embarrassment he licked a forepaw and sat under the Lawson's cypresses.

Smell enhanced his quieter moments and was a rich ingredient of his social life. Food smells produced purrs but not of the same intensity as the musk a tom or she left on the terrace. Such smells were created to luxuriate in, for the rolling and head rubbing and blind, lascivious, mouth-gaping surrender to it all. Smell was a sybarite dimension to a life of scrounging, hunting and fighting, and certain scents and odours could flood the whole being like a drug.

The ruins of Maylands garden wore the air of a place lost to time. Normally it was as quiet as a churchyard but the wind had whipped it into violent life when Ben ambled down to the earth beneath the chestnut tree, dug a hole and did his bits. Then he covered them and groomed himself. The undergrowth around him was shaking and rustling. He pushed through the hedge bottom and let his whiskers read the flux of wind. Eastwards spilled the townscape of roofs, chimneys, television aerials and trees. Gulls and songbirds drifted above it, a car horn blared and a train clacked over the railway crossing into Paignton Station.

Ben hesitated on the street wall. The whining telephone wires disturbed him but Winner Hill Road was deserted and he couldn't understand why the magpies were chattering in the chestnut tree. He wasn't to know that he was the cause of their alarm.

He dropped to the pavement and ran close to the parked cars.

For the young crow the day was the familiar dizzy trauma of insecurity. He opened his eyes and found his parents gone.

'Quaark,' he said, riding the nest of twigs tight against the sky.

The branch swayed six feet to the right and back again as regularly as the beating rod of a metronome.

'Qwaak,' said the fledgling, and his brothers and sisters

gazed at him from the bed of interwoven grass and animal hair in the bottom of the nest. Boughs rubbed together and squeaked and millions of pine needles whispered. The sky lurched and the land and sea tilted this way and that, endlessly.

'Quark,' the bird croaked, cocking his head and peering down through the foliage. Out of the hedge below came a black cat. Then the nest shuddered and sailed over Maylands' drive towards the edge of the roof, checked and swung back on the familiar arc.

'Quaaak,' cried the fledgling and he beat his wings. 'Quaak,' instinct registering danger.

But the cat had gone and the crow world was lifting and falling and the sky was vast and swift-scribbled.

Sometimes Ben ran under parked cars to avoid a dog or the milkman, and soon the road narrowed beneath a very high sandstone wall. Behind the wall was an overgrown corner of what was still known as St Mary's Monastery. A decade ago it had been a seminary for Catholic priests. Now the old chapel was the local Lions' club headquarters and the dormitory was a block of flats. The fields and gardens were part of the Council estate and the westward limits of Ben's hunting ground. Parts of it were shared by Sam, Silver and other strays and domestic cats. Some of his trails passed through the patches of toms who were capable of challenging him, but unless females were at stake travelling was usually uneventful.

Over the seasons the cats around the monastery had got to know each other and only newcomers were given a rough time. Pets were never a problem, but ferals from the small colony in Primley Wood could not resist a fight and where trails crossed toms would occasionally meet and eyeball each other. If this didn't sort things out violence would follow. But Ben knew most of the Primley toms. They walked the monastery paths at dusk and he chose to tread his trails at dawn or a little after sunrise.

He trotted past the two lamp-posts which stood tight to the wall about a foot apart and lowered his back to

17

squeeze under the gate into the garden of Ivy Lodge. Then he scampered up the path and crouched on top of the wall to stare about him, ears, nose and eyes busy. Woodpigeons crooned from the trees on the bank above and a whitethroat sent its melody clear of the songbird chorus whenever the wind dropped.

The morning held no aggressive smells so Ben burrowed into the undergrowth and began hunting among the flash and dance of leaves. But halfway along the path he stopped below an ash tree and the hair stiffened on his spine. Something was stalking him. Something was prowling in the grass by the bank of red soil.

Ben's tail swung and spiked out and his back arched. The ash tree beat about in the wind, and light and shade flickered over him. There was a roaring in the trees and big firework dazzles of sun blazing to brilliance between the leaves. Ben licked his lips and relived a fear he couldn't label. It was a gurgle of unease in his gut and it brought his whiskers back tight to his face.

'Why don't you come out?' he called. 'Come on. There's just you and me. Come and do it.'

'You wanna be crippled, Mousebrain?'

And Ben caught the black stranger's smell.

'What do you want?'

'Everything,' said the bleak voice.

'OK, so come and get it.'

'But you're only part of it.'

'And what are you, All-Mouth?'

'A shadow and the shadows are closing in.'

'Don't give me all that Wise Pussy hokum. Let's see your hooks. Let them speak.'

The stranger's laughter was drowned by the wind in the treetops and although Ben called repeatedly there was no reply. He ran up the bank to stand below a group of twisted holm oaks but the stranger refused to show himself. Ben flattened to scrabble under a horizontal root and run on to the wire netting fence and the gap by one of the posts. The ground was carpeted with dead evergreen leaves. Moving lightly over it he glided up the four foot

18

high wall at a point where the coming and going of cats had stained the stonework brown. Then from the nearby bramble thicket came a chuckle.

'Look behind you, Wormbreath. There's a shadow following you and shadows have hooks. You can't get away, believe me – they'll get you. They'll get you. You can't run from your shadow.'

A blur of legs brought Ben into the brambles but all that remained of the stranger was his stink. Ben ranged about for a while before returning to the path, his hunting forgotten. More leaf-litter saw him up on a lower bank and on into the grass and seeding dandelions in front of the old seminary. To his left the windows of the council flats mirrored the sky but Ben was still fretting about the stranger. He half-hoped the black tom would step out of the shrubs like one of the shadows he kept on about. A jay screeched and small birds alarmed, but he walked across the carpark of the Paignton Lions' Club and sat down beside the yellow van and began to groom himself. Then he had a real problem. A mongrel was bounding up from the back of the council houses on the seaward side of the estate, barking and crashing through the grass and buttercups in his haste to attack cat.

Ben departed.

He spent the rest of the morning on the lawn by the summerhouse, dozing and dreaming. One of his dreams belonged to kittenhood and was bathed in sunrise colours.

'From blindness to blindness,' his foster-mother said, speaking from the dream. 'It's the way things begin and end.'

'Blindness?' Ben whispered, and he shivered and opened his eyes and stared between the grass stems at the butterfly.

The rain had woken him. The shower hissed down and passed as he ran to the bamboos and collected Silver's smell from the canes. Sunlight and shadow swam on the lawn. Everything glittered.

'Silver.'

Ben's maraow was flung at the sky and the jet trail which was turning from white to gold. A blackbird ripped off a warning cry but Ben leapt onto the birdbath and lapped rainwater . . .

Halfway up the rockery the white tom lay with paws tucked under his chest. He did not answer Ben for he was lost in thought and was taking the sun, holding it and returning it to the day in the softest of purrs.

Silver had blue eyes and a piercing gaze. He was lean, long of body and elegant, and there was a lot of cream-point Siamese in him, especially about the face and eyes. His coat was short-haired and the top of his head carried vertical bars of champagne, the same colour as his ears. His back and the nine rings on his tail were a darker champagne and his greyish-pink nose was claw-marked. At times he went cross-eyed but his appearance was deceptive. Weighing over fifteen pounds he was a ferocious fighter, although he seemed to have lost interest in street violence for its own sake.

He had said goodbye to Scarnose and was trying to understand what it was about the ginger stray that disturbed him. He did not mind the gush of small talk and the boasting but Scarnose was too eager to proclaim his loyalty and regard for Silver. He was too glib.

Clouds sailed over the brightness, a couple here and there increasing to legions. The steam train, leaving Paignton for Kingswear, hooted and before long the peacocks of Paignton Zoo were bugling their rain warning. Ben ran up the drive. Watching him, Silver relented and might have called out if the rain hadn't begun to fall. The shower was soaking his fur and he got up, shook himself, and trotted onto the terrace. Against the french windows he was out of the rain that was creeping seawards and easing. The sky was blue-patched once more.

Ben stepped round the corner of the house and halted at the sight of Silver sitting there, gazing out over the garden and roofscape.

'Join me,' Silver said.

The ferals touched noses in greeting and Ben shook himself before settling on his haunches.

'Did you fight the other night?' Silver asked.

'No, but Scarnose walked all over Mellow and his brother.'

'That Mellow,' Silver smiled. 'Some of those strays are good animals, Ben.'

The rain fell hard again, bending the flowers and bouncing off the leaves and the terrace. But it quickly passed and a rainbow arched over Torbay. The day was creating enough movement to mesmerise the toms.

Eventually Ben said, 'There's a stranger on our patch – a black tom.'

'So?'

'He's got a lot of lip and he's not like other newcomers.'

'What do you mean?'

'I can't put my paw on it. There's something about him that gives me a cold gut.'

Silver nodded and Ben's loneliness became an ache for Lucy. The wind cut through the firs and sunlight and shadow raced over the lawn, engulfing Scarnose. Carrying his tail relaxed in the pump handle position the stray hesitated for a moment before leaping up at a bee, missing it, swearing at it and trotting on to disappear behind the bamboos.

Ben grinned and wondered why Silver was frowning. Small birds swooped and landed on the birdbath and two pairs of cat eyes dilated and ears twitched forward. A cloud passed swiftly across the sun but the showery weather was out over the Channel now.

The toms strolled along the terrace to the front of Maylands and were watching the coming and going of the firtop crows when Scarnose reappeared.

He sprinted up to them and said, 'Button is dead.'

'How?' Ben demanded.

'A car, by the look of him.'

'Show me,' Silver said.

They ran down Monastery Road thinking of Button. He had been a loner who had often wandered off by himself, once as far as Berry Head and on another occasion to the edge of Dartmoor. But he had never explained why.

'Parson and Scrumpy found him,' Scarnose said. 'He was on the wasteland dragging his hindlegs. You should see his face.'

He stopped and lowered his head. 'He don't look like an animal. No. How did he manage to live so long in that state? Parson says he died trying to tell them something.'

'What?' Silver said.

They dawdled at the Winner Hill bend.

'Shadows,' Scarnose sniffed, and Ben's heart turned to ice. 'Shadows. He kept repeating it. Bloody shadows.' The ginger tom sighed. 'He was hardly breathing, Silver, but he kept saying it.'

Ben and Silver looked at each other.

'Shadows have hooks,' Ben said woodenly.

'I dunno about that,' Scarnose said. 'A man dumped him in a dustbin but the light had gone out in his eyes so he never knew about it.'

On the narrow path between the sandstone cottage and the building site, six dustbins stood in a row against the wall. Button was in the first one.

'Old friend,' Silver whispered, rising on his hindlegs to peer over the edge.

The grey tom lay on his side among the eggshells, broken parcels of potato peelings and empty cans. He was badly cut about the muzzle and eyes. Then Silver saw something which prompted him to clamber in beside Button and sniff about for a moment. When he rejoined the others his tail was swishing.

'Hooks opened his face,' he said.

'But his back!' Scarnose exclaimed.

'A car. Maybe he was running away from the owner of the hooks and was knocked down.'

Scarnose swore. 'Which cat?' he growled. 'Tell me. Tell me.'

'None from our patch or our streets,' Silver replied and his eyes contracted to slits. 'There were wisps of black fur under Button's hooks and the smell was new to me.'

22

'So, he went down fighting,' Scarnose said.

As if it makes any difference, Ben thought sadly.

They sat staring at the dustbin, and the wind whipped up the litter and set it fluttering around their ears.

'Tell me about these shadows, Ben,' Silver said.

4
Another Black Stranger

But what was there to tell? A black newcomer was using their patch and maybe he had caused Button's death. But why the constant reference to shadows – and why all the threats?

'Scarnose was right,' Silver said. 'I've seen fear before on a cat's face but not the look of stark horror Button was wearing.'

'The stranger I met wasn't frightening,' said Ben. 'He was different, odd, a bit crazy perhaps.'

'There could be another black cat walking our ground,' said Silver.

'And these shadows?'

'Could be anything or nothing. It's got you on edge so the stranger or strangers have scored. We're letting it get at us, Ben. Could be some sharp toms want to take over the patch. The set-up's perfect. We got the lot here and other gangs would jump at the chance to move in and grab it all. Stay with it, hey? And keep a clear head.'

For a week or more any marauding black tom caught in the neighbourhood was interrogated by the ferals but nothing came of the paranoia and things gradually returned to normal. Yet Ben could not separate the stranger from the shadows which clouded his thoughts. Only Lucy possessed the power to coax him out of the brooding silences and nightmares. It was heaven to bury his face in her sun-warmed fur while the hawthorn blossom pattered around them on the summerhouse roof and doves crooned. Often the silence between creatures that love each other is the language of souls.

The day was cloudless and the honeysuckle hanging on the south side of the summerhouse was loaded with scent.

Heat played on the garden and the dull roar of traffic crept up from the town. Half a dozen ferals lazed about on the roof, grooming each other and chatting. Old Sam slept but Jessie who was even older was watching Belle run her teeth like clippers over a hindleg while Lucky attended to the washing of her own tail. A frantic scrabbling of claws lifted the heads but it was only Scarnose hauling himself up to join them.

Lucy lay on her side and delivered a light chirruping greeting. Ben's eyes narrowed with pleasure at the sight of her. The umber of her ears was tufted black at the tips and her upper lip, chin and throat were white and her underfur was a soft ivory. The thick black lines emphasising the shape and loveliness of her eyes were so perfect they might have been drawn with kohl. Glossy black hairs dusted the crown of her head and her whiskers were white. Two of the toes on her left paw were caramel-coloured.

It was a pity Button wasn't there to enjoy the company of the shes, Ben thought. He had gone to become part of nothingness. Now he was less than one of the stones lying in the grass. But Lucy was curling and uncurling her front paws, and her coat was speckled with hawthorn blossom. She smelt of life.

'I saw one big black cat,' Scarnose announced. 'Not your Blacky, Ben. This one was big and I mean *big*. He scared me, yes – he really put the wind up me.'

'Where did you meet this heavyweight?' said Sam, a note of scepticism in his voice. Scarnose had woken him and he was bad-tempered.

'I'm talking to Ben,' Scarnose growled.

'That's your trouble,' said Sam. 'You talk but you never listen.'

'Have you gotta be senile to be heard?' Scarnose countered.

'When you're old you swap dreams,' Jessie chuckled. 'It's the way of things. And even strays get old.'

'So when I'm old I'll let you into my dreams,' Scarnose said.

'You'd better go while you can still walk,' Sam said,

puffing out his sepia-tinted fur. He spent most of the day asleep but still fancied himself as a street fighter.

Scarnose laughed.

'I mean it,' Sam growled.

'OK, OK. Don't get sour-gutted over nothing,' Scarnose said. 'This is serious.'

'The big black one?' Ben pressed patiently.

'And he is big,' Scarnose said with the emphasis on the 'big'. 'Listen.'

And the ferals faced him, holding their ears erect.

'I was mooching along through the litter on the hill when I bumped into a wall of black fur that exploded. One moment I was sniffing out scavenge then I was leaping about trying to dodge a ball of flailing hooks. In the end I ran up the pole to the wires on the top but if a car hadn't come down the hill the black thing would have followed me and ripped off my ass.'

'How big is big?' Sam asked.

'Bigger than any of us – a lot bigger, and you should see that smile. Wow! It turned me to ice. You know the dog that killed the pet she from up the hill, Ben – the thickset job with his short legs and gull eyes? Well, this black thing and his smile ain't much smaller than him.'

'Black shadows,' Ben mused.

'Who knows,' said Sam. 'But Silver will sort it out.'

'That Silver,' Jessie grinned and revealed a mouth full of gums. She had lost the last of her teeth two summers ago.

Ben sealed his eyes and his muzzle burrowed into Lucy again.

Night descended and stars appeared. Then clouds began to build up in the east. Alone in the garden Ben dreamed about his foster-mother, whose smile was heaven. At times he rediscovered that happiness by giving himself to the living world. It was tangled up with the breathing of scents, the running and belonging to the wind, rain and sun.

The grass whispered around him and above him. Life

was so strange. There were the dreams and the waking and the loneliness. Feeling restless and insecure he marched around the garden scenting things at rump height. Then he sharpened his claws on the chestnut tree and loitered with intent at the mouse runs. Moths danced about his head and he flattened his ears. The drop in atmospheric pressure registered around his whiskers and in his gut. The air was heavy and sticky. He licked his lips. The stars were going out and the sky over the bay was black. Then rain pummelled the leaves and the earth, blurring in a cloudburst. The first peal of thunder sent Ben sprinting the wrong way, around the back of Maylands to the vegetable garden and the cold frame. Scrumpy and Parson had got there before him. During a lull between thunder claps they heard Scarnose cursing from the old water tank next door. Each flash of lightning made the toms crouch and quiver but the rain roaring into the leaves drowned their cries.

Across the bay the clouds poured, emptying themselves and hurrying on; but lightning continued to fizzle after the rain had ended and the final bolt struck Scarnose's lair. A moment passed before the ginger tom lurched out, his fur spiky and tongue protruding and his tail as stiff as a fishbone.

Ben, Parson and Scrumpy collapsed in a heap of laughter and rolled about kicking their legs and yarooling hysterically. Scarnose fixed his wild eyes on them before spitting threats and flying at Parson.

'Crow-eater! Blowfly Meat! Volebits! I'll hook out your tripes. I'll rip off your head!'

His rage would not be denied and Parson had no choice but to engage him and protect his vitals from thrashing hindfeet. Back and forth they tottered and the blackness retreated landwards leaving the sky above the sea pale and starlit.

Ben departed to sit on the street wall under the chestnut. Stars gleamed on the sea and the dark-leafed gardens waited for cats behind their hedges. Then all the gulls of

Torbay became airborne at the same time. Calling and screaming they climbed high to wheel in dense flocks.

A sea mist rolled in and the bottom of the sky disappeared. Three nights had passed since the thunderstorm and Lucy was rarely out of Ben's company. He was touched by her devotion.

The house called Fairview in Monastery Road provided good scrounge. Apart from the Jack Russell the family had a cat of their own which the gang trusted. Often half a dozen animals fed on the shed roof above the backyard. Barnie, the doctored black tom with his dead blue eye and amiable disposition, had befriended Ben and would leave a little of his breakfast for the feral.

After scrounge it was pleasant to bask on the shed roof, grooming paws, slicking back the whiskers and swapping small talk. Here among the ivy, brambles and honeysuckle which partly concealed the tiles, Lucy approached him. But he stared through his anxiety, hardly noticing the dead mouse she placed as a gift at his feet. She purred and kneaded the honeysuckle leaves in a slow dance of contentment, raising her short muzzle every once in a while to breathe his smell.

5

Dancer

Leaping from the nettles beside the fence at the back of Maylands, Ben hooked out one of the blackbird's tail feathers but the bird flew off on a staccato cry of alarm. Lucy licked a paw before walking at his side down Monastery Road. The sea had flattened to a blue calm and the smell of frying food wafted from the town's takeaway kitchens. Heat wavered on the tarmac.

A boy sat on the Winner Hill bench drinking coca cola. Keeping an eye on him the cats managed to dodge the empty can he tossed at them as they nipped by in a low, crouching run. Swerving into the rubble drive of Orchard Patch they ran up onto the grass in front of the bungalow. Three apple trees grew on the lawn above a herbaceous border and a hedge of box and privet. The warm soil against the privet was attractive and Ben and Lucy soon selected a spot for sunbathing. Lucy was purring and he ran his eyes over her snub nose and upward curving mouth. Then he sniffed the privet leaves.

Lucy was neatly bunched beside him, her left ear twitching off a fly, her flanks rising and falling. Bees droned along the flower beds and Ben's glance settled on the spider that was descending on a thread from a twig. Then he jumped, raised his hackles and growled. A pair of yellow eyes stared back at him from under the privet and he smelt the tom cat stink which had become part of a recurring nightmare. But now the smell told him the black stranger was hurt as well as unfriendly.

Mastering his anxiety Ben said, 'Was it an accident?'

And Lucy turned to see who he was talking to.

The reply was a rattling maraow of spite and the eyes in the privet became narrower.

29

'This is Silver's place,' Ben continued. 'Are you badly hurt?'

He smelt blood and the other thing which was both puzzling and alarming – a sort of decay which wasn't physical. Shifting his position he could see the stranger lying on the dead leaves. He was large and muscular and his round pug head was covered in a mesh of scratches. The right ear was so badly torn it flopped like the limp ear of a Jack Russell.

'You were in a fight?' Ben went on.

'Why don't you get lost?' the stranger grated. 'Who asked you to interfere? Who? Maybe you think I'm easy stuff now, hey? Maybe you think you can take me.'

'You're hurt,' Lucy said. 'We want to help.'

'Yeah. OK, so get out of here. That'll help.'

Ben's even temper made him charitable. 'Look, Hardhooks,' he said. 'You must have taken a hammering or you'd be at me or away by now. We can get you some food and lick those wounds clean. You gonna shut up or do we go?'

'You really mean it, don't you,' Blacky said in a baffled voice. 'What sort of gang d'you belong to – a load of ga-ga old pets? I'm a stranger. I could be a spy or somethin' but you wanna help. OK – so what's the catch?'

'Wouldn't you do the same for us?' Lucy said.

The black tom shook his head and laughed. 'O yeah, yeah – Dancer's famous for his good deeds. Big-hearted Dancer, they call me. Dancer-do-good-deeds. Kittens love me. Dogs smile as I pass by. I'm all sweetness and light. Dancer, the bringer of good times.'

'Where you from?' Ben said.

'Over the hill over there and down along and back along and keep your nose out of my bloody business.'

'A wanderer,' Lucy said, fighting for self-control.

'I get about a bit and I'm no good with fancy words. A rough life gives you a rough tongue and sharp hooks. And there's no sharper set of hooks than mine, except – well, it don't matter.'

'Can you move?' Ben asked.

30

'I can stand up to pee,' Dancer grinned and Ben walked slowly up to him and sniffed his head.

'What have you done to this ear?' he murmured.

'This 'ere what?' Dancer said provocatively.

'Leave the idiot alone, Ben,' Lucy snapped. 'Let him get on with it.'

'Only jokin', pet,' said Dancer. 'To be honest I could use some scrounge. Ain't had no grub since yesterday or the day before.'

'Keep your mouth shut and lie up here and we may get you some,' said Ben. 'But if Silver finds you all you'll get is aggravation.'

'Uh-huh. So this Silver is your local tom tough?'

'He is The Cat,' said Ben.

'Aren't we all?' the stranger grinned.

Ben and Lucy had formed the habit of sitting quietly by the dustbins in the lane at the top of the building site. Almost without fail at dusk the brown door of No. 5 across the way opened and a woman brought food to the cats. She knew they were ferals and liked to watch them crouching over the bowl eating with big deliberate bites. Often she felt drawn to the door, knowing they would be at the nearest bin, not as beggars but as free creatures confident in their dignity.

'It might be better if we left Dancer to look after himself,' Lucy said. Outsiders, even wounded ones, were regarded with suspicion by the gang.

Ben nodded. Instinctively he knew a badly injured tom was no threat to his back street status, but he also shared Lucy's doubts. Any cat lacking the blood was unwelcome.

'When he spoke I got the sinking feeling, the same as I got when I was told Button was dead,' Lucy said.

'Lucy,' Ben said kindly. 'If a bad thing's going to happen it'll happen whether or not we help the stranger. He's hurt. D'you really want to leave him under the hedge to die?'

'No. I'm sorry. It's just that he scares me – and what about Scarnose's big cat?'

'One tom at a time,' he smiled and licked her nose.

The valerian clinging to the wall near the bins smelt of Silver but the scent was stale. Other toms had added their pungency – Mellow, Scarnose, Scrumpy, Sam, Parson and, Ben frowned, Dancer. That loud mouth is taking a lot of liberties, he thought but they returned to Orchard Patch carrying chunks of boiled liver in their jaws. Ben wasn't fond of that particular sort of scrounge but Dancer was famished and wolfed the bitter meat. Bluebottles buzzed around the wounds on his head.

'Could eat a tortoise – shell and all,' he chuckled. 'You always live this well?'

'There's plenty of scrounge and scavenge if you know where to go,' Lucy said.

'Your Silver's got himself a patch and a half,' Dancer said and he stretched slowly and winced.

'Stiff ain't the word,' he groaned. 'But I gotta move on or certain cats will start wonderin' and worryin'.'

'Relatives?' said Ben.

'Better than relatives – friends, loads of friends. A traveller picks up friends like a stray picks up fleas.'

'And you have a patch?' Ben said.

'Patches, not patch.'

'How come you're lost and cut up?'

'Curiosity. I always poke my nose in where it don't belong. Show me a dustbin and I got to lift the lid. Show me a tree and I got to climb it. Show me a road and I'll walk it. But I must've walked for lots of days and nights before I come to your town. After the boring countryside the lights and houses bucked me up. Lights mean scrounge and warm doss and street fighting. I'm a glutton for punishment but no tom, not even your Silver, could see off six hardcases. I did a couple but the rest come at me, mob-hooked, at least eight of them.'

'It was six a moment ago,' Ben grinned.

'Six, eight, sixty-eight, I wasn't counting. When you're fightin' for your life numbers ain't important. These 'ere toms cornered me and worked me over. But I won't forget 'em. I'll have my day and bloody soon, too.'

'Where did this amazing battle take place?' asked Ben.

'By the sea. The smells hooked me and I came running. I should've known a patch so rich in scavenge and scrounge would belong to Jack the cat and his heavies.'

'Fancy's patch,' mused Ben. 'He doesn't give much away. You're lucky. Strangers have been crippled down there.'

'Yeah – but not this tom. They left me for rat-bait and I lay like dead until they cleared off. All I wanted to do was get to somewhere quiet and lie-up till this lot healed. But I met the dog. He came up on me sudden and had hold of a back leg before I could show him my hooks. Then – *shhhnick!*'

The violence had left Dancer's eyes although his gaze was still cold. High against the sun swifts ranged.

'Let's begin,' Lucy said.

They licked the deep, infected scratches on his head and opened the wounds. Then Ben set his healing tongue about Dancer's hind leg while Lucy attended to the broken ear. An hour later the job was done.

'There's got to be a catch,' Dancer said and Ben turned his back on him, so angry he couldn't speak.

'Only jokin',' Dancer said. 'Look, you've done me a good turn and I've got a long memory.' He fidgeted and shuffled as if he had revealed a weakness.

'Get some sleep,' Ben said. 'We'll take you to a safe spot tomorrow.'

Dancer nodded and lowered his chin to his front paws.

'He's more than a bit crazy,' Lucy said.

The ferals were walking up Winner Hill Road with light, quick steps. Their ears were back and they were intent on getting to Maylands unobserved but a blob of vanilla ice cream under the bench distracted them. They lapped at it, lifting their heads now and then to scan the approaches. Apart from the crow combing the bottom of the hedge beneath Maylands' firs the roads were deserted. The suburbs slept in the heat which seemed to have muffled the noise of the traffic and was flickering over the tarmac. The bungalows, semi-detacheds and rows of terrace houses with small front gardens were very English provincial.

The nightmare had sucked him into one of those back-waters of terror which are inky and bottomless. He sputt-ered and kicked and surfaced from it like a kitten escaping the ritual drowning.

'Always a white claw of a moon and the long dark street with a little pile of snow in the gutter. Then I'm in the water.'

Lucy shook her head, wondering what he wanted her to say. But her companionship was enough and dusk blunted his misery. It carried him into a time of day that he loved. Then it was safe to hunt the scent paths and mooncroon in defiance of all he couldn't understand. The darkness wasn't impenetrable but it would cover Dancer's move from Orchard Patch to the monastery garden.

'Into a trap,' Dancer grumbled, but catching Ben's slow hiss of disapproval he added, 'So lead on. I'm as hard as they come and I'll go down fightin' – head high, hooks flashin'.'

'Stop bleating your bloody drivel,' Ben growled. 'Where are your shadows with hooks? C'mon – where are they? Why aren't they here helping you?'

'Who's a touchy tom, then,' Dancer grinned. 'If I was fit you wouldn't be mouthing off like that. You'd be on your belly eatin' my bits.'

'If you were fit you'd be elsewhere boring other cats.'

'OK, so let's go,' Dancer said.

When he was bedded down on the leaf litter among the roots of a holm oak, the Golden Lily Chinese takeaway and the brown door scraps hardly met their own needs. Wearily they plodded back up Winner Hill and sat on a garage roof overlooking Paignton. The sky was starry and lights twinkled out in the Channel, down in the streets and along the seafront. But the brightest lights were in Lucy's eyes.

'Whenever I look at the night from up here,' she said, 'I feel there's something waiting where all the lights end.'

The long dark, Ben thought. Maybe Dancer had got the itch to chase after something he couldn't put into words. Maybe that was why he was running. Silver sprang noiselessly onto the wall beside him but didn't speak for a while. Both Ben and Lucy were startled and lowered their eyes.

'Take me to the stranger,' Silver said eventually in a low voice.

But when they arrived at the monastery there was just Dancer's stink under the tree. The black tom was travelling again and Silver's tail beat the tempo of his anger.

'You should've told me, Ben.'

'I was going to.'

'At once. He could have had something to do with Button's death.'

'Not him. This one's a talker not a doer.'

'He didn't do so badly against Fancy's mob.'

'But he's not the sort who would give an old cat a bad time,' Ben said. Inwardly he cursed himself for being soft. Dancer had asked a lot of questions and used his eyes.

Silver turned his piercing gaze on him and he blinked and licked his chest fur. Cats can see in the dark unless the blackness is total. A kind of mirror at the back of the retina multiplies the light filtering through the pupil, so a ghostly world lay about the ferals. Things which were indistinguishable to the human eye were palely visible to them.

Ben swallowed. It required great willpower to face Silver but he managed it by concentrating on something else. He thought about hunting. Lucy preferred to sit and wait rather than creep up and down the hedges and gardens. Sooner or later, she said, a bird or mouse ends up on your hooks. Why was it never that simple? Bringing front and hind paws together he arched his back until every inch of his tough little body was quivering. How did Silver know about Dancer?

'In future, Ben,' Silver said, 'I'd like to know the moment a stranger sets foot on my patch. You shouldn't have to be told.'

'Dancer was badly hurt,' Ben said. 'All we wanted to do was help him. I forgot about old Button.'

'You can't expect Ben to act like you, Silver,' Lucy said protectively.

'You trusted the stranger and he's betrayed you,' Silver said.

'Not necessarily,' said Ben. 'Maybe something scared him off. Maybe Scarnose's black tom is involved.'

'This Dancer saw me,' Silver said and Ben nodded while coldness flooded his heart. 'He saw me and let out a cry that cut me open. It was the sort of cry a cat gives over another cat's dead body.'

'You met him?' Ben said.

'Not exactly. I came this way and suddenly I felt eyes on me, cat's eyes. When I turned, the black tom was standing under this tree and he let loose the cry. I should have challenged him but I was too shaken. No living animal should hear a cry like that. So I came looking for you, Ben.'

He stared up at the sky.

'Now I can feel your shadows closing in.'

6

Catmint High

The leaves took on their summer shapes and the days grew longer. The shrill of fledglings under the eaves of Maylands ceased as the young starlings left the nest. Sometimes the weaker birds fell to the cats. It was the hard face of spring which blossom and flowers only partly concealed. Among the seeding grass life passed to life with a flash of claws and teeth. But the crooning of collared doves continued to lend a drowsiness to afternoons of heat and scent as the ferals moved about their territory or slept.

Silver had voiced his fear and it had raced through the gang like cat flu. Animals literally jumped at shadows and even the bravest toms were loath to leave the home ground. Scarnose pretended he didn't care about what Silver called 'the before the storm feeling', that hollowing of the gut. His absence from the stalking trails was conspicuous, though, and it was left to Silver to tread the boundaries of the patch. He scent-marked with chin and head, rubbing against twigs and gate-posts as well as spraying his signature on walls and tree trunks and scratching up the grass.

Bats were weaving their flight patterns above the wild corner of the monastery when he came over the wall at dusk. His ears twitched at the cries and laughter of children in the council house gardens. He wasn't stalking and moved through the thicket with a curious stiff-legged gait, something between walking and running. A spider's web wrapped itself round his muzzle and he pawed at it and sneezed. Then he was under the holm oaks, scuffing through the dead leaves to climb the bank and the wall and come on to the Lions' Club carpark. And he knew the stranger would be there waiting for him.

It was Scarnose's big black tom, and the sight of him sitting behind a grin on the tarmac lifted the hair on Silver's spine. He set down his paws with great deliberation and the stranger approached him in a similar manner. Soon they were face to face, locked in the eyeballing.

'Dancer got it right,' the stranger said. 'You are the white tom – the one Skeets keeps bumping into in his dreams.'

'This isn't a dream, Ratbits,' Silver said. 'But it may turn into a nightmare if you don't get your ass off my patch.'

The chirping of sparrows fell through his words and lowering his head he flung another full blooded maraow at the stranger, who merely smiled. All the domestic cats within range cocked their ears and for a moment or so hated their homes and the trappings of petship. The mooncrooning awakened mysterious desires, and claws were unsheathed and sunk into rugs and armchairs. Silver's cry had opened a window on a world lost in the far distances of time, when humans crouched miserably in caves and cats ruled the woods and heaths.

'You're all wind, Whitey,' the stranger rasped.

'And you, Ratbits? What are you?'

The stranger walked slowly and stiffly around Silver and Silver changed his position accordingly. His adversary was a good sixteen pounds of muscle and bone. His dirty black coat had been sepia-tinted by the sun and he was a thickset, pugnacious-looking creature. His ears and nose carried battle scars, and either his head was too large or his ears were abnormally small but the effect was brutal. The scruffiness of his fur, the fixed manic stare and the equally manic grin created an air of aggression which Silver had never encountered before.

'I'm a shadow, Whitey, and I'm heavily into violence.'

Ice stirred in Silver's entrails.

'I love violence,' the stranger crooned. 'I love it.'

'Don't we all? Silver never walked away from a fight.'

'I could murder you, Whitey.'

'With words?'

They met sideways on, caterwauling. The spitting and hissing and coiling of muscles was followed by the hump-backed circling and glaring, the raising of paws and the shooting of hooks. Then came the sparring, the lunge with paw and head, the explosive hissing and the sly feint. Finally both toms backed off without engaging and sat and stared at each other. Violence crackled between them.

'You're a big overweight she,' Silver said.

'But this is just for laughs, Whitey. You belong to Skeets, and the shadows are coming as sure as night.'

Silver looked at the toms gathered around the carpark. There was Ben, Scarnose, Scrumpy and others from the Maylands gang as well as a scattering of local strays.

'Got a message for Skeets, Whitey?'

'Tell him he's a loser.'

The black tom laughed and shook his head. The wind whispered, the trees stirred and settled back into silence again.

'Ben,' Silver called. 'This is the thing that attacked Button. Maybe there's a dustbin handy for him.'

'Two against one, hey?' the stranger muttered, but he kept on grinning.

'Three,' Scrumpy said, pacing forward to catch up with Ben and Scarnose as they advanced. Then the other toms followed suit and the stranger ran.

'Let him go,' Silver said. 'He may be leading us into a trap.'

'But he's responsible for Button's death,' Ben growled.

'OK. There'll be other opportunities to get even.'

'Why did he think we'd hit him mob-hooked?' said Scrumpy. 'It's always one against one. Where does he come from?'

'Who cares?' Scarnose cried. 'I want him now. I want him.'

'All you want to do is shoot off your mouth,' said Silver.

'And what about you?' Scarnose growled. 'You had the chance to take off his face. And what did you do?'

Silver caught him across the muzzle with a set of hooks and Scarnose sneezed and rubbed a paw over his nose.

'Get back to the garden, all of you,' Silver said. 'And call in the shes.'

'What's happening, Silver?' Scrumpy asked.

'The others will tell you. Leave me alone now. I want to work this out.'

'What if the black one returns?' Scarnose said.

Silver's whiskers bristled and his tail swished. 'Go,' he said in a low voice.

But what was Skeets? A feral – a cat? Half-dog – some sort of unimaginable animal? The blackbird delivering his hysterical alarm call was joined by others. The stammering complaint drilled into Silver's head and he laid back his ears and trotted off. Below the metal steps leading up to the side door of the Lions' Club he found a sandwich. The spam was sun-baked and curled at the edges but Silver ate it. Wanderers were one thing but these ferals had no fear. Maybe there were just the two black toms trying to con their way onto the patch. Single ferals were often strange. The blackbird din still rang in his skull. Darkness closed slowly and he walked through the light beneath the street lamps, his head jerking up every time a moth fluttered by. It had to be a couple of odd-balls on the loose. But why all the chat about dreams and shadows? What were the strangers after, apart from stirring up trouble? Scarnose had never stepped out of line before.

Silver stopped and pressed himself against the wall and the giant figure of a man trailing smoke from his mouth passed on the other side of the road.

Cats spend well over half their lives asleep and old cats like Jessie and Sam slept for even longer spells, like kittens. During the day, the Maylands gang usually found places in the sun and took cat-naps or curled into circles of deeper sleep. Ben and Lucy caught the morning sun on the terrace. They had drunk the fresh water put out by the lady and they had made half-hearted attempts to catch the crow fledgling which could flap into low trees but not all the way back to the firtop nest. Its parents were too noisy and aggressive for the ferals and in the end sun and sleep won.

The trouble was the dreaming. Often it was so bad Ben woke up mewling and Lucy would lick his face while he stretched and flopped back on his side again. For a while he lay somewhere between unconsciousness and waking. Then he was gone and his eyeballs were twitching under the lids, his muscles were jumping and he was panting. Soon his whiskers, tail and ears were quivering and every so often a paw kicked out and he uttered little chattering cries.

The dream road was always long, dark and cold and he was walking it alone. But something was after him. The shadows had fierce yellow eyes and gleaming fangs but ahead was a solitary street lamp and he began to run for it. In the gutter the lamplight fell on a little heap of snow. Two crows were hopping around it and Ben loosed a deep-throated cry of anger and sadness.

'Why the sadness?' he asked Lucy, blinking in the sunlight.

'Dreams are funny,' she said. 'I don't understand mine.'

'It's that dream all the time. The long dark.'

She groomed the loose hairs from his back before sitting beside him and gazing across the garden. The sun shone on the sea and metal flashed on cars passing in front of the Festival Theatre.

'It's always so dark in my head and so light out here,' Ben said.

They had eaten a thrush killed by a car in Monastery Road but both were restless. The sparrows scrumming down at the birdbath put them on edge until Sam tried to catch one and ended on his back, staring up from between his hindlegs and mouthing curses.

'Poor old mouse,' Lucy laughed.

They strolled around the edge of the lawn. The day was still hot and cloudless and Ben could hardly bother to see off one of the council estate toms who foolishly decided to push his luck. A steam engine hooted and the traffic din blurred to a distant roar. They wandered on past the sundial and Sir Francis Drake until they reached the corner where the catmint grew. It would be a couple of weeks before the dense clump of plants flowered, but many of the stems were already eighteen inches high and the hairy grey-green leaves exhaled the mint scent which no cat can resist.

Ben and Lucy pushed in among the mint and began to tread, kneading the stems and leaves to release a stronger scent. It was their drug, and like the other members of the Maylands gang they visited the plants regularly in season for a catmint trip. Now they lowered their heads to chew the leaves they were crushing beneath their paws, and released the essence of the plants. Their mouths were half-open in snarls of delight and their eyes narrowed as their feet lifted and fell, trampling out the source of their pleasure. Totally absorbed, they placed their noses to it and opened their eyes wearing expressions of stupor. Then Ben was rolling in it, rubbing his face and body in the leaves and maraowing softly while Lucy beat out the rhythm of her own catmint high.

Ten minutes later they were grooming beside the pond and the firtop crows were scolding them. The young crow was in a nearby hawthorn, rasping off cries of insecurity. The birds reminded Ben of his dream and the black birds beside the pile of snow on the long road.

7

First Blood

'The crazy black one is still around,' Scarnose said. 'His scent's on the hoarding.'

'What's that?' Jessie asked, and raising his voice Scarnose repeated what he had said.

'Well,' the old she observed, 'he's a cat. So maybe he's lonely.'

'Him lonely!' Scarnose snorted. 'He killed Button.'

'A car killed Button,' Jessie lisped.

She was a fifteen year old, long-haired grey with more than a touch of Persian about her. She had copper-coloured eyes and a lovely disposition although she walked with difficulty and weighed less than six pounds. Her coat was matted with burrs and the skin hung from her knobby backbone. Her claws were too long and hooked because she never visited the scratching posts. Sometimes she had to be freed after stapling herself to a plank or piece of wood.

'Cats don't kill cats, Scrumpy,' she chuckled.

'I'm Scarnose,' the ginger stray bawled and the ferals laughed.

But the situation was no joke. A large crazy tom prowling round the patch lent a new dimension of peril to an existence fraught with hazards.

'He has to be confronted,' said Ben. 'Properly.'

'And you'll do it?' Sam said.

'Yes, if I have to. This is our patch.'

Sam nodded his approval. 'And this Skeets thing?'

'If he's a cat he can be brought down by hooks. But that's Silver's affair.'

'And what do you make of these shadows?'

'I've had an empty gut ever since I tangled with Dancer.

43

It's not him or the big black one that worry me. Sometimes I get the sort of feeling that comes with the smell of approaching rain – you know, when your blood tells you something is going to happen.'

Again Sam nodded sagely but Louise, who was close to having her kittens, swallowed and licked her lips.

'Don't worry, Louise,' Lucy murmured. 'The strangers won't hurt us.' She smiled at Ben but he was inscrutable. 'Tell her, Ben. They won't hurt shes.'

'These toms are different,' he said.

'Bloody different,' Scarnose growled.

A cool spell preceded a return of typical June weather. The sun blazed down, the swifts screamed and the May-lands ferals celebrated the birth of Louise's kittens. Things seemed to have returned to normal and the black strangers hadn't made an appearance since the Lions' Club incident.

Louise had four kittens. They were born blind on the wood shavings under the table in the summerhouse and their uniform ginger colour betrayed Scarnose's paternity.

'Little flowers,' Old Jessie chanted, and Louise wore a smile of contented motherhood from the purring half circle of warmth she had thrown round her litter.

Belle, Lucky, Rainbow, Rita and Pepper gathered to lick the kittens but the toms remained aloof and trotted off when the lady brought food and water for Louise. The Rut was over and passions had subsided along with the desire to mooncroon. Only Ben and Silver remained truly alert. For them the streets were shadowed with menace and they walked ready for any unpleasant surprises the bends might hold. If Ben was absent for long Lucy called incessantly from the darkness that was moth-haunted and nervous with the flicker of bats. When he joined her she gave him an affectionate bite on the ear.

During one of his evening prowls he heard Silver's deep cry of greeting and met the white tom in the middle of Berry Road outside the Lions' Club.

'One of the shes from the wood was attacked last night

down in the trees over there,' Silver said. He nodded in the direction of the monastery garden. 'Apparently she was badly mauled.' He sighed. 'This is bad news, Ben. I have never heard of a tom really hurting a she.'

'Was it Smiley?'

'Who else?'

They walked down Monastery Road and stopped when a hedgehog came snuffling out of a garden. Both toms sat before the little animal until Silver patted it and licked his paw to disguise his bewilderment. The prickly creature was one of life's enigmas, like the stars and the wind.

A boy on a BMX bike sent them scampering over the gravel into the narrow alley at the back of the houses which faced Colley End Park. The old black tom, Barnie, who lived in the Jack Russell's house sat on the wall watching them with curiosity and friendliness. Behind the gate the terrier growled until the smell told him it was Ben. The Jack Russell, whose name was Jamie, was accustomed to seeing the black and white tom on his shed roof.

The alley stank of cats but Simon, the doctored tom from No. 15, did not challenge the ferals from the top of his wall. He had been roughed up by Scarnose in the past and respected the strength of the gone-wild and born-wild inhabitants of Maylands. Smokey, a small grey and white she from Bayview, mewed at them but was ignored as the ferals squeezed through a hole in Maylands' fence and trotted to the foot of the walnut tree.

'There's something you should know, Ben,' Silver said when they were seated. 'Apart from the scratches on Button's head there were teethmarks on the nape of his neck. They were wounds inflicted by the killing teeth, the sort of puncture marks we leave on the necks of mice.'

He drew back his top lip and fully revealed the bared canines like long ivory daggers. 'Button's attacker was trying to kill him, Ben.'

'But what cat would do that?'

'A black one, maybe. A shadow. I don't know. I never knew such cats walked the streets.'

At the summerhouse, Sam told them Jessie was ill.

'What with?' Silver asked.

'Age, mostly. She has a stomach-ache and diarrhoea and has been eating the grasses that cure these things. Poor old dab.'

Ben liked the way Jessie joked about her deafness. The rheumatism in her joints and her toothlessness meant she had to be cared for and the shes would bring her scrounge and small creatures taken on stalking expeditions. She was not wise in cat ways like Sam or Silver but she commanded respect and was loved by all.

He found her dozing on the settee. Under the table the noisy purring of Louise rose from the nest of kittens.

'How are you, Mother?' Ben said.

'What brother?' Jessie smiled, half-opening her eyes.

'Don't confuse things.' Silver grinned at Ben and he added: 'Are you well, Jessie?'

'Not really, but I can't grumble. I'm gettin' on, you know. It's a long time since I had my last lot of kittens. Still, Louise has done a good job over there – with the help of that Scarnose. Bless their hearts. I love kittens.'

They left her to sleep and came out to take the evening air.

'We'll have to hunt down Smiley,' Ben said. 'This can't go on, Silver.'

'OK, we'll start now. You go down the hill to the wasteland and I'll go up the hill to the big house and trees. If you meet him let us all know in the usual way and I promise every tom on my patch will come running. Good luck, Ben.'

But the building site yielded nothing except Lucy's scent and the faint stink of a tom Ben couldn't identify.

Then the neutered Siamese, Trixy, who lived behind the brown door of No. 5 met him at the bottom of Winner Hill Road. The cats were on friendly terms.

'One of your shes, the little tabby, is in trouble,' Trixy said and cold was hollowing Ben's gut again. 'She was running down the street past the flower beds with a tom on her tail.'

'A black tom?'

46

'No, a grey heavy with white paws and a white tip to his tail. I've never seen him around here before. He looked mad.'

'Thanks, Trixy.'

The car speeding through the bottleneck nearly aborted his pursuit but Ben grimaced and ran down Church Street and searched Slaughter House Lane before returning to the pavement outside the bakers. Her body scent lay between the parked cars and the Coach House Inn but it was almost masked by the tom's pungency.

Ben swore through his clenched teeth and ran on to Palace Place and paused once more to read the air at the lychgate of the Parish Church. Then he heard a low moaning cry coming from the rear of the churchyard. It was Lucy and Ben was bounding along the path by the sandstone wall of Paignton Hospital.

She was trapped against the door in the east wall of the yard. Crouching before her was a thick-set tom, steel grey and ragged of ears, his tail lashing.

'Waowl,' Ben cried as he streaked in and out of the gravestones.

Fur-spiked, the grey feral swung around showing his teeth in a snarl that wasn't totally convincing. There was an air of naked fury about the black and white tom bearing down on him which suggested this went beyond eyeballing and the rest of the ritual.

'Maybe you should know . . .' he began, rounding his baleful eyes. But Ben didn't want an exchange of threats. He was sick of strutting and posturing and windbagging. He saw Lucy cowering against the gate and he wanted the solid physical satisfaction of hurting one of these sinister strangers. He wanted blood.

The full weight of his charge sent the grey tom reeling. Then the stranger was on his back spitting and snarling and trying to fend off Ben and counter with swift raking blows from the hind feet. But Ben was fighting mad and ripped open a grey ear and clawed the grey muzzle in a flurry of claws and fangs before leaping off to gather himself for another strike.

47

The stranger cringed, averted his eyes and backed away but Ben hit him again, doing further damage to his face. When the grey escaped he fled without a word across the churchyard into Church Lane.

'Another shadow?' Lucy mewed, rubbing against him. The kittens stirred inside her and she was restless.

'One that bleeds,' Ben smiled. 'Did he hurt you?'

'He didn't have the chance,' she said, eyeing corners as possible nurseries in response to what was going on in her belly.

Ben placed his nose to her nose and licked her muzzle. It was quite dark now and pacing slowly through the churchyard they were rebuked by a blackbird.

'Aw shut up,' Ben growled.

The ceaseless zink-zink-zink went through his brain like nails.

8

Storm Warnings

'Don't let's go back to the garden,' Lucy said. 'Why don't we lie-up here? It's close to good scrounge and it's practical. Everything up there revolves around the strangers and Louise's kittens.'

The swifts were climbing the sky above the church tower and screaming as they went. Through the hazy half-dark the stars glowed.

But scrounge wasn't remarkable. The Central Fish Bar was closed and the people away on holiday, and a dog frightened them from the Golden Lily. Providence provided a little food outside the lychgate on their return. A drunk had dropped most of his Kentucky Fried Chicken near his vomit and the ferals carried it into the churchyard to eat.

An old tabby called Dolly lived in the yard. She occasionally slept in the vestry, but preferred her couch of dead leaves under a sheet of corrugated iron against the east wall beyond the graves. She was skinny and independent and her mind was wandering, but she had survived nine of her thirteen winters living rough. Only her lungs had suffered.

''Ere,' she wheezed, catching sight of Ben and Lucy. 'I doan like yer friends.'

'Which ones?' said Ben.

'That black Dancer and his mate, Slippery Jim.'

'The grey one,' said Lucy and she shuddered.

'Yes, him with the woodpecker laugh and frosty eyes.'

Moonlight slanted between the trees onto the head-stones, and something small panicked and ran through the grass. The cats' ears were instantly erect and their pupils dilated. The ghost world spread around them. It was a world of silver grass and pale shadows.

Dolly pushed out her forepaws and lifted her rump in a luxurious stretch. 'This Dancer told Slippery Jim that someone had gone for Skeets. Who's Skeets?'

'Cat Nasty. The one you saw in kittenhood nightmares, Mother,' said Ben.

She yawned and nodded, her mind elsewhere.

'Are you hungry?' Lucy asked from the start of a purr, and again her beauty and gentleness touched Ben.

Both young ferals licked the top of the old she's head, winkling out the odd flea and despatching it. Then they left her on a flat tombstone to groom the rest of her scragginess and visited the mouse runs. Before the night was very old they had laid four kills at Dolly's feet and she was fairly snoring out the purrs.

'You'm prapper lil dears,' she wavered. 'Fancy treat'n old Dolly to all this.'

'Where's your water?' Ben asked.

'Here and there. I don't go thirsty, oh no, and scavenge idn too hard to come by, but I do appreciate these lil treats. I idn too hot on the stalkin' these days. Too rocky on me legs.'

Ben and Lucy hunted then slept curled together among the buttercups under the giant lime tree. But they were awake at dawn to tread the scavenge trails. In Church Lane a posse of gulls was going through the litter and they lifted on angry squawks as the ferals came bounding at them. But vegetable chow mein wasn't to Lucy's liking and they trotted on to Church Street and the chip wrappings which sparrows, starlings and more gulls had already subjected to surgery. Unexpectedly, the bottom of Winner Hill presented them with a bonus – a complete hotdog. The sausage had rolled clear and there wasn't too much sauce on it. Ben had a bit before pushing it towards Lucy who ate and purred at the same time.

The morning was perfect. Sun washed over the roofs and brought a warm flush to the sandstone walls. Birds sang and jackdaws jangled out their cries as young ones were encouraged to abandon the chimneypot nests. Although the cats did not know it, it was Saturday and the litter in Winner Hill Road was at its worst over the weekend after the busiest nights in Torbay's pubs and clubs.

They lingered at the bend by Winner Hill Garage and put their noses to the silver cartons which had held the King Prawn chow mein and fried rice. From the garage roof came the scrabbling of claws, an angry mewl and the screaming yodel of gulls. Two herring gulls were swooping and yelling until Dancer appeared and looked down at Ben and Lucy.

'Hi, you gentle souls,' he laughed, and ducked as a gull skimmed his head. 'There's a young gull up here but I wouldn't recommend trying to hook him. These bloody big birds don't half hurt.'

'Come down and try these for size,' Ben growled, lifting a paw and shooting his claws.

'No thanks. Too busy at the moment, but I tell you what,' and Dancer sniffed and ducked. 'It won't be long before you have the chance to use them volehooks on some really tough opposition.'

'Like Slippery Jim?' Lucy said.

'OK, so you caught Slippery by surprise. Big deal. Me and Smiley won't be no pushovers. And the other top toms are murder. If I was you I'd run while you can still walk – if you know what I mean.'

'Maybe I'll come up there and hook out your tongue,' said Ben, trying to pick out the way onto the roof.

'Gotta go,' said Dancer. 'Friends are waiting. Why don't you join us, love?' he called to Lucy. 'Try playing with the winners.'

'Get lost,' Ben said and Lucy leaned against him to print her body scent on his.

It was approaching the summer solstice and the hedges were hung with sweetbriar and dogrose. The seeding grass waved in the wind that came off the sea like the draught from a furnace. Glittering green and blue dragonflies

51

clicked and rustled over the lilies of Maylands' pond. Evenings heightened the fragrance of the honeysuckle and the apple scent of the sweetbriar. Bees and flies swarmed around the borders and the elderberry flower.

'What's up?' Scarnose said.

They discovered him sitting in the shade of the bamboos that evening, swinging a paw and cursing whenever a moth bumped against his head. The shrilling chorus of the swifts agitated the cats and they blinked and scowled until the birds were so high their cries no longer played on the nerves. Bats were squeaking along the avenues of warm air and ghost moths danced in the light from the french windows.

'A meeting,' Ben said.

'What, now?'

'Now, by the shelter. Silver wants to speak to us – all of us.'

'Lead on.'

The ferals and most of the strays had gathered under the chestnut tree facing the summerhouse where Silver sat on the roof. In the twilight his white elegance was especially attractive.

'What's the problem?' Scarnose said, uninvited, and the ferals glared at him.

'You shut your mouth till Silver asks you to speak,' said Sam.

'OK, OK, so I'm all ears.' Then, realising he had gone too far, Scarnose mumbled, 'Sorry, Silver. I only just woke up.'

Silver ignored him and said, 'Some of the toms who call themselves Shadows are on your patch. You'll have to be careful when you walk the hunting grounds. As you know, Ben saw off a grey heavy who was coming it strong with Lucy and I had an exchange of words with the one called Smiley. This Dancer has been shooting his mouth off all over the place. So if you see any more strangers, you tell Ben or me.'

'Then what?' said Scarnose. 'This is our patch. No one

muscles in by prancin' about dropping threats and scaring shes. Only hooks count and we got the best.'

The toms growled their agreement but Lucy noticed two of the shes, Pepper and Lucky, glance at each other and grin. When the meeting broke up she approached them and said, 'Have you been speaking to the strangers?'

Pepper was a sleek black and white youngster. She shook her head and laid back her whiskers.

'You're sure?' Lucy persisted.

'Yeah,' Lucky said. 'C'mon, leave us alone. You've got a tom. We don't want no aggravation.'

'The newcomers are dangerous.'

'Aren't they all till they flash their hooks and Silver gives them the bad news,' Pepper said.

'It's not like that this time,' Lucy said. 'There are lone wanderers who are looking for ganglife and a family. And there are these Shadows who are after somethin' else.'

'Yeah, their kicks at the expense of our toms,' Lucky sneered.

She was an insolent tortoiseshell with large eyes and a tomcat swagger.

'You've been warned,' Lucy said.

'Don't nag, Lucy,' Pepper said sheepishly.

At twilight the blackbird hysteria seemed to concentrate on Maylands. The cock birds threw their rattling screams from treetop to treetop as if the neighbourhood was seething with cats or the garden exhaled menace. When they stopped the silence fanned by the heat was hostile. It remained so when Scrumpy ran into it at dawn looking wild-eyed and shaken.

'They've gone off with the big black and the big grey,' he panted, clawing up onto the summerhouse roof.

'Who?' Silver said.

'Pepper and Lucky,' Lucy yawned.

'Yeah – them two,' Scrumpy growled.

'But why?' Silver said.

'Vanity,' Lucy replied, sitting up and stretching. 'The Shadows only had to flatter them. They're empty-headed enough to listen to sweet talk.'

'Some of us better go and look for them,' Ben said.

'No,' Silver said firmly. 'The Shadows will be expecting us to do that. Maybe Lucky and Pepper won't come to no harm.'

Ben narrowed his eyes and gazed at him, wondering what was the real reason for Silver's reluctance to act.

9
Skeets

Three mornings later Pepper came limping back to Maylands, her ears ragged and bleeding and bald patches on her back and hindquarters. There were no rebukes or retribution. The little stray was too ill to scold. Protectively the shes gathered round her, applying their tongues and dispensing sympathy while Silver and his toms looked on. Only when she was ready was she coaxed into giving an account of her misfortune.

After sneaking off a little before dawn Pepper and Lucky ran up Monastery Road and met the Shadows at the Lions' Club carpark.

'A wise decision,' Dancer grinned, walking round them in a slow circle of appraisal. 'There's no future with losers and Whitey and them are yesterday's cats.'

Smiley sat watching and listening, and Slippery Jim polished his claws with his tongue and glanced slyly at the shes.

'Where are your own shes?' Lucky asked.

'Everywhere,' Dancer chuckled. 'Now you're our shes. What's your names?'

They told him and Smiley's smile grew bigger and Slippery Jim dredged up a chuckle that made the shes lay back their ears. He really did sound like a green woodpecker.

The mating was fierce.

'As if we weren't animals,' remembered Pepper. 'And this Smiley just sat there watching – him and his awful grin.'

'But how did you get the scratches on your face and the chunks out of your ears?' Lucy asked.

'Listen,' Pepper shuddered.

The shes were shepherded through the Council estate, across Clifton Road and up into Primley Wood.

'Jo-Joe's patch,' said Ben.

'Not any more,' said Pepper. 'It belongs to the Shadows. Poor Jo-Joe. He was crawling down over the meadow between the trees and the white house. And he was in a terrible state – blind in one eye and covered in scratches and bites. His gang didn't stand a chance. They're all gone now.'

Up by the trees at the top of the sloping field the Shadows were sunbathing.

'How many?' Silver wanted to know.

'Lots. More than us. All toms. No shes.'

'And Skeets?' Silver prompted.

'Oh yes – he was among them.'

The ferals looked at her intently and she swallowed but could not control the spasm of shivering that racked her body.

'Himself,' she whispered.

'Is he big?' Scarnose asked.

'Big as the killer dog who chopped Betsy last winter. I've never seen a neck like his, nor legs so powerful.'

She closed her eyes and continued in a low trembling voice. 'He's more than a tom, much more. He's all my worst dreams and terrors and bad feelings, and he has these incredible yellow unblinking eyes.'

'And he's black,' said Silver.

'No. He's sandy with small ears and big teeth. But it's his eyes that frighten me. They look through you like – like we look out over the houses to the sea and the lights on the sea in the evening when our minds are somewhere else. They are utterly without feeling, Silver. Dead eyes with light in them but a colder light you couldn't imagine. Beside Skeets, Smiley and Slippery Jim are kittens. He is the Big Crazy surrounded by Crazies and the sight of him loosened my bowels.'

The feral toms gave each other sideways glances. Pepper's words had confirmed everything Ben had felt in his gut. Sam looked up at the bird in the top of the

56

chestnut tree. It was the kestrel tiercel whose mate was tending fledglings at their nesting site high on the façade of the Lions' Club. Watched by the old tom it flew swiftly over the back gardens to the ledge on the top of the chapel and deposited the vole at the falcon's feet.

The flutter of wings and the cries of the kestrel eyasses brought Skeets' eyes briefly up from his reverie. Then he submerged once more into dreams, teasing the small bird with a playful paw as he sang slowly and softly through clenched teeth, 'When the red, red robin . . . comes bob, bob, bobbing along . . .'

But the sparrow was dead and its lifelessness was of no further interest to Skeets. Petulantly he flicked it away and licked his chest fur. The group of toms sprawled close at hand on the leaf litter were alert for any change of demeanour. The singing and happy preoccupation with teasing the life out of some unfortunate creature could suddenly explode into sensational violence. Like Skeets himself they knew nothing of his brain tumour. As far as they were concerned he enjoyed being a bad-ass. Bullying and cruelty were necessary to his temperament. Maybe the tumour wasn't entirely to blame for his unpredictable behaviour. He had been an abnormally aggressive young-ster. Orphaned in kittenhood, he had been raised by a half-crazy, wild-tempered mongrel bitch whose puppies had been drowned. Without playmates or companions of any sort Skeets had been schooled in violence, and ever since the traumatic days under the spell of his foster-mother, he had been haunted by a vision of a white cat striding confidently across dreams which grew out of the pain in his head. His mind was never blank like his eyes.

With a mew of distress he went to the hazel bush and stood up on his hindlegs to suck at the leaves. Then he dropped to the ground and savaged his tail before throw-ing back his head to yarool. His body quivered, his eyes closed and he collapsed into unconsciousness which lasted less than thirty seconds.

'Where does he go in his head?' Skiffle whispered.

'He's chasing that bloody white tom,' said Slippery Jim.

'But he's down the road,' said Dancer.

'And in Skeets' head,' Smiley said.

'Skeets can't be afraid,' said another tom. 'Skeets don't know the meaning of the word.'

'Yeah, but he's superstitious,' said Smiley. 'You wanna ask him about it, Boomer?'

'Do me a favour! What he says goes.'

'When the red, red robin . . . comes bob, bob, bob-bing,' Skeets groaned, climbing to his feet. His coat was covered in red dust. 'Bring me the little tabby she,' he said suddenly.

'She's gone,' Smiley said. 'Gone back to Whitey.'

'That Whitey,' Skeets sighed. Then a movement among the roots of the holm oak set his nose twitching. Lucky was cowering there, too exhausted and bruised to move.

'Hullo, Pretty,' Skeets purred. 'And who are you?'

'Lucky,' Dancer said, thinking no name could be more inappropriate considering the circumstances.

'Come to Skeets, lovely lucky little Lucky. Don't be shy. Come on. Come on. There's things to do.'

Burying her muzzle in her forepaws Lucky began to cry like a kitten mewling for its mother.

10

Like Dogs

For nearly twelve months, Skeets and the Shadows had been wandering in a south-westerly direction from the large town where he had spent the first four years of his life. He had begun with three toms – Smiley, Dancer and Slippery Jim, and a lean old stager called City. But on the way they had picked up other misfits and delinquent strays and the gang was now thirteen strong, a number Skeets liked. Some of the most violent and vicious cats in the West country shadowed him because he could dream up happenings beyond the bounds of even the most vivid imagination. It was he who had ordained that no shes would travel with them.

'Shes are dispensable,' he announced. 'We find, take, use and discard. Where the sun rises out of the water I'll meet the white tom and the pain in my head will go. Between that moment and this there's just the kicks.'

Recalling the Shadows' response, he sat swaying in a cat-nap while the sea breeze bent the treetops and rocked the grass. Dead leaves fell and were sent flying again. A cloud drifted over the sun and without opening his eyes Skeets said, 'Where is the little Pretty?'

'Gone,' said Smiley. 'She went in the night. But soon we'll have a whole new batch of shes. When do we take the garden?'

'What garden?'

'The place where Whitey's gang is lying up.'

'Where else?' said Boomer, the overweight ginger.

Skeets was smiling as he turned to face him and Boomer quailed because he had never seen such a murderous chill in the yellow eyes.

'Surely you weren't intentionally sarcastic, Boomer?

Tell me I didn't detect a note of criticism and arrogance in your remark. Surely you weren't questioning my authority? Surely you weren't? Surely not. Tell me I imagined it all.'

He ambled over to Boomer, carrying himself lightly for such a large animal. Like a dream coming apart the swifts dived between the trees and the block of flats, shrilling all the way. The noise corkscrewed in Skeets' head but the smile stayed intact.

'You are Boomer,' he crooned. 'Good, honest, loyal Boomer. What would I do without such celebrated heavies as you, old son?'

Boomer licked his lips, grinned and nodded. Then a sandy-coloured paw lashed out and four hooks ripped through the ginger tom's right ear and the other sent swinging from the opposite direction left four horizontal lacerations on his muzzle.

Blood flowed and Boomer flopped back on his haunches sneezing and blinking.

'But, Skeets – ' he began.

'But nothing,' Skeets smiled, gripping Boomer by the scruff of the neck and shaking him in his powerful jaws before thumping him down to work at the soft underparts with hind paws.

When it was over he panted, 'There, a lesson in survival, Boomer. Mouth shut – peaceful life; mouth open – aggravation. Right?'

'Yeah, right Chief. Right,' Boomer groaned.

Skeets lowered his head until his nose was a leaf's thickness from Boomer's nose.

'Do you really understand, Sparrowbrain?'

'I understand, believe me. I'm a big-mouthed idiot.'

'And Skeets is leading you to the end of the rainbow?'

'To rainbow's end,' Smiley said. 'Skeets has the vision. Skeets provides everything – scrounge, kicks, and now the patch with it all.'

'But everything isn't available,' Skeets chuckled. 'Give me a little live something to amuse me, Boomer. Get me a vole. And Boomer—'

'Yeah, Chief?'

'You don't get me a vole and you can kiss goodbye to an ear.'

Softly Skeets began to hum the tune of his Red Robin song.

On Maylands' terrace the toms and shes were mesmerised by the dance of the ghost moths. It was twilight but a blackbird sang from the top of the chestnut tree and the breeze washed the medicinal smell of the bay into the flower scents. Gulls cackled on rooftops but the song-thrush in the Lawson's cypresses sat quietly on a second brood of nestlings.

The ferals had eaten the tinned food and drunk from the water bowls. All of them were resigned now to the conflict promised by the Shadows. Lucky's pitiful return strengthened their resolve, although her account of Skeets and the other Crazies dismayed them. But she had been welcomed back into the family and taken off to sleep in the summerhouse.

'Using shes that way is shameful,' Sam said.

'They're like dogs,' said Lucy. 'Lucky is in a terrible state. I think I'd better go to her.'

'I want her, Pepper, Jessie, Louise and the kittens gone from here as soon as possible,' Silver said.

'Gone where?' Lucy enquired.

'Somewhere safe.'

'Like Dolly's patch,' said Ben. 'Tonight, Silver?'

'Yeah. When the town's quiet we'll move them.'

'A good idea,' said Sam.

Scarnose and half a dozen strays came up the rockery and waited to be invited onto the terrace.

'You lot can watch the back fence, the gates and the road,' Silver said. 'Put one of your best toms halfway up the hill, Scarnose. Tell him to come running if any of the Crazies head this way.'

'And we'll fight here?' said Sam. 'We know the garden, so we have an advantage.'

'But they are Crazies,' said Parson.

61

'Then we must be Crazies,' Ben said.

'Like dogs,' Parson muttered. 'Maybe we oughta join the shes.'

'Maybe you oughta eat my bits,' Scarnose growled. 'Let's go and no more lip.'

A moth thudded against his head and became trapped in an ear, and Scarnose writhed and kicked in his desperation to dislodge it. By the time he had succeeded the ferals were tottery-legged with laughter.

'Why does it always happen to me?' he complained, leading his toms off the home ground.

It became dark and the wind freshened. The ferals at their vigil were watchful and silent. Behind wisps of high altitude cloud the stars littered a moonless sky. The light had been switched off in the lady's bedroom but to cat eyes the dark corners of the garden were pallidly visible. They waited, some sitting, others crouched with paws tucked under chests and pupils dilated. After midnight the shouting and laughing of young people leaving the clubs began. It lasted for a half hour or so and faded into silence broken by the soft rush of wind in the trees. A hush descended and several nostrils rounded and contracted repeatedly to trap individual scents. Then a long drawn maraowl climbed into the night.

'That wasn't mooncrooning,' said Sam.

'It came from the big house on the hill,' Ben said.

'And it was like the cry Dancer gave when we met up there back along,' said Silver.

The ferals had heard it before, that long wavering wail of grief for a dead animal.

'For us?' Ben asked.

'No, Ben,' Silver said. 'Just for me.'

Heads dropped and he added, 'I think it's time we took the shes to Dolly's place.'

The lamplight at the bend of Winner Hill Road a little above the entrance to Orchard Patch emphasised the blackness of the shadows. Progress was slow, for it was dictated by the pace of old Jessie. The fit shes walked in single file. Lucy, Louise, Rita and Belle each had a kitten swinging by the scruff of the neck from their teeth. Sam led the way and Ben and Silver brought up the rear, constantly stopping to check the darkness behind them for alien tomcat smells.

'Nothing ahead,' a voice whispered from the foot of the hoarding.

'Thanks, Trixy,' said Ben. 'You look after yourself, OK? Keep out of the way of Skeets' mob.'

Kittens dangling from their mouths the shes trotted down Church Street and through the lychgate.

'Where to now?' Sam whispered.

'Follow me,' Ben said and he led them to Dolly's lair.

'So many visitors,' mewed the old she, emerging from her corrugated lean-to.

Lucy placed her kitten on the ground and said, 'We have to hide these and their mother and a couple of friends. Is it OK if they stay here?'

'Of course. And didn't I hunt with your foster-mother? And didn't I play nurse when she was absent? Is my heart a stone that I could forget an old friendship? Bring those little dears in here where tez snug and warm. You shes up one end, Louise and her kits in the middle and me this end.'

'And us back to the garden,' said Sam.

But Ben's heart sank as he ran back up Winner Hill Road. The Crazies had dynamited their world and the old life was slipping away from him. A dog howled, voicing Ben's loneliness.

'Bring Scarnose's toms to the garden, Ben,' Silver said. 'I want us all on the terrace where we can control things.'

It's a game to him, Ben thought. Like the street fighting and the mating and life itself. We play it and kittens are born and old cats die but the leaves fall only to come again. What does it mean? I am running down the long dark but where am I going? Where does it end? Why does it end? Why does it happen?

He called Scarnose and the other strays and padded down the hill some distance behind them, and they were entering the silver gates when he was ambushed. Smiley and Boomer dashed out of Huccaby's drive but Ben nipped between them into the alley at the back of Monastery Road. Ahead was the brick wall of Fairview with Barnie perched on it.

'Who are they?' the old tom growled.

'Enemies,' Ben said. 'I got trouble.'

The Shadows hit the wall and ran up it but Ben and Barnie caught them with a barrage of blows from forepaws and exposed hooks.

'They're big,' Barnie said, watching the Shadows retreat to make another dash. 'And this time we haven't got surprise on our side. I think we need help. Follow me.'

They came down the old wooden stepladder into a concrete yard and with their pursuers' claws raking the side wall Barnie nudged Ben towards the back door.

'Through the cat flap,' he grunted.

Ben hesitated. He had never been in a house. 'If it's gonna be OK,' he said.

'It's got to be better than this,' Barnie grinned. 'Hurry, or I'll lose my ass.'

A moment later they were in the kitchen of Fairview and Jamie the terrier was rising from his basket opposite the fridge to inspect them.

'Ben's with me,' said Barnie. 'He's a friend.'

'Ben who?' the terrier said in a language only Barnie understood.

'Ben the tom from the garden over the way.'

'Oh him, he's my friend too.' The dog was more asleep than awake. 'What does he want? Milk? A bite to eat?'

Smiley took the cat flap with him in his eagerness to get at Ben. He was wearing it for a collar when he skidded over the floor tiles to be confronted by the terrier, who was still not fully awake but very angry.

'Skeets preserve me,' Smiley cried, and entering the hole in the door behind him like a torpedo Boomer crashed into his rear, pushing him closer to Jamie and disaster.

'More friends?' said the dog.

'Enemies,' Barnie said. 'They're after your food.'

'Yeah?'

Avoiding Smiley's hooks Jamie bowled him over and bit a hind leg. The landing light went on, then the hall light and Smiley screeched. But Boomer was already halfway out the door with Ben's hooks scoring his rump when human footsteps pounded down the stairs. Breaking free of the Jack Russell, Smiley tried to escape but the cat flap collar became wedged in the aperture and Jamie's teeth did a lot of damage to the squirming hindquarters before the kitchen light was snapped on. A loud voice called the dog to heel and the man of the house wrenched open the back door and let Smiley out into the night still wearing the cat flap. Smiley pawed desperately at it and was free, only to be bowled over and bitten again by the dog before he shot over the gate.

The yarooling and barking was astonishing and lights were coming on in most of the neighbouring houses. In the confusion Ben said goodbye to Barnie and slipped away to return to Maylands through the gardens.

The story of Smiley's collar amused the ferals and strays on the terrace.

'So, they can be outsmarted,' Sam said.

'Yeah, by a gutsy old pet,' said Ben. 'Believe me, I was lucky. Barnie is as sharp as hooks. He did all the brainwork and the dog did all the fighting.'

'But it'll make the Crazies think twice before they set foot in our garden,' said Parson.

'Will it?' Ben said. 'I wouldn't count on that. We haven't got a resident dog and Smiley will be dying to get his revenge.'

'So? We're ready, aren't we?' said Scarnose.

'You haven't seen that Skeets or some of the other Crazies in action,' said Ben.

'Neither have you.'

'But I listened to Pepper. That lot do fight like dogs.'

'So why didn't Smiley see off Jamie?' Scarnose countered.

'You bloody fool,' Ben growled.

'But he's got a point,' said Sam and Ben gazed at him in disbelief.

In the last hour of darkness two of the Primley Wood ferals called from the gates and Scrumpy escorted them to the terrace. Frogs were singing in the pond and an insomniac gull was walking back and forth across the roof talking to her chick.

'You heard?' said Jake, a ginger tom. 'Our gang's finished. Jo-Joe's gone. It's all over, thanks to them Crazies. They destroyed us, blew us apart.'

And his grey companion nodded. 'Them Crazies are more dog than cat.'

The Maylands toms glanced at Ben.

'We never had a chance,' Jake continued. 'They came through the trees and worked us over like we was kittens. Charlie's badly hurt and so's Jo-Joe. The last I saw of Charlie was outside the big house by the field. A woman came out the door and bent over him. I think he was dying.'

'They are over the top,' said the grey. 'They get high on aggro like we get high on a green scent trip.'

'And they took our shes,' Jake concluded.

'What do you suggest we do?' said Silver.

'Run,' Jake said bluntly.

11
Lull

A chainsaw that was busy two streets away snarled through Lucy's thoughts. She abandoned the cat-nap and watched the stray she, Rainbow, come bounding through the long grass. The kittens within Lucy stirred and she mewed. Her siblings were asleep around her on the terrace and the sun stood in the bottom of the sky above the bay. A garden warbler sang from the hedge below the horsechestnut where his mate was feeding the nestlings.

Walking along the terrace Ben paused and let his ears register the song before he dropped the mouse at Lucy's feet. Instantly she was up, tail raised and curled at the tip in greeting. She was glad to see his ears perked and his whiskers fanned out in enquiry.

'Everything's OK,' she said, but a commotion at the far end of the terrace woke all the cats.

Parson had caught a cock starling and attracted by the racket the bird was making the firtop crows swooped at him, cawing and beating around his head with their wings. Ben and Scarnose chuckled. Then the hen starling flopped down in front of Parson and fluttered about as if she was injured. So Parson released the male who promptly took flight followed by his cunning little mate. Every blackbird in Maylands saluted the escape with their staccato cries.

'Hey,' Scarnose cried above the laughter. 'It's the cool cat himself. No wonder he's all skin and bone if that's the best he can do.'

'It was just a bit of fun,' Parson grinned self-consciously.

'Yeah, yeah,' said Scrumpy.

The swifts were lower in the sky and there was some grey creeping across the blue although the cats could not smell approaching rain. The garden was in a sun daze and things were coming apart in the heat which carried street smells. The cats were uncomfortably warm and the sweating pads on the bottom of their feet left damp trails of pawmarks when they strolled about the terrace. The older animals panted out their body heat but a sultry noon was responsible for Rita and Maria quarrelling. Before anyone could intervene the shes were locked together in a squawling, kicking tangle.

'So what's up?' Scarnose asked as they separated and eyeballed.

'Wind your neck in, Mouseparts,' Rita growled. The eight pound she was a grey and white patched ball of fury.

The toms laughed and Scarnose grinned and turned away.

'No more digs at me, OK?' Rita said to Maria, who nodded and began to groom herself.

During a mid-afternoon prowl about Scrumpy and Scarnose were ambushed by Smiley and a black and white heavy called Wayne who had a bald patch on top of his head. The attack happened in Monastery Road opposite No. 23. The usual exchange of curses led to a fight between Scrumpy and Wayne. Scarnose could only crouch and watch, paralysed by Smiley's chilling grin. Badly bitten, Scrumpy might have fared even worse if a woman hadn't come out of a nearby house and thrown a saucepan of cold water over Wayne. Some of it caught Scrumpy too and both toms ran in different directions.

Scarnose lowered his head, shaking with laughter in spite of his own predicament.

'You see how easy it is?' Smiley chuckled. 'There's the Shadows and there's all the other cats. We're the élite, friend, and Skeets, not your white hero, is The Cat.'

Scarnose slowly backed off.

'No need for alarm, friend,' Smiley continued. 'You look like a real tom. Maybe you're lending your hooks to the wrong gang. Maybe you should have a word with Skeets. We're taking over this patch but that could be OK for you if you're smart.'

Scarnose turned and crept away.

'See yuh,' Smiley called after him.

Chesting the lawn grass Scarnose joined the gang on the summerhouse roof. They were following the sun and it was their afternoon place. Sam and Mellow were busy licking Scrumpy's wounds and to conceal his embarrassment Scarnose attacked his own chest fur with his teeth to winkle out grass seeds.

'Smiley ran,' he said, intercepting one of Silver's glances.

'Good,' said Sam. 'So they can get the wind up.'

'Knock it off,' Scrumpy groaned. 'The cat that took me was as hard as rock. I didn't stand a chance.'

'But Smiley legged it,' said Scarnose, unwilling now to look Silver in the face.

'What d'yuh do?' Scrumpy sniffed. 'Piddle on him?'

'It may have been the car coming up the road,' Scrumpy admitted lamely, and several curious pairs of eyes fixed on him.

'One thing's certain,' said Sam. 'This Skeets is playing the old game.'

'Cat and Mouse?' said the black stray, Henry.

'What else? And I *don't* like being the mouse.'

The dream of the long dark pulsed at the back of Ben's mind as he watched Silver. Despite the heat the group of ferals and strays were alert. They stood or sat, staring about them. They were all there, Ben noted – Sam, Silver, Rainbow, Rita, Lucky, Lucy, Maria, Belle, Scarnose, Scrumpy, Parson, Mellow and Henry. It had never happened before, this gathering of the Maylands gang.

The sun illumined Lucy's ears and lent a radiance to the white inner hairs. Like the rest of the gang she carried some of the day's beauty in her soul. It was the sheen on her coat and the roundness of her body which told of the life lodged in her.

69

12

The Battle of Maylands

'What we gonna do?' asked Scarnose.

He was striding back and forth across the terrace watched by Ben, Silver and Sam and a group of shes including Lucy.

'Pull out,' said Silver.

'You mean run for it?' Scarnose said.

'Yeah. Tonight.'

'But what if Skeets don't hang about? What if he decides to take us now?'

'What if the moon drops out of the sky?' Sam said mysteriously. 'What if cats grew wings?'

The other glanced at him, irritated by his Wise Tom gibberish. Silver's fox-shaped head, with its blunt muzzle, lifted and he sniffed the morning. His ears were stiff and erect. Heat swam around him as it struck the flagstones.

'Tonight,' he said. 'When it's dark. I reckon the Crazies will wait for the town to go dead before they do anything. We'll go down over the gardens, not down the hill. But we'll scent-mark the hill first.'

Sam sighed. 'I'll miss this place. I've been here a long time.'

'But we'll be back,' Silver said. 'Skeets wants me, not the place. Maybe he'll get bored and move on. Ferals like him don't have a place.'

A Flymo in a neighbouring garden began to chew through the hush and the cats' ears flattened, but it was more tolerable than the blackbirds' incessant din or the cackle of the gulls. A lazy sea breeze stirred the shadows and wafted scents and smells over Maylands. Yacht sails were bellying out on the bay and the glare of the water had Ben blinking and averting his eyes.

'Wuhhhhh-warrr-wuhh,' the Flymo snarled.

Ben persuaded Lucy to join him in a romp on the lawn which was now a flower-choked hayfield. He loved her liveliness and noisy purring. She was an extension of himself and all his deepest feelings flowed into her. As if nothing has changed, Sam mused, gazing down on them. The collared doves crooned and the garden warbler sang and the Flymo continued to bring someone's lawn under the thumb. It was just another summer's day with the garden hoses hissing and the sprinklers busy on grass which was never allowed to get untidy. The wild roses had flowered and fallen but the floribundas had opened among the elderberry corymbs and briar.

Tiring of the game of chase and mock fighting, Ben and Lucy lay in their separate hollows in the grass. He was on his side, right paw curled, left paw extended and supporting his chin. She was also on her side, tail between hindlegs, licking a foreleg then angling her head to clean her chest fur. Silver sat on his rump against the summerhouse door, hindlegs thrust out and parted, forelegs hanging at his sides, his head lowered for his tongue to clean his stomach fur. Belle and Lucky slept on the summerhouse roof – Belle in a circle of contented warmth; Lucky sprawled full-length on her side with her back pressed against her sister.

Sam licked a forepaw and rolled over on the terrace. The joy of life brimmed his eyes. Strangely he could recall the taste of his mother's milk. The butterfly dancing through the sunlight was part of his memory of kittenhood. He stood up and shook himself. He did not want to abandon the old place, not at his age. And the heat was too much. Bounding down the rockery he walked across the lawn and settled in the shade of the bamboos.

Not far away Skeets was happy. It was a long time since he had had a fit and the Shadows were amazed at his cheerfulness. Often after brief good humour he would rocket off into violence. They were waiting for him to drop to the ground, twitching and yarooling, lost in his dream of the silent white tom and the water that ran to the bottom of the sky.

The enormous sandy cat lazed on the tarmac of the Lions' Club carpark and tried to hook the flies which buzzed around his head. Close at hand were Smiley, the old ratter, City, and Dancer. Slippery Jim and a couple more toms were stretched out under the holm oaks and everything was peaceful until Wayne trotted up from the council houses carrying a chicken carcass in his jaws.

'Lucky you got a big mouth,' Smiley said.

'Where's my share, Wayne?' Dancer added.

'Go eat ratbits,' Wayne snarled. He dropped his scrounge and settled before it and began to lick it.

'Good stuff?' Skeets smiled.

'Yeah,' Wayne said, ripping off a chunk of flesh, skin and bone and holding his head on one side to crunch it. 'Yeah – good stuff. This is a good place, Skeets.'

'Enjoying it?' City asked.

Wayne grinned and grabbed another mouthful. The rest of the gang eyed him hungrily with growing resentment. Then Wayne started to choke. His eyes stood out and he clawed at his mouth, shuffling backwards in a crouching position, neck and head extended. Skeets was suddenly alert and darting forward.

'Garrg,' Wayne gurgled.

The others trotted over to sit in a semi-circle before him.

'He said "garrg",' Skeets chuckled, looking quickly to the left and right before returning his gaze to Wayne. The bald spot on the unfortunate's head, caused by some kittenhood infection, seemed more ridiculous than usual.

'Help . . . me . . .' Wayne gasped.

'But it's your scrounge,' Skeets laughed and his cronies were spluttering and shaking as Wayne rolled and kicked and beat at his muzzle, ripping his mouth.

'Garrg.'

'Garrg,' chorused Skeets and the Shadows, and moments later Wayne was dead.

72

'Poor old thing,' City said quietly. 'There are better ways to go.'

'He had a brain like an empty eggshell,' said Slippery Jim.

'Garrg,' chortled Dancer.

'But now we're down to twelve,' Skeets frowned. 'Thirteeen is the magic number. Thirteen hard toms.'

'I think I got us a useful replacement for Wayne,' Smiley said.

'Garrg,' Skeets laughed. 'Garrrrrrrg.'

'Killed by a chicken,' said Slippery Jim.

'A dead chicken,' said Smiley.

'Wayne was never gifted up top,' Dancer observed.

Skeets had stopped laughing and his eyes were blank.

'A new number thirteen,' he whispered. 'That is good. That is an omen, my friends. But will he be loyal and true and would he walk through fire for the sake of Skeets and the Shadows?'

'I do not know,' Smiley said patiently. 'I haven't your vision. But I think I oughta sound him out.'

'Yessss.' Skeets' voice broke and rose and wavered to a mindless yarool.

Here we go, City thought. Or there he goes.

'Smi . . . lee,' Skeets yowled, keeling over.

'I'm here,' Smiley said, but Skeets was writhing and kicking into his dream until he fell through starlight to the garden. There was the rooftop, the hedge and the sea beyond. But the white tom had gone.

'No! Naow! Naowowowow!' Skeets screamed and Smiley winced. Then he groomed himself and slunk down Monastery Road, his haunches rolling. A patter of feet told him City was on his tail.

'Is this the end of the big walk?' the old tom asked. He was a lean, dusty creature, white with black patches and a tail that a rat had taken a chunk out of at the base.

'Could be. It's all here – the place, the water, the white tom.'

'What if Skeets loses out?'

'Skeets don't lose. We don't lose. Don't forget it.'

73

Smiley's fierce loyalty didn't surprise City but he was old enough to step out of line and get away with it.

'You think Skeets will be OK in his head after we take over the patch and Whitey's gone?' he said.

'He's all right in the head now.'

'Yeah?'

'Yeah. You know that, City. He's been good to you.'

'And I'd kill a dog for him if I had to, only – '

'Only what?' Smiley said, turning.

'Only I'd like a patch of our own with good scrounge, shelter, loving shes, peace.'

'What about the kicks?' Smiley stopped.

'I'm just an old cat who wants to sleep in the sun and stare up at the moon.'

A little warmth returned to Smiley's smile. 'Skeets will look after you.'

'Like he looked after Wayne?'

'Garrg,' Smiley chuckled. 'He was all self and he wasn't in at the beginning. Skeets never trusted him.'

City nodded and said under his breath, 'We're being watched. Up on the wall, in the flowers.'

Smiley sat down and lifted his eyes. Scarnose gazed back at him from the valerian.

'Number Thirteen,' Smiley crooned. 'Wanna come down?'

'Do I look crazy?' Scarnose growled.

'No. You look like a cat who can take care of himself.'

'I'm a stray,' Scarnose sniffed.

'But you wanna be a winner?'

'I am a winner.'

'OK,' Smiley said. 'We're recruitin' winners so why don't you walk up the hill to the big house and have a chat with Himself.'

'And lose an eye?' Scarnose said.

'Give yourself a break. The Shadows aren't open to any old tom. Skeets wants you in. Think about it and take a stroll – up. No hassle. No tricks. After tonight it'll be too late to do deals.'

It was a pensive Scarnose who returned to Maylands

and searched out Silver. Seen from the drive the white tom on the summerhouse roof flickered like a flame in the heat shimmer. He was alone, facing the sea, his eyes closed.

'What is it, Scarnose?' he murmured.

'The other day when Scrumpy was roughed up by that Crazy,' Scarnose began, but it was difficult to continue.

'Go on,' Siver urged.

'I was scared. I *didn't* do nothing. What they did to Button, you know, it – it . . .'

Silver nodded but his eyes remained closed.

'I ain't a coward. It's just that I'm not sure of myself when I'm with you.'

The pale blue eyes with their dark blue pupils opened and narrowed to vertical slits.

'It's been that way from the beginning, Silver. I know you don't trust me so I go over the top trying to be Hard Hooks. But it don't work.'

'Why you tellin' me this?' Silver asked kindly.

'Smiley just asked me to join the Crazies. Looks like he's got a low opinion of me, too. Only, I wouldn't rat on the gang. Ben and Lucy are my friends and I loved old Button. I'd rather lose a leg than cause you any aggravation.'

'And now what?'

'The Crazies will make their move tonight. Maybe while you get the shes and Sam to Dolly's place me and a few other toms can bring a bit of trouble to Skeets.'

'A diversion? That sounds good,' Silver nodded. 'Come up and we'll chew it over. This Smiley sounds like the brains behind the Crazies. Maybe we should be thinking about knocking him off the gate.'

A black shadow separated itself from the shadows under the Lawson's cypresses, glided over the wall and ran up through the garden next door to the ground behind Monastery Road. And a little later Smiley, who was lying under the yellow van in the Lions' Club carpark, grinned and stretched.

'All this warble and twitter,' Skeets yawned. 'I nod off

75

only for the bloody birds to wake me up again. What are you grinning at, Smiley?'

'I got you a Number Thirteen.'

'Ahhhh. Already I feel a sense of completeness returning.'

'This ginger, Scarnose, is on the edge of Whitey's mob. He's only got stray status and I'm pretty sure he'll come over to us.'

'That is excellent news.' Skeets stretched.

'Yeah, he'll be a real asset. He knows all the paths on the patch and the strengths and weaknesses of Whitey's mob. And he'll lead us to the shes.'

'Then bring him in.'

'He'll come by himself, soon,' Smiley chuckled.

'Yeah,' said a scornful voice. 'And tomorrow it'll snow.'

'There had better be a good reason for this interruption, Dancer,' Skeets hissed.

'I just left the garden,' Dancer said. 'Scarnose was boasting to the white cat Silver about how he had fooled Smiley. No way will the ginger one raise his hooks against Silver's gang. But he'll try to fix you, Skeets.'

Smiley kept smiling and said, 'That's a pity.'

'Garrg,' Skeets laughed, thumping the ground with his tail and fixing his baleful yellow eyes on Smiley.

'When the red, red robin . . . comes bob, bob, bobbin' along . . . along . . .' he sang softly through clenched teeth and Smiley was alarmed. He licked his lips and arched his own tail and lowered his belly to the tarmac.

'There'll be no more sobbin' . . . when he starts throbbin' . . . his own sweet song . . .'

The silence behind the last word was the sort of nervous silence that closes behind a speeding express train.

'No one's fault,' Skeets said woodenly. 'They all try to deceive the Shadows. They all try to stop me reaching the white crowbait. They're all against me.'

'We're not, Skeets,' Smiley said.

'Call the others,' Skeets said, his pupils dilating. 'We hit them now. They're waiting for darkness so we'll give them darkness.'

Smiley, City and Dancer raised their voices in a chorus of maraows which sent local domestic cats on cringing runs for home. Shadows elsewhere pricked their ears and homed in on the calls, quivering with excitement.

Sitting on the little wall behind the fuchsias just beyond the silver gates, Parson also heard the war cries and he ran for the summerhouse crying, 'The Crazies are coming! The Crazies are coming!'

Cats rose to their hindlegs all over the lawn and heads popped out of the grass.

'Where?' Silver demanded when Parson stood before him.

'I dunno. But they're coming. I heard their calls.'

'I heard them too,' Maria said.

'So what,' Rita growled. 'Let's give 'em hook. There's enough of us.'

'Shut up,' said Sam, scrambling up the side of the summerhouse to join Silver.

'Do we go now?' Ben asked, looking around for Lucy.

'Collect the rest of the gang,' Silver nodded. 'Scarnose, get your lot and meet us here as soon as you can. Scrumpy, you watch the fence at the back. Parson, the gates. When you see them you yell.'

'Try to stop me,' Parson grinned.

'Lucy,' Ben cried. 'Lucy!'

The other shes came running but the little tabby was not among them. While the gang assembled Ben ran about the garden mewling his alarm and all at once she was darting out from under the conifer hedge and bounding high through the grass to greet him. They pushed their noses hard together and she lowered her head to rub it against his chin. Then he drew his tongue over her muzzle and ears in long slow licks.

'I was over there looking for a safe place to have the kittens,' she purred. 'I heard all the calling from the big house and our garden. I can guess what's happening.'

The new life within her kicked.

A screeching yarool spiked their fur. They swung

around to see Scrumpy trying to shake off two of Skeets' toms as he fell down the rockery.

'Get onto the sun roof,' Ben cried, nudging Lucy's rump. 'Go quickly and don't worry about me.'

'But I can help,' she protested.

'Think of the unborn kittens.'

'I can't. I can only think of you.'

'Lovely Lucy,' Ben said gently. 'Please go.'

And he was off to Scrumpy's aid.

The two Crazies were engrossed in their torment of Scrumpy when Ben attacked the hindquarters of the ebony self whose greasy coat had earnt him the name of Chips. Ben was all muscle and hooks and Chips screamed and tried to squirm free, but he was thrown to one side and his belly raked by thrashing hind feet. Then his muzzle and ears were clawed from a flurry of blows.

Scrumpy and Slippery Jim were a knot of limbs and heaving bodies but Slippery Jim was in control until Chips crashed against him and sank his hooks by mistake into Slippery Jim's head, opening it to the bone. Yarooling and spitting, the grey heavy frantically pawed at his wounds and Scrumpy took the opportunity to bite one of his hind feet. Then three more Shadows came down the rockery and Ben and Scrumpy ran.

Maylands was strewn with fighting cats. On the terrace four separate duels had the lady shouting from her bedroom window. Rita and Maria were proving more than a match for Dancer when reinforcements arrived from the Monastery and he could regain his composure. The shes bolted.

'Them shes givin' you bother?' Skiffle smirked.

'Eat maggots, Frog-gob,' Dancer snarled and Skiffle's deep chuckle provoked one of Slippery Jim's woodpecker laughs.

Running for the summerhouse roof and Lucy, Ben was confronted by Boomer and Skiffle. Leaping higher than the grass he saw Lucy cowering before Smiley but was dragged to the ground before he could do anything. Boomer's grip on his back leg was like a gin trap. Jackknifing, he savaged the white and ginger patched tom but Boomer took it all on his shoulders and carved wounds above Ben's eyes. Blinded with blood Ben tried to dodge the strikes, his whole being straining towards Lucy.

But Lucy was gone and Smiley was after her.

'Where you running to, pretty?' he sang. 'You can't run from your own shadow. C'mon, c'mon. Ain't I good enough for you? Ain't I the tom? Take it easy. I'll be good to you. Smiley will take care of you.'

She landed awkwardly in Winner Hill Road and Smiley laughed as he dropped onto the pavement a couple of yards behind her.

'So, where do we go from here?' he teased. 'C'mon. The garden and everything in it's ours. You are ours. When Skeets gets hold of Silver he'll murder him. Your Silver is blowfly meat.'

But Lucy could only think of Ben and the unborn kittens. She hissed at Smiley and slowly backed off, the hair rigid on her spine and her back humped.

'Don't be frightened, sweetie,' Smiley crooned. 'Smiley is good to shes. C'mon, c'mon.'

Parked two gardens away down the road was a navy-blue furniture van. The back doors were open and the ramp was down. All the bits and pieces had been loaded save one armchair which the foreman had set aside for his teabreak.

'OK, run,' Smiley laughed, pursuing her along the pavement. 'I like games. But you ain't goin' nowhere, sweetie. You're mine!'

The men were halfway down the garden path with the armchair when she scampered up the ramp and squeezed under a sideboard amongst the jumble of furniture. Smiley swore and hesitated, but the men were at the gate now and the foreman was coughing on his cigarette. Smiley swore again and returned to the battle.

The armchair was slotted home between the dining room table and the sideboard, the ramp was raised and bolted into place and the doors were closed with a bang.

Lucy lay trembling in the blackness. Then the engine started and the van moved off.

Ben and Sam finished up on the pigeon loft in Winner Hill Road and were joined a little later by Parson and Scrumpy. All were tattered and bloody.

'Have you seen Lucy?' Ben asked.

No one had.

'Maybe she's with Silver,' Sam said. 'I saw him and Scarnose fighting off some Crazies while Rita and Maria and the rest of the shes went down over the gardens towards the road where you get your fish scrounge, Ben.'

'Yeah,' said Scrumpy. 'She'll be with them. What we gonna do now?'

'Stop them Crazies from following the shes,' said Sam. 'If they get to Dolly's place the kittens are finished.'

The four toms trotted to the black and white house, Dan y Craig, opposite Maylands. The back garden fell to some steep wasteland, where old houses had once stood, and Winner Street at the parking lots near the Golden Lily takeaway. A group of Shadows jumped onto the pavement below Maylands and faced the four, yelling their challenges across the road. Smiley was bristling with rage and frustration but Squib was in no hurry to tackle the tom whose eyes blazed from his bandit mask. A man with a slight limp came out of Dan y Craig and seeing Scrumpy's pitiful state and old Sam crouching in the gutter angrily scattered the Shadows. Smiley, Boomer and Chips climbed the wall back into Maylands and Slippery Jim, Skiffle and City ran up Monastery Road.

'Let's go,' Sam said, dashing down the path beside Dan y Craig.

'But Lucy,' Ben cried.

'She'll be with Silver and the others,' Parson said, barging him in the rear. 'Go on, run.'

Ben knew it was a mistake but he went out of blood-commitment to his kin.

'Lucy,' he mewled, but Lucy was travelling away from

Paignton along Totnes Road in a juddering noisy gloom
that terrified her.

13

Lucy Alone

The air became warm and sticky and the sky overcast. Swifts were screaming low over the rooftops of Torbay and the cats felt the approaching storm before the rain fell. A rumble of thunder above the darkening sea was followed by the first drops. Soon the deluge was hissing into the shrubberies of Maylands and drumming on the summerhouse roof.

Skeets emerged from one of his fits to collect his senses and consider the situation. He lay on the summerhouse settee with the Shadows at his feet. As the rain eased, the sky brightened and eventually the toms went out into the garden.

'When the red, red robin . . .' Skeets began, only to break off and add pensively, 'D'you know, we're actually walking through my dream? Doesn't that blow your mind? It's the ultimate green scent high.'

He walked across the lawn and raindrops beaded his fur and whiskers.

'This was Silver's place. In my head he sits on that roof there and stares out over the town to the water and the sky. Already I feel better. Come on – let's really make this our home patch!'

The afternoon sun behind the houses touched the Winner Hill side of the lawn and the hedges and trees. The toms ran into it, blotting out the scent of Silver's gang with their urine, whooping and yarooling in an orgy of macho pride. They scratched up earth and grass and savaged flowers. They chased each other round the bird-bath and sundial and Slippery Jim got onto the head of Sir Francis Drake which he casually sprayed. Another shower did not dampen their enthusiasm or wash away the pungence. They dashed up the drive and marked the boundaries of Maylands, flying at any domestic cats unlucky enough to stray into their celebration. Then they gathered at the walnut tree and sank their claws into the bark, rising on hindlegs in a noisy scrum.

'But we still aren't thirteen,' Smiley observed.

'No matter,' Skeets said indulgently. 'That'll take care of itself. Whatever it is that's looking after me will look after that.'

Slippery Jim, Dancer and City glanced at each other but feeling Smiley's eyes on them returned to the scratching post.

'Tonight we're gonna find this Silver and finish him,' Skeets said.

They had paraded back to the summerhouse and he was sitting imperiously on the roof looking down on the Shadows.

'I want him crippled and broken. The dream will be perfect when he's finished. It must end and begin here.'

The next heavy shower sent them scampering for the interior of the summerhouse and the tantalising smells of the shes.

'Don't fret,' Skeets said, and City wondered why his smile never reached his eyes. 'We get Silver and we get the shes. We get the lot.'

Then they slept until dusk. The light from the french windows fell across the terrace and the recluse was calling the clan to supper. Standing at the broken window of the summerhouse Smiley could smell food.

'It's got to be their scrounge,' he said.

'So let's collect,' said Skeets.

Wet and bedraggled they crept up the rockery and watched the lady dolloping food from tins onto dishes. Light glinted in the ferals' eyes but they were hungry and edged forward when the lady retreated to her chair.

'You are shy tonight,' she murmured. But these weren't 'her' cats and for a moment she was bewildered.

'Where is Snowball and the old one with the long grey

83

fur? Where's the frisky black and white one and his Dick Turpin mask? And where's my lovely little tabby she?'

City prostrated himself at her feet and licked the fingers she extended.

'There, there. You're lovely, too. Are you friends of my cats? I'll get some more food. I wouldn't want any of you to go without.'

'This is the place,' City purred when the french windows had been closed and the downstairs lights turned off.

'And Skeets is The Cat,' said the sandy and white patched tom, Reekin.

'Yeah,' Skiffle agreed, shaking his head. 'This is the end of the rainbow.'

Then it was night and Skeets watched the next shower run in from the sea and clouds cover the stars.

'Naow, Silver,' he suddenly wailed, burying his claws in Reekin's neck. 'Naow. Naow,' and his cold yellow eyes were on Dancer.

'Take it easy, Skeets,' Reekin mewled. 'Take it easy.'

'But the white tom's not here, Skeets,' Dancer said placatingly.

'Yes, yes of course,' Skeets sighed, releasing Reekin and studying his claws before sheathing them. 'Yesssssssss. And I'm here in his place, in my dream. But where is he? Where?' His voice rose.

'He ran off,' Slippery Jim said and the others groaned at his stupidity. 'Well, I mean,' Slippery Jim fumbled on, 'I mean – who wants to stand up to Skeets, hey? Who?'

Skeets screamed and Slippery Jim shrank from him.

'Some of you go and find me a Silver. When the streets are quiet go and get the shes. Give them aggravation. Have fun but whatever you do bring me the white tom.'

Then he smiled and said softly, 'Me and City will go and find a warm little four-legged thing to play the Go-and-come-back game. Yesssss.'

The squall hit the garden but Smiley and four Shadows were already squeezing through the hedge to drop into Winner Hill Road.

'This way,' Smiley said, shaking the rain from his eyes.

The furniture van cruised through the afternoon along the Devon roads and lanes heading for Tavistock, and when Lucy's fear had subsided she explored her new environment. The unborn kittens' activity added to her restlessness. But not in here, she thought. Please, not here, not here. Oh Ben. Misery drove her to the armchair, where she buried her face in her paws.

Rain beat against the van and it bumped and lurched until suddenly it came to a halt and the engine was turned off. Lucy flattened herself beneath the sideboard.

Presently the back was opened and the men began to move the furniture out and into the bungalow. When they were gone Lucy made her escape and came down a short drive onto the Tavistock-Two Bridges Road. Rain had fallen heavily and traffic sizzled by, throwing up spray which made her recoil. She sat on the grass verge, close to the hedge, sniffing the rain of the approaching shower. Her whole being responded to the pull of home. It was as powerful as water tugging at a dowser's rod and the source of this spiritual magnetism was the east. It was the Heart Place speaking directly to the heart and Lucy set off towards Dartmoor full of optimism, even though the burden of unborn life she carried was constantly making itself felt.

The evening, the traffic and the rain, and the strangeness of the place with its few houses and the countryside spreading before her to the sky, were alarming. Dusty puddles were skirted but great clouds swelled and billowed above the high ground and each downpour released the scent of dark green foliage. The cattle crying through the rain startled her, but the sound belonged to the natural world like the birdsong and the rush of wind in the trees. Then a numbing surge of unhappiness brought her up sharp and she stood at the roadside crying, 'Ben. I want Ben.' Only the kittens moving in her womb could eclipse her sorrow. She was close to giving birth and their welfare was uppermost in her mind. Instinct was taking over.

Drenched by the downpour, she came past Lodge Wood and on to the crossroads to begin the long haul up Pork Hill. The shower swept by and the darkness faded, with the sky brightening to blue. The sun shone on Whitchurch Common and the granite of Cox Tor was holding it like a beacon.

She gingerly crossed the cattle grid at the top of Pork Hill. On the right was a carpark and half a dozen cars lined up at the best vantage point for views over the Tamar valley to Cornwall. Lucy trotted among the vehicles and nosed out part of a discarded corned beef roll which she ate greedily. Other scraps of food lay close to the litter bin.

Back at the roadside a coach roared by, drenching her in spray. She sneezed and the kittens kicked. Mistrust of the great open place and its creatures swelled to fear, but she ran on, sloshing over the waterlogged turf and crouching when a convoy of military vehicles overtook her. Ahead yet another shower was falling. This is Cloud Country, she thought. This is where the rain comes from.

Beyond the carpark were huge horizons, although the sun had vanished from the common. Dark vertical drifts of rain sailed over Cox Tor and Middle Staple Tor and all at once her condition and plight were pressing heavily on her spirit.

The road wound downhill past the stone quarry to the Dartmoor Inn and Lucy knew her time was close. The pub lights were on and people were standing with drinks in the doorway watching the showers build up and advance. But no one saw the little rain-spiked tabby dash around the back of the building with an air of quiet desperation.

Lucy ran to the disused shed and entered through a missing panel in the door. The interior was dark and dry and for a she in labour the pile of sacks in a corner behind a stack of old wooden crates was a godsend. She was purring as she trod the sacks into a nest. Rain pattered on the roof before hammering down to remind her of happier times in Maylands' summerhouse.

'Oh Ben,' she said sadly.

Three black and white kittens were born and Lucy licked each of them clean and bit the umbilical cord before eating the birth sac and the afterbirth. When it was all over she settled down to some serious grooming while the kittens lay within her purring warmth, drawing milk from her nipples.

By the time she was ready for sleep Lucy was lost in maternal bliss.

Driven by hunger she appeared at the back door of the inn and cried for food. Then after two successful visits, the woman followed her to the shed and the nest of kittens was discovered. But her behaviour told the people she was a feral cat. She refused to be stroked, and her ears were always laid back and she would crouch warily even when receiving scraps.

So it was decided to leave her alone although food, milk and water were regularly put outside the shed door. Sometimes the scraps were taken by the fox that had her lair in Longash Wood above the nearby River Walkham. Despite her smallness Lucy showed no fear of the larger animal whenever their paths crossed. The vixen had cubs and was bold in her efforts to feed them. At dusk she was a frequent visitor to the back of The Dartmoor Inn.

Lucy was never away for long. Apart from pub scrounge the moor behind the inn yielded mice, voles and young rabbits, but while her young were blind she spent most of the time suckling and grooming them. Yet behind the joys and anxieties of motherhood she would suddenly feel the tug of home and ache for Ben and the old places.

14

Exodus

She wasn't in the churchyard. Ben trotted between the headstones, calling her in deep cries until Silver appeared at his side. The rain drove into their eyes and they blinked and shook their heads so hard their ears clacked. The coldness in Ben's heart was pumped out with every beat into his limbs. His legs felt heavy and weak and his body was an ache of misery.

'You'll be returning to the garden,' Silver said. It was a statement of fact.

'Yes, and if she's there I'll bring her back here.'

'Good luck, Ben.'

Luck, Ben thought, loping up Church Street into Winner Street. The car takes you by surprise and you're lost to the world. You eat the meat near the chicken run and it kills you. The dog's teeth close on your throat. You get ill and weak and fade away. Your luck runs out and you're gone.

He walked under the chain at the parking lots and climbed up through the walls and vegetation to the garden of Dan y Craig. Then, with the wind sweeping the rain along Winner Hill Road, he hauled himself up the wall into the shrubbery by the bust of Sir Francis Drake.

Maylands reeked of alien tomcat. The shower which was tailing away to let in the sun once more had not diluted the pungency. Stealthily he approached the summerhouse where the smell was strongest, and sprang onto the window ledge in a great, silent leap. She was not among the sprawl of sleeping toms. His nose confirmed it.

Then he ranged about the garden before running up Monastery Road to the estate and another fruitless search.

The strays and pets he met acknowledged him but he didn't linger. Finally he returned along Winner Hill Road and down to the building site. A fierce shower beat against the hoarding until the sun and silence returned. Trixy came to him as his low cries rang over the gardens. Cars in the Winner Street narrows passed with little roars of noise.

'She isn't here, Ben,' Trixy said. 'Look,' he added when Ben's head dropped, 'she's probably hiding somewhere safe. Maybe she went somewhere new but she'll come back.'

'Yeah, OK – that's it,' Ben grunted. 'If you see her, tell her we're at Dolly's place. But if we're gone when she comes, tell her to stay there and wait for me. Dolly will shelter her. You do that, hey, Trixy?'

The siamese nodded and they touched noses before Ben ran swiftly down the Winner Street bottleneck.

Dusk gathered and the showers continued to ghost across the bay. Lights were bright then blurred and the largest and brightest flashed on Berry Head.

As soon as it was dark, the Maylands' cats assembled at the great stone cross in the Parish Churchyard and Silver addressed them.

'We'll be back,' he said. 'But now the old ones and kittens must be taken to safety.'

'Where?' Mellow asked.

'We'll find a place if we travel towards the flashing light.'

'To Button's place?' Mellow sneered.

'Maybe. If you don't like it go your own way.'

'And if you think it's OK now, shut your gob,' Rita growled.

'All of you can stay here,' Dolly said. 'You're welcome. There's bags of room.'

'We need somewhere the Crazies don't know about,' said Silver. 'Look what they did to Jo-Joe's cats up the wood.'

'Let's go – please,' Louise said, standing protectively over her brood.

'I'll lead with Scarnose and Scrumpy,' said Silver. 'Shes and kittens in the middle and Ben and the others bringing up the rear. Parson, you and Rainbow drag along behind and keep your eyes open and your noses busy. If we get separated, meet on Fancy's patch.'

'I could make my own way if you left me a young tom to do the guiding,' said Jessie.

'No, Mother,' Silver said. 'We go together. We are family, all of us,' he added, gazing around at the strays. 'All of us are family now.'

'That's great news,' Scarnose laughed. 'Me and my new brothers and sisters are gonna get roughed up together. Thanks, Silver.'

It was good to depart with tails up, Silver thought. Scarnose was turning out to be the sort of big-hearted street fighter any gang would welcome into its ranks. Sam was impressed and Ben was grinning despite his heartache.

'Button went to the flashing light,' Silver told Ben as they strode shoulder to shoulder to the iron gate on the south side of the churchyard. Rain gusted down and was spent before the cats trotted into Bishop's Place beside the tall sandstone walls and Coverdale Tower.

Silver raised his voice. 'Button found somewhere peaceful by the flashing light, didn't he, Mother?'

'Yes,' said Jessie, wobbling slightly. 'Plenty of cover, plenty of food. Are we going there?'

'Perhaps. Maybe it's too far for you.'

'We'll see,' Jessie said. 'Maybe we'll find somewhere on the way. Who knows? Between sunset and sunrise things are exciting. You bump into them or they grab you.'

'And I told Dolly to keep Lucy with her if she shows up, Ben,' Silver said. 'She'll be OK. When we're settled you can go back for her.'

Ben nodded and fought the need to reveal his innermost feelings in a long maraowl of distress. Where was she in this cool, rainswept night with the shadows full of hooks and the moon gone from the sky?

'Let's go, then,' Silver said, reading his thoughts.

The kittens mewed as they dangled from the mouths of the shes who trailed behind Jessie down Bishop's Place. The cats were strung out in untidy single file. They kept to the shadows wherever it was possible, relying on the toms in front and behind to concentrate on danger. Now and then a kitten squirmed and cried out.

The wet night had kept most holidaymakers off the streets, and the seafront pubs were crowded. The gang crossed Palace Avenue in front of the cenotaph and came along the pavement to New Street. Ben groaned, for he felt the exodus was a betrayal of his love for Lucy. The night was empty but he splashed through the puddles without a backward glance although his heart was breaking.

Silver brought them past the Rates Office and over Totnes Road into Midvale Road by St Hilary's School of English. Rain pelted down and they pressed against the wall until the worst was over. Then they hid under a parked car while a couple of men smelling of beer passed. Parson and Rainbow were fifty yards behind, checking to look back for pursuit.

'It's a good night for it,' Sam said.

They entered Curledge Street and gave Jessie a breather in the yard of Austin's Sale Room.

'There's not a lot of scent on the air,' the old tom sighed and his gut gurgled. 'I'm bloody hungry, Ben.'

At the junction of Curledge Street and Dartmouth Road they met a sporadic flow of cars.

'Me and Scarnose'll cross first, then we'll call you when it's safe,' Silver said. 'We'll shout out your name and you come running.'

'I won't,' said Jessie.

'Totter across in your own time, Mother,' Silver smiled.

The wet, stony smell of the road lifted on the spray of passing cars and the gang held their breath until Jessie had meandered through it onto the opposite pavement. In

91

twos and threes the rest of the tribe joined her in the narrow alley that linked Dartmouth Road to Station Lane. A grey pet tom met them head on under the railway embankment by the signal box and was questioned by Silver. Then the gang turned left at Sands Road, came over the railway crossing and walked the pavement towards the sea. At St Andrew's Church they heard Parson's yarool of alarm and stopped. Moments later Parson and Rainbow bounded up to Silver.

'The Crazies are coming,' Parson said. 'They're sniffing around in the alley where you stopped – five of them. One of you marked the wall.'

'It was me,' Sam confessed. 'I did it out of habit. I'm sorry.'

'Not your fault,' said Silver.

'I should bite my own ass for being so stupid,' Sam growled.

'I could do it for you,' Scrumpy offered.

'Cut the yap and get the shes into the garden over there,' and Silver nodded at the churchyard. 'Move them quickly. We haven't much time. Scarnose, you and a couple of others go scent mark all the way down the road. When you catch sight of the Crazies, hide. Don't come out till you see us.'

Louise set down her kitten. 'And us, Silver? These kittens and old Jess?'

'You stay here,' Silver said, leading them up the church path to the laurel bushes beside the hall. 'Get down on the dry leaves and keep those kittens quiet. Lie on their heads if necessary. One squeak out of them and the Crazies will have you.'

Pepper and Lucky lowered their eyes.

'And what do we do?' Ben said, his blood boiling.

Silver smiled. 'We run for the salt water and Fancy's patch.'

'And?'

'Fancy's mob will join us.'

'But we can't be sure of that,' said Mellow.

'We can't be sure we'll wake up when we go to sleep,' said Sam. 'We can't be sure night will turn into day.'

The toms yawned and caught some of the new shower on their tongues. Heavy drops smacked on the laurel leaves and flower beds, filling the night with dark summer smells.

The running shes and toms scrambled over the wall into Sands Road.

'Show yourselves,' Silver cried. 'Cross over and go with the pavement.'

'Bloody running away,' Rita fumed.

'Yeah,' said Scarnose. 'Because we don't want to end up like Button.'

'You look like Button already,' she snapped back.

'And you look like Button's mother.'

'Who the hell's she?'

'She got run down by a car when I was young,' Scarnose laughed.

'Funny – yeah!' Rita growled. 'You're a comedian, Scarnose. Maybe you'd like a matching scar on your ass.'

Ben glanced back. A posse of small dark shapes was closing on them.

They galloped past the small hotels and guest houses, startling a group of old age pensioners returning from a seafront pub singsong. The showery spell was over and the sky from Roundham Head to the horizon was an immensity of stars. Swinging right at the bottom of Sands Road the Maylands gang weaved in and out of more holidaymakers and shot over the wall into the grounds of Torbay Gentlemen's Club.

'Under here,' cried Scarnose's voice and the cats crept under the parked cars. The club windows laid their rectangles of light on the ground.

But leading the chase, Smiley had seen the last of the fugitives leaping the wall and his smile became gleeful.

'What do they call a pile of Mousebits, Squib?' he chuckled.

'Tell me.'

'Silver's mob,' came the reply and Slippery Jim loosed his lunatic yaffle.

One by one the Shadows jumped onto the wall and sat facing the carpark. The street behind them was quiet because of the rain; and it was an hour till the pubs closed.

'Do we have to come and hunt you out like the mice you are?' Smiley said, addressing the parking lot.

'Come down and lose part of your face,' said Silver.

'That's a fair offer from a cat who's lost his brains and has less guts than a sucked egg,' Smiley said.

The ritual exchange of insults amazed Ben. He was itching to claw flesh, and when Dancer strutted close to his hiding place he was out and into action before the Shadow could unsheath his hooks. The waraow of pain and surprise fired the rest of the gang into a display of aggression which amused the heavies each side of Smiley. Parson, Scrumpy and Mellow were savaged by Boomer and Squib, and Slippery Jim tore open Rainbow's muzzle as she and Rita leapt out of the eyeballing. Only Ben, Scarnose and Silver held their ground with Smiley and Dancer reluctant to take on the white tom.

Ben displayed a viciousness that brought Dancer to the crouching, submissive position but it did not save him and he was badly cut about the face. Then Smiley attacked Silver and Scarnose was caught by Boomer as he tried to help the shes.

Sensing the initiative was lost Silver turned and clawed Boomer's haunches, swivelled and flailed one of Smiley's ears with a full set of hooks.

'Run,' he cried. 'Follow me. Now. Naow!'

Ben and Scarnose fought a brief delaying action while the others poured out of the grounds onto the deserted prom and through the arch to the harbour.

'Not that way,' Silver bawled as Pepper broke to the left at the pleasure boat stands.

They scampered up the slope past the lavatories and along the pavement opposite The New Pier Inn. The noise of the customers singing in the music lounge flattened their ears to their skulls. On the seaward side beyond the railings and wire netting boats bobbed at their moorings in the harbour.

Overtaking Ben, Dancer realised he had been allowed to do so. He had a glimpse of mad blue eyes before his cheek was torn open from the corner of his mouth to his ear.

The Maylands cats streaked on with tamarisks and garden benches on the right and the black waters of the harbour down below the crag to the left. Bearing left they ran past the aquarium and Paignton Yacht Club to the dinghies on the hard outside Browse Brothers Shellfish Factory.

Smiley brought his Shadows to heel in front of the aquarium and watched the Maylands cats taking up positions on open ground.

'Well?' Slippery Jim said, his tail lashing.

'You really wanna make the decisions, you old she?' Smiley growled. 'I sniff out a situation before committing myself to hooks.'

'Smiley's right,' said Dancer. 'This is the patch of Fancy. Him and his lot did me back along. Then the tom who just opened up my face went and nursed me back to health. It's nuts.'

'Life's full of little unexpected twists, ain't it?' Slippery Jim chuckled and Dancer glared at him.

'We don't wanna bite off more than we can chew,' Smiley murmured.

'They got three real heavies at the most,' Boomer said. 'Silver, the ginger stray and the black and white hardcase who gave Dancer aggravation. The rest are Mouths-on-legs and shes.'

'Don't piss on the shes,' Smiley said. 'Some of them are capable of takin' out your eyes, especially if they've got kittens.'

'But we're on top,' Slippery Jim said. 'I reckon Skeets would be down there showing them his hooks.'

'You wanna put that to him if we slip up?' Smiley said.

'They're on the run,' said Slippery Jim. 'We always hit cats on the run. It's the Shadows' way.'

Smiley licked his lips, wondering why his gut was contradicting his brain.

'OK,' he muttered, and he walked casually down towards the shellfish factory with his toms behind him, tails scything arcs of menace. But when they reached Harbour Sports they became aware of three cats walking parallel to them among the craft on the quay. Smiley halted. His instinct hadn't betrayed him after all, and he scowled at Slippery Jim whose hair was stiffening. But Smiley could use words like the best toms used hooks.

'Listen,' he crooned. 'There is aggravation and there is violence so black it blows your mind. We trade in that special thing. You wanna sample some of it, walk over here.'

'Yeah,' Squib snarled. 'C'mon. Come and lose your eyes.'

The leader of the harbour ferals was the happy-go-lucky grey and white patched tom, Fancy. His mob lived on scrounge from the shellfish factory and the Harbour Lights Restaurant. They were skilled ratters and grabbed seagull fledglings despite the efforts of dive-bombing parent birds.

Fancy stepped out of the shadow of a motor cruiser and paused to groom the inside of a forepaw.

'You with Silver?' he said between licks.

'We're after Silver,' Smiley replied.

'You're the mob that took his patch?'

'So what's it to you?'

'Silver's done me a favour or two.'

'And you want a share of his war?'

'Maybe.' Fancy grinned as he recognised Dancer. 'How's things, Blacky?' he crowed. 'Come for another working over?'

Dancer hissed at him but Fancy was not impressed.

'Tut tut,' he said. 'Here we are, bargaining, and you lose your temper. Maybe I oughta present you with a set of hooks.'

'Maybe I oughta – '

'Shut your mouth, Dancer,' Smiley said.

96

'Listen,' Fancy continued, as though they had been interrupted by nothing more than the buzzing of a fly. 'I put it to you straight. You're on my patch, uninvited. You offer aggro when I'm short of four good warriors. They're away after scrounge. So, do you leave still wearing your tails or do I and my brothers here join up with Silver's mob and make things difficult for you? That's the situation.'

'And you're a reasonable tom,' said Smiley, recognising the chance to retreat with dignity. 'OK. We leave.'

When reports of the episode reached Skeets it would swing things in his favour. If they got a thirteenth Shadow, he reflected, maybe their luck would change. Why was it a maybe world? They had Silver's patch but the white tom was still on the loose and he had some rough friends. Yes, a tactical retreat was wise and Fancy had given him a street fighter's way out. This Fancy would make a good number thirteen. The real problem, Smiley mused, was getting Silver back to the garden. It needed another of those Maybes to swing things for them.

The Shadows walked away and the Maylands gang cheered, but Fancy was bristling when he confronted Silver.

'Is this polite?' he said. 'Is this an act of friendship? Do I look as if I want Crazies hanging about my patch? Silver – is this the act of a blood brother?'

And unable to keep up the pretence of anger he burst out laughing.

'Old friend,' Silver chuckled. 'How did you manage it? It was great. You were great.'

The two toms met nose to nose and rubbed the length of their bodies together in an exchange of scents.

'They may be crazy,' Fancy said, 'but they're about as streetwise as blind kittens.'

'You underestimate your presence,' said Silver. 'You look like a tom no cat in his right mind would want to mix it with.'

'Yeah, and these cats *aren't* in their right mind,' Fancy grinned. 'But you are welcome here, Silver. I'm sorry you got problems, and I'm sorry them Crazies have got your patch. You want help and we'll give it. Bring in your shes and kittens. My patch is your patch. Take whatever scrounge you require.'

'You hear this?' Silver cried to his followers. 'You hear this tom speaking from the heart? C'mon. Come forward and pay your respects. This is no ordinary cat.'

'Yeah, well, let's not go over the top,' Fancy purred but he accepted the gestures of gratitude and allegiance from Silver's ferals. The strays maintained a respectful silence and distance.

'And another thing, Silver old buddy,' Fancy said later as they shared the tasty scrounge outside the Harbour Lights Restaurant. 'This Skeets and his heavies can be taken and I'm the cat to do it. My toms have stoneheads and hooks like – like – well, there ain't no hooks like ours. So let this Skeets come. We've done one of his Crazies and seen off the rest. So let him come.'

Ben raised his head from the food bowl and looked at the honest boastful creature beside him. The words had such a hollow ring. Then he shivered and gazed at the stars and wondered if they were gleaming in Lucy's eyes.

'Why wait for Skeets to come?' he said. 'Is your heart really in this running, Silver? The good life is in the garden and the streets we know. The flashing light was the end of Button's dream. He went looking for something but he didn't find it and he always came back to us. I would like to return and fight for our patch. That would surprise Skeets. He expected us to run. But maybe you scare him. Maybe the last thing he wanted was one final rumble.'

The three toms strolled along the quay and jumped onto the sea wall that overlooked the bay. They sat in a row grooming themselves and watching the lights of Torquay twinkling in the clear night air.

'Ben's right,' said Fancy. 'You got everything on your patch – scrounge, shelter, status, the lot. You can't just chuck it away without a fight. Anyway, this Skeets and his Crazies will come after you. If you gotta fight, do it on the turf you know.'

98

Silver nodded. Over the water the lights winked and danced and just for a moment he was a kitten again, curling into his mother's warmth.

'Look,' Fancy went on. 'Me and my toms'll help. We'll throw in our hooks and our muscle. Then we choose our time and bite ass.'

'And you agree, Ben?' Silver said.

'Yeah, I like it. Dump the shes with Louise and the others and collect them after we've taken the garden.'

'When?'

'Tonight. Now.'

'*Waraow*,' Fancy cried, throwing back his head and closing his eyes.

'OK, then,' Silver smiled. 'The Crazies are divided. Smiley's lot are lying up close by, waiting to see where we'll go tomorrow and Skeets is probably dozing on my roof. Round up the mob, Ben. How many toms can you count on, Fancy?'

'Four, including me.'

'I thought there were seven of you,' said Ben. 'You told Smiley back there you were short of four warriors.'

'But I meant one,' Fancy chuckled. 'I tell lies, Ben, when it suits me. Maybe I was counting my shes, too. But they won't be coming. I need some cats to stay here and look after the patch. Strays try to move in all the time, so you gotta show muscle.'

They returned to the sheds by the Shellfish Factory and broke the news to the rest of the gang.

'Now that's how it should be,' said Scarnose, although Sam was less enthusiastic.

'We could be playing into Skeets' hooks,' he said. 'If I were you, Silver, I'd put a lot of darkness between me and the Shadows.'

'He ain't you,' Rita crowed. 'Them Crazies had better watch their eyes when I get among them.'

'How can they watch their eyes?' Scarnose said. 'How can you watch things you see with?'

'If one's out on the floor the other one can watch it,

stupid.' And Rita shot her hooks. 'I ain't staying with the pretties doin' nothing. I'm fightin'.'

'OK, listen,' said Silver.

But all they could hear was the slap of waves on the hulls of the moored vessels and water sliding up and gurgling down the nearby slipway.

'What?' Rainbow whispered.

'The town's dead,' Silver smiled. 'Let's go.'

Scrumpy and Rainbow glanced nervously at each other but followed Silver up towards the street lights.

15

With the Sea Mist

Smiley and his toms were stalking on Roundham Head when Silver and Fancy moved their cats off the harbour-side. They had agreed to leave Louise's group at St Andrew's Church although Fancy had no doubts about the result of the coming conflict. He was an animal who took everything life flung at him with little complaint.

A mist rolled in from the sea and the Three Towns vanished. The cats ran through it over the wet streets, crouching whenever a car sent the long beams of its head-lights into the smoking gloom. Loneliness hit Ben and his head dropped. She wasn't part of the night that swirled around him. It was as if his heart had been cut out.

'Bear up,' Silver whispered, bumping gently against him.

'I must look in at Dolly's patch,' Ben said. 'I gotta know one way or the other.'

The mist was thicker now. It billowed among the houses and between the metal bars of the Parish Church gate at the head of Church Lane. The cats saw Ben race into the graveyard while they trotted to the lychgate to wait for him. Lucy's scent was not on the mist and although he called her repeatedly he knew she wasn't there.

'I hab'n seen her,' said Dolly's tired voice.

'If you do,' Ben cried, 'tell her we're at the garden again.'

No Lucy. Transfixed with misery he stood in the grass among the headstones and loosed one clear, long miaow of sorrow. Why were there trees and flowers and other cats and no Lucy? The others gazed at him but said nothing. Many things went beyond words.

They ran on, crowding around him to blanket his distress, but by the time they had left Church Street to cross Winner Street he had mastered his unhappiness and undergone a change of mood. They sat on the pavement before the Pocket Book Shop waiting for Silver to take control.

'Me and Scarnose and you lot,' he nodded at a handful of toms and shes, 'will go up through the steep place and the garden to the wall at the back of the shelter. Ben, Fancy and the rest had better go up the hill and over the hedge. When I yell you all come in and rumble. OK?'

'OK,' they chorused.

Was it the long dark of his street dream, Ben wondered as he led the way through the bottleneck and up Winner Hill Road. The mist had lent the night an opacity which he explored with his whiskers and nose. The dream of the running overlapped the dream of the street and he groaned. They were at the hedge and he was clawing up it to crouch there until Fancy and a couple of harbourside toms joined him. What happened didn't matter. If all the stars never shone again it wouldn't matter, if Lucy had gone from his life forever. He swallowed. Her image was stalking him and he laid his nose to the wet vegetation.

High above the mist, a jet airliner roared across the sky. It was one of those sounds he could never fathom. Was it some great bird calling as it flew by? Then Silver's cry set him running and rage choked him. He was grim as death when he came upon a Shadow on the edge of the bamboos. It was the dirty grey and white patched Scrag who had half an ear missing and walked with a slight limp, having been bitten on the left hindleg by an alsatian.

Cats glided past Ben in search of other Shadows. Only Rita remained at his shoulder, growling her anxiety for action.

Scrag raised his hair, his back and his spiky tail. His good ear began to fold back at the tip and his whiskers twitched forward. In the fog he was a daunting creature but Ben saw him merely as something standing between himself and Skeets.

'Wot you up to?' Scrag growled. 'You tired of livin',

hey? This is Skeets' patch. You wanna lose your tail and everything you got dangling under it? You wanna – '

And Ben broke all the rules. He too was swollen and spiked with madness but he came crabwise through the eyeballing, his breath exploding from his nostrils. Scrag's facial expression changed instantly but it was too late to placate the black and white tom. They grappled and there was a snick of claws on Scrag's nose followed by his sneeze and cursing which soared to a screech when Ben tore at his head, ripping out little chunks of fur and flesh. A moment later the spitting, growling and yarooling were over and Scrag broke to fly for the hedge with Rita fastened to his hindquarters. She did more damage before Scrag turned and cuffed her off and went through the hedge.

Ben and Rita ran on and found Fancy and Scrumpy questioning City on the terrace. His fleabitten agitation touched Ben. He looked what he was – an old, worn-out, underfed, neglected stray. Fancy had roughed him up and he crouched there with the blood from a wounded ear dribbling down the side of his head.

'You want some more?' Fancy growled, pacing forward in the mist.

'Yeah – like I want an ass full of wasps,' City groaned.

Ben smiled and said, 'He's had enough, Fancy.'

'OK, it's your patch,' Fancy said cheerfully and he went off in search of more violence.

'So you can be beaten,' Ben said, gazing without malice at City.

'Oh yes,' the old cat whispered. 'Some of your toms will win the odd scrap. It's the way it happens. You and Whitey and him who just done me over – cats like you can put it across the Scrags and Reekins and maybe even the Smileys. Then you come up against Skeets.'

'He's that good?'

'He's mad. OK, we're all a bit crazy but Skeets is really right over the top. He's on a violence high all the time.'

'Why d'you run with him?' asked Rita.

City shook his head. 'For the kicks. I was alone. I came

out of a big town by a big river so many summers ago I can't remember, and I picked up with Skeets who was walking towards the sunrise. Skeets meant regular scrounge and safety from other toms that wanted to test their hooks on old meat like me. The Shadows was company and I had a gut full of going it alone. When you're old and you ain't got friends, who will look after you when you're sick?'

'And you think Skeets will look after you like we look after Jess?' asked Ben.

'No, I was kiddin' myself. I knew that before I saw the way him and the rest behaved when Wayne choked on a bone.'

'Where is Skeets?'

'Stalking, talking to the darkness, killing something – who knows? He's just away. You find him tonight and he'll kill you. He's got one of his moods on him.'

'And the others?'

'In the shelter, I expect, and Bang is probably lying up round the corner at the back. What you gonna do with me?'

'Nothing. You can stay here if you like.'

'You mean it?'

'Yeah, he means it,' Rita said. 'Ben's all heart.'

The old tom stood up and stretched. 'It's a good way to end the journey,' he said. 'But go carefully, my friends. When Skeets gets all the Shadows together and they go into action there ain't no cats what can stop them.'

Ben left Rita with the old tom and crossed the lawn to the summerhouse. Silver, Scarnose, Fancy and the rest of the gang sat under the window.

'They're inside,' Scarnose whispered, but Ben's head was bobbing as he gauged the distance. After a shift of paws to attain perfect balance he sprang and touched the window ledge once before hurtling into the darkness beyond. Fancy and Scarnose both leapt together in their eagerness to follow him and became wedged in the gap.

'Stupid,' Fancy rasped, biting one of Scarnose's ears before they dropped back onto the lawn. Three Shadows landed among them and streaked off into the mist. Ben had scared them witless and now Silver's gang drove them up alongside the conifer hedge to the vegetable garden where Bang was yawning awake.

'What's up?' he cried, and found himself staring at Fancy's eyeballs.

There was no time to run and in any case the Shadows were in a blistering rage. This didn't happen to Skeets' toms! The mooncrooning wavered between the two gangs, creating a hullabaloo that woke the neighbourhood. But the mist hid everything. Erupting from a garaowl Silver smashed into the nearest Shadow. It was Bang the feral with a talent for removing any sort of dustbin lid. He was as mean as he was heavy and Silver couldn't drag him down. In fact, he might have done considerable damage to the white tom if Rita had not fastened herself to his face.

'Hey,' Skiffle growled. 'What sort of rumble is this?'

'Our sort,' Rita hissed.

Spluttering and snarling Bang extricated himself from Silver and Rita and scowled at them from the cabbages and stands of mallow. Insults roared from him like fireworks.

'You better dig a hole, Whitey, and get in among your bits. When we return you can kiss your tail goodbye.'

The cats stepped back from each other and became weird apparitions in the mist that curled and rolled around them. Fancy launched himself in a bodycurving pounce to land in front of Chips and leap onto the startled ebony self. All his hooks sunk into Chips' head and produced a wild screech of pain. Then Chips seemed to uncoil and Fancy was shaken off and slashed about the muzzle.

'Let's get out of here,' Scrag growled and the Shadows raced to the fence and clawed over it to tumble into the alley at the back of Bayview. Fancy and Scarnose were too wise to follow them.

'We won,' Scarnose grinned. 'We got our garden back.'

'And you think Skeets will give up now, do you?' Sam said.

105

'Who knows? We've seen off some of his heavies. They aren't that tough.'

'They are that tough,' said Silver. 'But we had too many hooks for them to handle. It'll be different when the others come back from Fancy's patch.'

'But we'll be ready,' said Scarnose.

'With more words,' Sam yawned.

'You can count on them coming back,' said City's voice from the mist behind them.

'Who asked you, House-toy?' Scarnose growled. 'I've seen more life in a pet tom with a collar and nothing swinging under his tail.'

'Let him speak,' said Ben. 'I told him he could join us. Fancy roughed him up.'

'He's not another Dancer, I hope,' Silver said pointedly.

'Who knows?' Ben was nettled and didn't try to disguise it. 'A tom is a tom. I can't get in their heads. I felt sorry for this one. He's a tired, lonely, old cat who just wants a bit of peace and quiet.'

'Well, he won't find a lot of that in this garden,' Sam sniffed.

'I don't want no hassle,' said City. 'If you say so I'll go.'

'Stay,' Ben said.

'Yes, stay,' said Silver. 'If you turn out to be OK you'll get your share of scrounge and shelter.'

'That's all I ask – a garden to sleep in, regular grub, a bit of a chat now and then with cats who won't suddenly turn on you like you was a bird or a mouse.'

'You wanna see some cool stalkin', old tom?' Rita called, and she trailed her body along the length of Scarnose. 'You gonna join me at the hedge by the shelter? I got the fastest hooks on the patch.'

'No thanks. I just want a kip,' City said and the toms chuckled.

'Come on, Belle,' Rita muttered. 'Let's mouse.'

'Want me to look after you?' Scarnose sniggered.

'Yeah,' Rita said, swaggering off under the cabbage

leaves. 'Me and Belle need you about as much as we need a bellyful of maggots.'

Scarnose licked first one forepaw then the other amid the laughter.

But there was no laughter on the parking lot outside the Lions' Club. Above Huccaby the sea mist thinned and the council estate stood in a clear starry sky. The moon shone down on the fleece of mist that covered all but the highest hills of Torbay.

'You gonna tell Skeets?' Bang asked Skiffle.

'Do I look as if I'm tired of the face I'm wearing?' Skiffle said.

They sat beside the yellow van.

'Whitey and his top toms aren't mugs,' said Bang.

'We could've handled them if Smiley and the others was with us,' said Scrag, and his pupils dilated as he caught a whiff of Skeets.

The huge sandy tom came sedately up through the trees and across the carpark.

'We're in the sky,' he announced, sniffing the mist and smiling up at the stars. 'We're above the clouds. But why aren't you in the garden?'

'Because Whitey's back,' said Chips in a strangled voice, like a cat being forced to eat a shrew.

Skeets stared at him.

'Back in the garden,' Bang added.

Skeets' eyes had narrowed and he was purring.

'We didn't stand a chance,' Bang continued. 'There was hundreds of 'em. They swarmed all over us. I dunno how we got away.'

'Yet you still have your tails,' Skeets murmured. 'And I see no obvious signs of wear and tear about your muzzles.'

Chips licked his lips and crouched.

'What did they do to Smiley?' Skeets said.

'Smiley wasn't there,' someone replied.

'Where was he?' Skeets demanded from a sepulchral boom.

'Lookin' for them who attacked us,' said Bang. 'They

must've doubled back and they've got friends – hard friends.'

Skeets turned away and laughed. 'It's perfect,' he said softly. 'The white one had to come back because he's always there in my dream, always looking out over the houses to the water and the sky. I had to bring him back or it'll be his dream. Smiley's little chase was part of the plan. You see, Silver could've vanished but he would remain in the dream forever. I had to get him back. I have to see him broken before the dream is mine alone.'

He laughed and began to sing the Red Robin song.

'Do we take them tonight?' Bang asked. His fur was damp with sweat and he wasn't fully convinced Skeets had let them off the hook.

'No, Bang. We don't. We don't. Silver has done us a favour. Don't you understand? We don't have to traipse around looking for him now. He is down the road waiting for the chop. I can have him when I choose. One night he'll walk into me and – '

He raised a paw and unsheathed his claws.

'It was a mistake to attack the garden. I should have known Silver would run. No one wants to tangle with Skeets. Now I can hang about giving him aggravation until I get the opportunity to pick him off.'

'Sounds fun,' Chips chuckled. 'Like the old game and you in control. It's real smart. Brilliant.'

'As always, Chips,' Skeets smiled and whipping round he bit Bang on the hindleg and playfully crunched bone. Then he sat bolt upright.

'No more unfortunate blunders, my sons. This game will be a creep about after dark – the threat followed by the hooks. We'll be the Shadows in the shadows and we'll take them on, one at a time, when it suits us. And we mustn't neglect the shes. They're all back now, all available.'

'We can have fun with them,' Chips grinned.

Skeets' teeth closed and he sang, 'There'll be no more sobbin' . . . when he starts throbbin' his own sweet song . . .'

108

'City's gone over to Silver,' Bang gabbled, hoping he had chosen the right moment.

'It doesn't matter. City is nothing, Bang. One night he'll end up on my hooks or Smiley's hooks. For him a garrg job was inevitable.'

'Do we look around for a couple more toms to make up the magic thirteen?' Scrag said.

'Of course. But first of all you go and collect Smiley.'

'But I dunno where he is,' said Scrag.

'Excuses, excuses. Use your initiative, Scrag, and don't come back without him unless you want to join City as a cat about to lose sight of tomorrow.'

16

Games

Making his way back to the harbour, Fancy called in at St Andrew's Church and broke the good news to the shes, and after a brief discussion they decided there was enough night left to cover their return to Maylands. The mist had gone and Venus shone brightly among the other stars.

Every so often the shes carrying Louise's kittens had to stop and lay down their burdens while they rested. This suited Jessie, who had found the evacuation a far greater ordeal than she would admit. Her hip-joints hurt badly whenever she took a step but her stoicism was typically feral and she tottered up Winner Hill Road without complaint. Scrag watched them from the roof of Winner Hill Garage but made no comment. He hoped Smiley had put two and two together and was heading for home. If not, something would turn up. It always did. The rough life was great, he reflected. Things just happened. A jet cut across the stars and his ears twitched. What was that? No one knew, not even Skeets. Was it some kind of bird that roared louder than a big car? He shunted the mystery into the back of his mind, rested his chin on his forepaws and dozed.

Dawn was breaking when the shes stood at last before the gates of Maylands. Pepper led them to the terrace and assisted in the grooming of the kittens. Louise was not the sort of mother that fussed over her brood but collectively the shes provided the warmth and purring essential to the kittens' well-being. They also hunted for Louise and encouraged her to suckle the small creatures but none of them could match Jessie's devotion. Extravagant demonstrations of affection were necessary to her. She had too big a heart to bank all her love in one animal. It extended to the entire family but the kittens had aroused a fierce maternal instinct despite her years and she fussed and crooned and licked the tiny heads at every opportunity. She was roaring out the purrs when Ben walked up to her and said loudly, 'Were there any signs of Lucy, Mother?'

'No,' the old grey she replied in her uncatlike voice. 'Have you questioned Dolly?' At times she sounded like a kazoo.

Ben nodded and sat down to stare over the roofs and TV aerials to the bay and the sunrise. Silver and a few ferals and strays were at the other end of the terrace, similarly engrossed. How soon the familiar ways repossess us, Ben thought. After the nightmare the sun was coming out of the water as if nothing had happened. But Skeets was real and he was still there like the trees, the grass and the house. But Lucy was gone and the pain of losing her was as persistent as the smell of the garden and the purring of the shes.

The sun rolled clear of the horizon and the cats luxuriated in its growing warmth. A blackbird sang melodiously from the top of the chestnut tree. The elderflower had withered and just one crow fledgling remained in the firtop nest. Rapidly the new day assembled around Ben. Other birds began to sing and presently a collared dove was crooning wheezily above the cackle and wail of adult gulls and the piping of their young.

A woodlouse crawled over the flagstones and a couple of cabbage-white butterflies straggled past.Why wasn't Lucy part of this, part of his living of it? The gentle easterly smelt of the sea. In the evening it would smell of chip shops and fast food takeaways. The town hadn't come alive yet. There was the sun and the sea, and the gulf between the horizon and Ben was the measure of his loneliness.

He pushed his front legs forward and yawned and stretched before going into the streets to look for her.

The slop and gurgle of water against the sides of the boats moored in Paignton Harbour was music to Fancy's ears.

111

He and his three toms sat in the flower bed on the sandstone headland opposite the post office stores and watched the sun rise.

'We got company,' the ginger tom to his right said from the corner of his mouth.

'Smiley?' Fancy sniggered.

'Smiley and some uncool cats.'

Fancy lowered his muzzle and shook with laughter. The Shadows were trying to hold their tails in the pump handle position and walk with a slow swagger which brought Fancy's ginger friend to the point of collapse.

'Hey,' he spluttered. 'You hard cases have a good night?'

Smiley gazed at him.

'You goin' back to Silver's patch?' Fancy chuckled.

'Your white friend lost out, All-mouth. He's yesterday,' said Smiley.

'Wrong again,' Fancy gasped between snorts and gulps of laughter. 'I'd give the garden a miss if I were you. We was up there last night – bitin' ass and helping Silver sort things out. You'd better believe it. You ain't got a patch and if you don't leg it you won't have a tail, either. Let me spell it out: Silver is back in his garden.'

The smile on Smiley's face was enormous.

'Back where we want him,' he whispered and he hit Fancy so quickly the grin was frozen to the harbour tom's face as he went down under a blitz of paws. Before he could recover Smiley wrecked his muzzle and ears and Fancy's toms received the same treatment from the other Shadows.

'Show your butt on our patch again and I'll gut you,' Smiley said. '*Our patch* – get the meaning? Silver's return don't change a thing. So, no words, no insults, nothin' – understand? You nod if you do. If you don't then I'll have to believe you need some more persuadin'.'

Fancy nodded and spat blood.

'Here,' the ginger tom gasped behind the Shadows' departure. 'They weren't jokin'. They can really perform.'

Fancy licked a paw and rubbed it over his nose.

112

'Put it down to experience,' he said. 'But I don't get it. What are those heavies up to? They can handle themselves, so why the sham? Why did they back off last night?'

'Silver had better put his act together,' Ginger said. 'Them Crazies let him go back to the garden and we were too thick to sniff it out.'

'You're spot on, Ginger,' Fancy said. 'We've been conned.'

'Who is this Skeets?' Ginger asked.

'What is he, you mean,' Fancy muttered, wondering if he needed the shes to lick his wounds.

A mile away across town Ben nosed out Dolly. She was asleep on a tomb under the dance of gnats. A wren sang and a milk float rattled up Church Street. Smells whirl-pooled but the aroma from the takeaway cartons which had been tossed over the hedge from Church Lane, prevailed.

He woke Dolly.

'No,' she said drowsily in reply to his question. 'She hasn't been here since you and her paid me a visit back along.'

'I don't understand,' Ben said.

'There idn always somethin' to understand. Cats disappear and it usually means they've run off or got knocked down by a car. The more you worry about it the worse it becomes. We wadn intended to know everything. I mean, where do the sun come from and why do the moon only come out at night? And what's snow and why do the light go out in your eyes when you stop breathin'?'

It wasn't Sam's Wise Pussy talk. Ben knew it. The old she was approaching the time when the light would go out in her own eyes. She was coming to terms with death.

'Walk softly, buyh.'

He came up through the streets more watchful than usual. Two Shadows ran up the bottleneck ahead of him so he sat for a while in the doorway of the Pocket Book Shop where a drunk had left half his fish and chips and a complete set of false teeth. Ben ate the fish and made his way up through the ruins of the old houses and garden of Dan y Craig into Winner Hill Road and Maylands.

'Who is it?' whispered an anxious voice.

'Ben.'

And Pepper and Rainbow emerged from the shrubbery looking relieved. Then Ben began to understand what it was like to live under siege. The Shadows were in possession of the council estate and were making life hell for pet cats and any strays stupid enough to lurk around the monastery.

'They're playing with us,' Silver said when Ben joined him, Sam and Scarnose on the terrace.

City regarded them from a respectful distance at the terrace. Jessie and Belle lay together on the rockery.

'We should've kept going the other night,' Silver continued. 'We should've run for the flashing light.'

'No,' Sam said. 'This is our place. We belong to it. If things are going to change it should happen here.'

'Maybe nothing will change,' Ben said. 'If we don't act like mice we can still give Skeets and the Crazies a hard time.'

'Yeah,' said Scarnose emphatically. 'Yeah. I ain't no plaything. I ain't no squeakin' bloody vole.'

'A vole's got a bigger brain,' Sam said. Much of his comment was inspired by indigestion.

Scarnose unsheathed his claws and grinned down at them.

'In the end,' he said, 'it's all about hooks.'

Ben paced through the jungle of geraniums, lavender and ivy-leaved toadflax to find Jessie. Petals fell from the dogroses in the hedges. Scarnose was wrong, he thought. In the end it was all about kittens and kin and the peaceful place in the sun. In the end it was the warmth he felt for Lucy and the way his life was complete in her company.

Jessie lifted her head and looked at him.

'My heart is breaking,' Ben managed.

'Yes, I know,' she said, without hearing his words. 'But Lucy is alive, Ben. I know it. I feel it. Just like we feel the coming storm in our bodies and you felt the coming of the Crazies so I feel she is alive. You'll find her. Keep looking. Keep thinking of her.'

17

In Cloud Country (i)

The days passed and the kittens' eyes were open. Returning from the stalking which was really necessary to her physical condition, Lucy would call to them and once in the nest she nuzzled them and suckled them within a trance of purrs. Then one evening, returning after a slightly longer absence, she sensed danger and smelt fox. The vixen had found her nursery and had killed and carried off two kittens and was about to enter the shed for the third when Lucy took her by surprise.

Darting across the yard, the little cat threw herself at the vixen and slashed at her nose and eyes. The ferocity of the assault unnerved the fox. She had never encountered such blind rage and aggression. Twisting and rolling on the floor she eventually freed herself of the cat and slowly backed away until she could run around the side of the inn, leaving Lucy to rush to her kitten maraowing her grief.

For a while the relief of finding him alive cancelled out her suffering. Then, as he settled into sleep, the ache for her two gone-forever kittens swelled to nausea. It kept clenching and unclenching in her stomach so that she had to swallow repeatedly. She was desolate, and the purring of the kitten she had christened Skip lent a poignancy to her distress. It drew her deeper into a situation that lacked reality. It couldn't have happened.

Lucy gave a long cry and let it tail away to numbness. 'Ben. Oh Ben. Help me. Help me.'

The sickness of it all was sloshing around inside her. She swallowed again and Skip kicked out and she lowered her muzzle to lick him. But even when the ache subsided to a rawness round her heart she was stranded on the island of her distress in a night full of menace.

Two small creatures that had come out of her body into life had been taken from her. She closed her eyes on the grief but could hear them mewling from a darkness beyond her reach, and called out to them. Then Skip was demanding to be fed and the nausea was no longer all-possessing. The kitten burrowed into her belly fur and she inclined her head to take in his scent. He was there, warm and beautiful, and she lavished her love on him with her tongue. For as long as she suckled the tiny tom she cried low, deep maraows until the life squirming on her nipple brought her beyond the first sharp pain of loss.

Night ended and she ate at the back door of the inn. Grief and the tug of home worked on her entire being, and when she had groomed Skip she gripped him by the scruff of the neck and set off for Paignton, trotting along the roadside towards the sun.

Beyond the River Walkham and the bridge, the road to Two Bridges climbed in a loop towards Rundlestone. Lucy's vision of the world was the cat vision. Her head was rarely higher than twelve inches above the ground and distance did not register as it did in humans, but the bigness of the moors and the sky alarmed her. It was full of the breath of green living things. Where were the houses which meant scrounge? Where were the familiar smells? Cars passed and some motorists slowed for a second to look at the cat with the kitten swinging in its jaws.

But Lucy trotted on over the turf and dried rabbits' droppings. To her left on the hilltop was Great Mis Tor; on the right was King's Tor and a small carpark fringed with trees. She stopped in a sunny hollow and suckled Skip. Then she rested and dozed before continuing.

Big fat white clouds came billowing over North Hessary Tor and its radio mast up ahead, to sail off across the sky. The larksong was ceaseless and irritating. Whenever one of the birds fluttered into view Lucy narrowed her eyes and her teeth chattered on little moans of bloodlust. Skip tottered around her, reminding her poignantly of Old Jessie and former times. She sighed and licked the kitten, who grizzled and tried to make off.

'This way,' Lucy said, gripping the loose skin at his neck and swinging him off his feet.

On the brow of the hill by Rundlestone two coaches full of tourists pulled up for the passengers to gawp at the tabby and her black and white kitten. Most of them assumed she was a local farm cat. They would not have believed she was an urban feral on an Homeric journey.

There was a turning to Princetown on the right but she ran straight on along the verge to the drystone wall. Now the cars were slowing down not for people to stare at her, but for a better view of Dartmoor Prison over the sheep pasture. Then Lucy met her first ponies and their foals. The half-wild creatures loitered at the verge to scrounge titbits from motorists although it was forbidden because ponies on the road at night often became car accident victims.

A mare slowly lowered her head and sniffed Lucy, who lifted her tail and rubbed her back against the pony's muzzle. Full of curiosity, the other mares gathered round the cat until she had had enough and was off again with Skip hanging from her mouth.

It was nearly noon and very hot. Her pads were damp with sweat and her coat was moist. Laying down the sleeping Skip she groomed herself in long deliberate licks, not only cleaning her fur but taking back the Vitamin D her glands were producing under the hairs. Her lower jaw ached a little and flies troubled her but as soon as Skip began to draw the milk from her body she was purring on the brink of bliss.

At the narrow Blackbrook River beside the road she drank, wondering why the water was trying to run away from her. Then she walked down the road with the heat rippling and cars wobbling in and out of it like objects in a mirage. After three more rests she was contemplating the scene below the dip at Two Bridges.

The road here was busy, for there was another right-hand fork to Princetown and the hotel at Two Bridges beside the West Dart was a popular tourist haunt. Lucy could smell scrounge rising from the building. It was a warm savoury smell that put her in mind of Winner Street and Church Street. Through a spasm of grief ran the cold ache of homesickness.

Hunger was enough to overcome her suspicion of people, so she marched off the main road along the old road and over the old bridge to the front of the hotel and the tables where tourists were eating bar snacks. Few hearts would have gone unmoved by the sight of the dusty little tabby and her kitten. Water was fetched for her and the lady from the Two Bridges Hotel brought out cooked meat on a dish and a bowl of cream. Cameras clicked and there was a lot of oohing and ahhing which Lucy played up to with arched back and erect tail.

'A farm cat,' someone said, and of course no one disputed it.

'Such a pretty little thing.'

Lucy ate so much she was sick but she lay on the lawn and suckled Skip watched by fifty or sixty human admirers. Camera-bearing tourists followed her a little way up and round the bend onto the B3212 Moretonhampstead Road. Lapwings soared and tumbled above the mires of Muddilake and a curlew cried as it landed among the reeds and scrub willow. And always, on and on, the larks sang.

There were other sounds and scents new to Lucy, and perhaps the most mysterious and disturbing was the metallic smell of bracken stems crushed by the hooves of cattle and ponies. A wheatear called from the drystone wall at Parson's Cottage and cars roared down on her and passed, leaving pockets of hush which soon filled with noise again. Feeling weary, she went through a gateway into the grounds of the Cherrybrook Hotel and settled under a tree for a catnap. Her jaws and teeth ached a little less than her neck muscles but Skip's contented slumber had her purring. Even the snarling whine of a helicopter could not break her reverie.

119

Catnapping and daydreaming Lucy eventually decided it was time to move on again. Three hikers, stooping under the weight of their backpacks, caused her to cross over and run close to the wall. Then a convoy of military vehicles had her cowering against the stones. But she was streetwise and knew the perils of straying from the verge. Pausing for a rest she hoped this was not the long road in Ben's dream. Her mouth was open and she was panting out her body heat. The play of sunlight on the road hurt her eyes, which had narrowed to slits. Gathering up Skip she tried to master her thirst and her misgivings.

Below Powdermills at Higher Cherrybrook Bridge, she left the road and trotted down to the Cherry Brook to drink and Skip nearly fell in the water. He was scolded and shaken and returned to her teeth before Lucy walked on. To her right was the conifer gloom of Bellever Forest and she felt she had come far enough for the day. Trees meant shelter, safety and prey; and she wanted a long sleep.

Beneath the firs was a dry litter of twigs and needles, ideal for a nest.

18

In Cloud Country (ii)

Strange noises woke her. A roe buck crossed the woodland path with a patter of hooves but the badger sow and her cubs were noisier. They snuffled and grunted through the trees and were off over the road to grub for beetles beside the Cherry Brook. The moon and stars shone and branches ticked and trembled in the hush. Lucy's tongue curled up over her nose and Skip kicked out with his hindlegs but did not wake. It was an alien, baffling world. Lucy sighed. Beneath unpleasant reality was the past and Ben.

'Oh Ben,' she murmured.

At the end of the walking he would be there in the garden. She smiled, recalling the bluebottle incident and his trick of letting them buzz behind his clenched teeth.

Skip continued to sleep as she crept away to sit in ambush at the vole runs. But a vixen calling her young from the depths of the forest brought her swiftly back to the kitten for the suckling.

'My beautiful one,' she purred, licking his head. 'My little dear. My lovely, my life.'

At first light she was carrying him along the woodland path that ran beside the road and he was growling his protests. Darkness was fading but car headlights remained on full beam and the vehicles travelled much faster than they did in the seaside town. Lucy trotted, her ears and nose busy and soon she reached the side road that brought her over the cattle grid back onto the Moretonhampstead Road again.

The day was already quite warm although the big clouds were still rolling off the hilltops. She crinkled and uncrinkled her nose to read the air but it held no menace. A

121

milk tanker rumbled by and picking the moment, she ran across the road and down past Postbridge carpark. Lights were on in the upstairs windows of the post office and Lucy hesitated as she caught the smell of food. Then she threw back her ears but the solitary walker struggling to adjust the straps of his rucksack seemed to pose no threat. He called to her, using the name most humans bestow on unknown cats – Puss, puss. But the generous portion of pasty which landed beside her was welcome enough. Skip mewed when he was set down and Lucy bolted the meal. The huge, lumpy figure of the man stood unmoving until she had finished and was gone.

She crossed the bridge spanning the East Dart, her nerves twanging as she was buffeted by the draught of a passing van. A few lights were on in wayside dwellings but she did not linger at the East Dart Hotel despite the tempting smells wafting from its kitchen. She walked the broad strip of turf under the beeches and came through Postbridge to rest at the entrance of the lane which led to a farm. Skip charged head down into a serenade of purrs to get at her milk. They were under the hedge and Lucy felt secure until her nose told her cats were nearby. Moments later a couple of young farm shes padded up to her and sat down to watch Skip feed.

'Where be gwain?' the black she asked in a broad Devonshire accent.

'Sunrise way,' said Lucy.

'Where be from?' asked the black and white she.

'Sunrise way,' Lucy smiled.

The farm cats nodded.

'I'm on my way home,' Lucy added.

'You baint a pet, be 'ee?' said the black one.

Lucy shook her head. 'Born free of a gone-wild mother.'

Again the two heads nodded.

'Hungry?' said the black and white.

'I wouldn't say no to some meat.'

'Wait yer and us'll bring 'ee some.'

They weren't absent for long and returned carrying chunks of boiled rabbit in their mouths.

'Tez the dug's,' Blacky laughed.

'*Twas* the dug's,' said her companion. ''Ee gets enough – creepin' round the man awl the time, 'im and they old sheep. Eat up and get strong. That babby needs awl the milk 'er kin get.'

They helped groom Skip and added their own low purring to Lucy's deep proclamation of life. Traffic passed. The sun climbed higher and soon Lucy was ready to depart.

'Walk with luck, li'l sister,' Blacky called after her.

Lucy waited for a car to rattle over the cattle grid before crossing it herself. Ponies were on the road and cars were slowing down but few motorists saw the tabby walking quickly over the turf below Merripit Hill. A couple of girls on bicycles stopped by Statts Bridge to watch her drink at the brook before she hurried on. Again the awesome spaciousness of Dartmoor filled her with unease. The white clouds appeared to rise from the hills and float over the empty green places. There was so much sky and the land seemed to go on forever. Part of it fell away on the right to Soussons Down Plantation, and trotting up the rise she was suddenly confronted by the Warren House Inn and her heart swelled. Buildings meant scrounge and shelter and a release from the threat of open moorland.

At the roadside facing the inn were hitching rails for pony trekkers. A couple of cars were drawn up on the verge and some people were turning binoculars on the old tin workings below Birch Tor. Between the tor and Soussons Plantation it was possible to see red grouse, ring ouzels and dippers. The spot was much favoured by bird watchers but the motorbikes arriving on a wave of noise disturbed Lucy and she trotted on to rest further up the road against the granite of Bennett's Cross.

The drift of cloud over Bush Down was restful. The long hushes between cars were broken by birdcalls, bleating and the fluted cries of pony mares. Lucy drowsed until the stink of sheep alerted her. A blackface lamb was sniffing her face and several ewes were showing an interest. She got up, stretched and gripped Skip. Winged

123

insects rising off the heather were saluted with a swat of the paw. A coach cruised by and two fighter jets roared low.

The difficult bend at the East Bovey provided the sort of perils that made her quail. Cars cornering too quickly came close to killing her but she flattened to the ground and crawled past the bad section until she could take to the turf and put her fears behind her.

At the top of the hill and the next bend an astonishing view over moor and in-country fields to Fernworthy Forest and Chagford lay in wait; but Lucy was concentrating on the traffic although it wasn't heavy. The Devon heartland was too big for one small cat and her kitten.

Resting and running she passed Leapra Cross, and a little beyond Lettaford Cross had no hesitation in turning right onto the B3344 road. The road was narrow and comfortable. The hedgebanks were hung with honeysuckle and the leafy greenness reminded Lucy of Maylands. Most of the cars slowed for the cat but once or twice she had to leap into the hedge and lie quivering as some vehicle thundered by.

At Barramor Bridge a gang of farm dogs chased her and she jumped onto the wall and crouched there until a man in a lorry saw her plight and drove the dogs off. Lucy was tired. The heat and the dust, the noise and the scares had got to her and Skip needed constant attention. But she kept walking, pausing only to cower from a car or to suckle her kitten.

Between Canna and Easdon Farm she halted frequently. Some free range hens frightened her but feeling the weariness heavy now in her limbs she walked up to the farm under Easdon Tor and looked for a place to sleep.

'Hullo, my dear,' crooned a husky voice and out of the garden in front of the house stepped a large ginger tom. 'Are you from down the road or over the fields?'

Lucy laid Skip at her feet and said: 'From the town by the water where the sun rises.'

Purring and wheezing the tom walked around her, tail upright, eyes narrowed. He had the long tread of a panther that ill-suited his flabby bulk. He was a fireside moggie and it was obvious to any cat that wasn't a pet.

'So far, hey? A long, long walk and you all alone and me prepared to offer you my – er – protection.'

'I don't need protection,' Lucy said.

'But your kit is so small. Anything could happen to him. He could, for instance, become a tomcat's snack.'

'And the tomcat could become blind, for the she would die with her hooks in his face. If my little one is harmed I shall commit murder.'

'But these harsh words are so unnecessary,' the tom said.

He was a domestic cat and it was slowly dawning on him that Lucy was nobody's pet. She was wilder than any farm she he had met on his amorous sorties.

'Yeah,' Lucy said, her tone hardening. 'So why don't you take your fat face and hide it before I open it with these?'

And she sprang at him with a flash of claws.

Hastily he backed away and licked his lips and nodded from behind a stupid grin.

'Perhaps, when you've rested – ' he said sheepishly.

'Get lost,' she growled.

'Rest and reconsider,' he crooned, but all his cowardice was revealed in obsequious retreat.

Lucy made a nest among some bales of hay in a shed and as soon as Skip was settled she fell into a deep sleep. Hours later she opened her eyes and found the night waiting outside. It was irresistible and she set off again by starlight.

19

Thoughts on Life and Death

Three pairs of eyes followed the flight of the peacock butterflies over the privet blossom. The crooning of collared doves filled the Maylands morning. Clouds drifted in from the sea and swifts were busy around the church tower. Other birds flew across the rooftops.

Sunlight flooded the garden but it could have been winter rain for all Ben cared. He got up and dug his claws in the summerhouse door. Silver and Scarnose watched, unable to understand what appeared to be a total change of character. Ben was touchy and eager to quarrel. Lucy was lost and as far as they were concerned nothing could be done. It was the way of the world. You had everything, then you had nothing. You ate, then you were hungry. You were awake, then you slept. The light shone from your eyes, then it went out and it was all over.

'What happens when the light in your eyes goes out?' Silver asked Jessie.

'It's the end,' Jessie said, frowning because it was a stupid question. 'Look at this,' she continued, rising awkwardly from the grass beside the summerhouse and flicking a dead vole in their direction. 'It's dead. No light in the eyes. It's finished. It's nothing.'

Ben was dead inside. He ranged around looking for trouble, hoping Lucy would appear to put everything right. The herring gull chicks on the roofs whistled but he took no notice of the occasional swoop by adult birds. He walked up Monastery Road to Berry Drive and took Reekin by surprise on the lawn in front of one of the council houses. The skirmish was resolved in less than thirty seconds and Reekin departed with one of Ben's

126

claws embedded in his cheek and his ribs bruised by strong hind feet.

'The black and white one is the fighter,' Smiley mused.

'Could he be persuaded to join us?' Skeets asked.

'No way!' said Dancer. 'Him and Silver are as close as my toes.'

'Well, who cares?' Skeets yawned. 'I'm gonna have the white tom. The others are mere playthings.'

The pigeons from the Winner Hill loft swept overhead on a rush of wings and the cats' heads jerked up.

'Next time this black and white wonder tom sets foot on my patch,' Skeets said, 'I want him hurt even if it takes all of you to do it.'

'We'll send him back to Silver with bits of his body missin',' Boomer laughed. 'Yeah – *garrg*.'

'Garrg,' Skeets chuckled and he imitated the frenzied retching of the late-deceased Wayne.

'That Skeets!' Dancer laughed, walking beside Smiley down Monastery Road. But Smiley thought he detected a note of uncertainty in his companion's tone.

'Isn't he The Cat?' Dancer added.

'Yeah,' Smiley said.

Approaching Maylands they quickened their pace, but from up in the hedge Rita and Pepper saw them and hissed insults.

'And we know what you really want,' was Dancer's parting jibe.

'Real toms,' Rita yelled. 'And there ain't none outside this garden.'

'Those shes are something else,' Dancer grinned as they ran on.

'Silver has a good set-up,' Smiley said.

'And Skeets will move in?'

'What do you think?'

'Maybe for Skeets the old game is enough.'

'He wants Silver finished and the garden ours.'

Smiley pulled up sharp and glared at Dancer. 'OK – you wanna get something off your chest?'

'No, no,' Dancer laughed. 'Nothing.'

'What Skeets says goes. That's the rule – Skeets' law.'

'You're on Silver's patch,' said a voice from the hedge above them.

'Silver's patch,' echoed a second voice from the same place.

'Yes,' breathed yet another a little further along the garden boundary. 'Get out of here, Ratbits,' in a trembling growl. 'Go on, run – or we'll hook out your liver.'

The hedge rustled and Dancer was suddenly enveloped in a drizzle of urine.

'Got the message?' a tom chuckled and the Shadows ran.

'They're doin' our thing,' Smiley snarled. 'Those flea-bitten failures are playing at Shadows.'

At Ivy Lodge they stopped to scent-mark. Then they strolled leisurely up through the wild garden to the Lions' Club.

'Skeets is havin' fun,' Slippery Jim announced from a leer. 'Down at the back of the houses over there. Follow me.'

But the yarooling would have guided them.

Skeets had trapped a domestic tom in a council house back garden. The pet was big and finely marked with dark tortoiseshell on white. He also had courage and stood his ground, although he recognised a darkness in Skeets that was uncatlike. And the smell of the great, sandy-coloured feral was offensive, like a man-made smell.

'You're wearing a collar, Toby,' Skeets crooned. 'Who's a pretty puss, then? Who's a cuddly Toby?'

Toby stared unblinking into the empty yellow eyes. Is there a way out of this without loss of face? he thought. There wasn't. Skeets needed to demonstrate his power to the Shadows who were gathering at the fence.

It was brief, ugly and vicious, charged with a violence that impressed even the seasoned street fighters. Toby was left staggering about trying to hold his face together, but the noise had brought people out of their houses.

'That bloody sandy stray,' a man said, gathering up Toby to pat the wounds with a handkerchief.

A boy in his early teens ran after the Shadows but they had scattered in the undergrowth by the time he reached the carpark. Two slightly older lads on skateboards were told about the council estate 'wild' cats and Big Sandy in particular. One of the skateboarders lit a cigarette and gazed thoughtfully at the trees and shrubs.

'I reckon we ought to do some cat hunting,' he said. 'You got your air pistol?'

'I sold it to buy the skateboard gear,' replied his friend.

The boy breathed smoke. It didn't matter. He would come alone and hunt the big wild cat. His airgun was really powerful and a lot of people were complaining about the monastery strays. He would make Toby a present of Sandy's carcass. Cat hunting would make a change from skateboarding and the amusement arcades.

Louise neglected her kittens but the other shes did not disapprove. It often happened. Louise was a rough and ready feral, nearly five years old, and she was even more promiscuous than her sisters. So when she went 'on the razzle', trailed by Scarnose and Parson, there was no comment. Jessie organised the nursemaids and several shes were eager to involve themselves in the kittens' welfare. They fussed around them attending to their every need while Jessie sang out in her twanging voice the songs without words.

Louise came and went as boredom prompted absences that became longer and longer, until Belle and Lucky took over completely as surrogate mothers. Both had lost kittens of their own through carelessness and illness but Louise's kittens had revived something deeply maternal in them.

Straying close to all the contentment accentuated Ben's unhappiness. Whenever he saw a tabby cat he would run towards it, belling his greeting call until his nose told him it wasn't her.

'Where can I look?' he cried from the steps linking Colley End Park and Winner Hill Road. It was a mewl of anguish which saddened Sam. He had come running after Ben for company and protection.

'Hey,' he said. 'Come on. This won't bring her back.'

'And next you'll say – don't be unhappy, don't feel sick and empty or lost. It'll be all right. Yeah, but it isn't now. If all the gardens and roads were Skeets I'd kill them.'

'And that would bring her back?'

'No, but it would make me feel good.'

The toms laughed and climbed the steps to the gate of the little vine garden, which lay open at one end above a high drop and was bounded on three sides by sandstone walls.

'Dancer,' Ben whispered.

He sniffed the woodwork and the fresh spray-marks before throwing himself effortlessly onto the gate and dropping to the tiny lawn. Newly planted vines grew on the walls and Dancer was sprawled in a corner taking the sun. Sam's awkward scramble up the gate woke the black tom, and he slowly bunched into the crouch position with a low waraow.

'What do you gain from this, Ben?' he said.

'The satisfaction of removing some of your flesh and fur.'

'The two of you?'

'Me 'n you. The way it always is.'

'And you think you can manage it?'

Ben swaggered up to him and pushed his face into Dancer's.

'Words won't help,' he rasped. 'This is where the talk ends.'

The awful certainty behind the statement prompted Dancer to give a nod. Then the hooks flashed and he was submissive at Ben's feet.

'Why d'you chase aggravation?' Ben said. 'Why stick with Skeets? OK, there's a time and place for this sort of thing but why can't you just enjoy the sun and the shes and the scrounge?'

'Skeets is The Cat,' Dancer said defiantly, looking sideways up at Ben with his head on the ground.

130

'Yeah – and Silver is The Cat and Smiley is The Cat and Fancy is The Cat. So what? What is so great about being The Cat?'

'We are all The Cat,' said Sam. 'Just as the leaves are the tree and the grasses are the field.'

'OK OK, please, no smart talk, not now,' Ben said. 'Look at you, Dancer. You don't want bother. You want the street fightin' for the shes and you want the prowls and the freedom of the patch. So why this stupidity? You ain't a Crazy like the rest. You got the streets up by the big house. For most cats that would be enough.'

'Skeets wants it all and I'm running with Skeets.' But there was little conviction in Dancer's newfound bravado.

'Get out of my sight while you still got a tail.'

Sam moved off the gate onto the wall and Dancer was gone behind the shudder and rattle of the woodwork.

'Skeets'll win,' he called when he considered it safe. 'You wanna know why, Ben? Because you and Silver are too soft. When it comes to the crunch it's not about heart. It's about hooks.'

'But what does Skeets really want?' Ben mused a little later, as he and Sam sat at the open end of the garden looking out over the old part of town to the trees of Victoria Park and the bay. 'He had our patch but he surrendered it. Now him and the other Crazies are hanging about making life difficult.'

'Nightmarish,' Sam yawned.

'We're just part of a game he's playing – him and Silver. I've lost Lucy because of it and that makes me bitter.'

'But you didn't take it out on Dancer.'

'It didn't seem worth it.'

'But if we start cutting up the Crazies at every opportunity we'll bleed Skeets useless. If Dancer meets one of the shes or me when I'm alone d'you think he'll hesitate before he throws hooks?'

'All I can think about is Lucy.'

'Well, try to think clearly. Letting him go with his tail held high was a mistake.'

'Maybe. We'll see. Why don't you go to sleep?'

131

'I'm always asleep. I'd rather see fur fly.'

'So long as it ain't yours, old mouse.'

'I've lost more fur than you've had mice,' Sam said irritably.

'I know. Get your head down and I'll make sure you don't lose any more.'

Sam smiled. 'You keep on your toes, Ben. Skeets is a killer.'

20

Whispering Grass

Slippery Jim's woodpecker laugh rang through the trees: '*Wa-wa-wa-wa-wa-wa-waraow-waraow.*'

Terrified pet cats heard it and lurked on their home ground.

'Why does he keep doing that?' Smiley snarled.

'Because it turns him on,' Boomer said. 'It's his thing and that's what this is all about.'

'Yeah,' Chips agreed and Reekin also added his grunt of approval.

The evening easterly was shaking the tops of the holm oaks and sending down a few dead leaves. The Shadows had collected in the carpark and Skeets sat facing them on the roof of the yellow van. A moment later they were joined by Squib and Skiffle.

'Eleven of the best street fighters on the scene,' Skeets smiled.

'Should be thirteen,' said Dancer.

'Should and Is don't always sit together, Dancer,' Skeets said.

'True,' Reekin said. 'We should be stuffin' ourselves with the best scrounge and layin' our choice of shes. But we ain't. We won this patch with hooks but Silver still holds the garden.'

'They got the sort of patch the Shadows should have,' said Chips. 'From there they control the streets down below and the best scrounge. Every stray she can lie up with them. They got it made.'

'Haven't they,' Bang sighed.

'Live hard, fight easy,' said Skeets, lifting a forepaw and examining his toes.

'OK, so we're doing that,' said Scrag. 'But you said

this was the end of the rainbow, Skeetsie. You said we'd find it all here. This was supposed to be the Big Food Bowl at the end of things.'

'And it is, it is,' Skeets crooned. 'Do any of you go hungry? No. And you got status. You're the tops. Cats get out of your way. Cats run when they see you coming.'

'Yeah,' Scrag chuckled. 'Like that black and white bundle ran from Dancer. Like – '

'Pleasssssssssse,' Skeets hissed. 'No sarcasm.' And he began to hum the Red Robin tune.

Scrag swallowed noisily and stared about him for support but the lowered eyes told him he had gone too far. Skeets was still the darkness at the end of the blind alley.

'Don't worry, Scrag,' Boomer said. 'Skeets will give us Silver's patch in his own good time. Skeets don't fail.'

'Streetwise tom,' Skeets beamed.

'But maybe we oughta hit them now,' Slippery Jim offered. 'They've settled in and must be feelin' nice and safe and cosy.' He unsheathed his hooks and wagged a paw.

'All them shes,' Skiffle said dreamily.

'And what does Smiley think?' Skeets said in a gentle voice.

'I'd like to see us in control of the garden,' Smiley grinned. 'But you're The Cat. It's your decision. If we don't put it together this time it'll be hard to pull off again.'

'Ever smart and loyal, Smiley,' said Skeets. 'So this is what we'll do. We'll hit them now, tonight.'

A murmur of surprise and excitement rippled through the toms.

'You see,' Skeets went on, 'they think they know my mind. They think I gotta stick to one plan. But I got loads of plans. There's the stalking and the terror, the demand and menace, and the loitering with intent at the cat trails. They are a band of stupids. So we do the dirty. It's what we're really good at. But whatever happens, remember the garden is ours even if we don't live in it.'

Slippery Jim laughed and Skeets winced. 'Let's go,' he said.

They ran down Monastery Road as high wispy mare's tail clouds veiled the moon and a mackerel sky spread over the Channel. Rita was leaving Colley End Park to cross Monastery Road to the silver gates when she saw the crowd of small dark shapes coming through the lamplight. Dashing into Maylands, she lifted her voice to warn everyone.

'Crazies,' she yarooled. 'The Crazies are coming.'

There was a mad scramble of half-asleep cats to get out of the summerhouse.

'Not again,' Sam groaned. 'That bloody Skeets.'

'Everyone out except Jessie,' Silver called.

Ben and Scarnose crashed through the grass and met Skeets and Smiley head on. The rising wind set the grass whispering.

'I want the white one,' Skeets hissed. 'Just him and me and the garden up for grabs for the winner.'

'We fight,' Silver said, appearing at Ben's side and he added under his breath, 'No matter what happens, Ben – we fight, all of us. We don't surrender any of our patch.'

So it began in the whispering grass with the smell of rain on the wind. Other scents and smells swam across the garden and constricting rings of excitement drew the watching animals closer together beneath the waving heads of grass.

'This is the end of the road, Silver,' Skeets said and the coldness closed around Ben's heart. The sky was darkening and the wind growing stronger and the grass was hissing now.

He closed his eyes and walked the long dark road towards the heap of snow in the gutter. Then Silver's rising proclamation of fury snapped him out of it and he was back in the night that was alive. The dark object to his right behind a jerking screen of grass was the sundial. Then all the smells were tomcat and he was choking on the thrill of it.

Silver and Skeets held their ears erect. Their tails were

135

thrashing and their pupils had narrowed to knife slits. Locked in the eyeballing neither had gone on the defensive, neither would quail from the staring which had brought the two pugheads close together, face to face; neither would concede an inch of ground. They were almost touching noses, breathing the hot stink of each other's cathood and growling as if their guts were on the boil. The two wills strained and heaved somewhere behind thought and Ben waited for the outcome which none of the onlookers could predict.

The rush and hiss of the wind in the grass ruffled the fur of the motionless toms, both of whom seemed reluctant to press home the attack. Their fur was spiked and their faces were masks of hatred but Ben sensed a curious stalemate of the spirit, as if both ferals had recognised something self-destructive in the encounter.

Then, without a sound, Skeets keeled over and lay as if he was dead. The grass curled at the tips and danced over his body. With the wind furrowing his fur none of the cats could tell if he was still breathing.

'It's a warning,' Jessie called to the Shadows in her haunting voice, and she staggered through the grass stems. 'It means get out of here while you can still walk. There are things looking after Silver which you'll never understand.'

The wind rose behind her cry.

Smiley leapt forward and stood over Skeets and the flash of moonlight vanishing behind cloud briefly lit his grin.

'No one touches him,' Smiley growled, but the other Shadows were backing off when City cried out from the terrace.

'Fancy and his toms are here.'

With that Skeets got to his feet as though nothing had happened and turned and walked away. The Shadows fell in behind him and none of the Maylands gang were prepared to follow. The oddness of the incident had baffled them.

'Did the light go out in his eyes?' Parson asked.

136

'Did it?' Scrumpy echoed.

The cats looked at each other in the gaps of light with the clouds building up and the trees beginning to roar.

'I dunno,' Ben said and he didn't care.

'Of course it didn't,' Sam snapped.

A strong gust flattened the grass and they saw the Shadows swarming up the rockery onto the terrace. An even stronger gust made the fir trees boom and Skeets suddenly came back into the moment. He turned and maraowed and the Shadows watched him as uncertain as ever of his next move.

'Why are we running?' he panted.

'You had one of your turns,' Smiley said. 'You was open to Silver's hooks.'

'But we should press home our advantage now,' Skeets said.

'Fancy and his mob are coming. If they hit us and Silver hits us we're in big trouble.'

Skeets groaned. 'I was somewhere else and the pain in my head was the white cat. I tried to get at him but he just sat there laughing at me.'

'Sat where?' Smiley asked.

'There,' Skeets nodded.

Silver was on the summerhouse looking out over the rooftops to the sea. The roar and quake of the garden trees matched Smiley's confusion. He had another glance at Silver and swung around.

'We gotta go, Skeets. This is not the right time.'

'OK, we go. You're smart, Smiley. You knew. The others wanted a rumble but you knew Skeets' master plan – which is?' And he broke off and beamed expectantly at Smiley.

'To stalk and terrorise and pick off, one by one,' said Smiley.

'Yessssss. I should have heeded you and stuck to The Plan.'

'It's a great plan, Skeets,' Smiley said. 'But we oughta get out of here now. This place and that white tom give me the creeps.'

Rain fell but didn't come to anything and the sky cleared and the stars shone. In the garden, the wind was juggling the leaf glitter and throwing light around on the lawn. Silver and his top toms marked the terrace, spraying over any evidence of Skeets' visit. Then they sat in a row watching the lights of ships in the bay and out on the Channel.

'The light did go out in Skeets' eyes, didn't it?' Scarnose said.

'If it did,' said Ben, 'he couldn't have got up and walked off.'

'But maybe that's what makes him The Cat,' said Mellow. 'You can't fight that.'

'The light didn't go out,' said Silver.

'You're the only one who's sure of that, Silver,' said Scarnose.

'I'm sure because it didn't happen. It doesn't happen. It can't happen.'

'You mean it hasn't happened up till now,' said Scrumpy.

'Cut this out, hey,' Silver said sharply. 'He's just a tom like you and me.'

'No, he isn't,' said City's voice.

The old cat was in the shadows at the far end of the terrace.

'You got something to say,' Silver rapped, 'you come and say it.'

City ambled up to them and sniffed the empty food bowls. 'Skeets ain't all there,' he said, grinning at Silver. 'He's a headcase and he has these blackouts when he goes off into dreamland. But I never saw him drop like that before – not in a fight.'

'That's a relief,' Scarnose breathed.

'But you were wrong on two counts,' said City. 'He don't only go to sleep in a hurry when no one's expectin' it, but there ain't no light in his eyes to go out. He's got the deadest eyes you'll ever see. When there's no warmth in your heart there's no light in your eyes.'

Ben turned his own golden eyes on Silver. There was

138

an odd side to the white tom's nature and to recognise what it implied was to become part of it.

21

To Hay Tor

In clusters the stars were going out but Lucy didn't care what was happening in the sky. She trotted down the lane to Heatree Cross and continued straight on past the sleeping cottages. Small creatures panicked in the hedges and something large and clumsy broke from the undergrowth behind her and padded off in the opposite direction. The occasional muffled scream or squeak sounded the end of a victim as fox, badger, stoat and weasel plundered the night. The scents of this alien darkness intrigued her. Cattle, ponies, sheep – the smells mingled with the subtler smells of wild creatures.

She crossed the cattle grid by the telephone box and stopped to do her bits in the wayside mush of beech leaves and mud. Rain ghosted through the leaves above her in a short-lived shower whose scent lingered on the drystone walls. Emerging from the trees she was frightened by a herd of pony mares and their foals walking round the bend to meet her. The scent of crushed grass was on their breath.

Seeing the dark little thing running among them, one kicked out and her hooves narrowly missed Lucy. Skip was crying by the time she set him down and groomed her damp fur. The wind was bending the foxgloves on the hedgebanks and cutting through the treetops.

Gathering Skip firmly by the scruff of the neck she went on her way, apprehensive but never uncertain, her whiskers alive to the darkness that flowed around her. The sky was brightening in the east when she killed a young rabbit. She had abandoned Skip for less than a quarter of an hour but he was mewling when she returned. She fed some of the rabbit to the kitten and ate the rest

140

of it in big gulping bites, then looked round for water. Down off the open moor at the roadside was the grave of Kitty Jay, a young girl who had committed suicide in the nineteenth century and had been buried in unconsecrated ground at a crossroads. Over the years, someone had always put flowers in the jar by the unmarked granite headstone. Now the wind had scattered the foxgloves, and sticking her head in the jar Lucy drank the water which had a queer earthy tang. Then she lay on the grave and suckled her kitten.

The light in the bottom of the sky continued to strengthen around the silhouette of Hound Tor and the tabby ran towards it, coming along the road under Swine Down. A milk tanker thundered by, rocking the wayside vegetation with its draught. Lucy slowed to a walk, the kitten steady in her jaws, and presently she was passing Swallerton Gate and the grey cottage. The fartastic humps and towers of Hound Tor reared from the sweep of common ahead but she came right with the swing of the road and was soon under the beeches of Hedge Barton. A bank and drystone wall hid the fields to the west but Cripdon Down was open on the other side.

A dog fox crossed her path but hardly spared her a glance. Lucy bristled and growled from her throat and paced on. Her heart was thumping and the scare had heightened her awareness of the morning. She sifted through scents and dwelt on any sound that hinted at danger. The movement of birds produced a corresponding movement of her head.

Down the hill she came, keeping close to the drystone wall beneath a row of mature beeches, and during her crossing of the cattle grid Skip was sick. So Lucy took him to a wayside hollow and cleaned and comforted him before trotting along the edge of Bonehill Down with the drystone wall of Holwell Down to her left. But Skip was crying pitifully, so she found a gate onto Holwell Down and came over the lowest bars to a place against the wall where she felt free to lavish all her attention on the kitten. Lapwings were climbing and falling on their cries between

141

her and the little nameless tor. A raven croaked from higher up in the sky and some sheep walked over to her, full of curiosity. But Lucy was purring again and the sun was rising. She licked the dew and grass seeds off her coat, glad Skip was asleep; and before long she was also asleep with the morning growing around her and larksong washing over the landscape.

Skip woke her. He was mewing and she waited to see if he would begin retching as her tongue worked on his head. Then she nuzzled him towards her nipples and her purring mellowed. The sun was above the little tor and the great clouds were in motion. Watching them break up the blue and hold the gold flush of sun Lucy sank into a catnap. She would have preferred to be travelling again but although Skip appeared to have got over whatever it was that had been troubling him, she was reluctant to move until she was certain.

Traffic was building up but there were never a lot of cars on the Hound Tor road. A horn bleeped and the first coach of the day rumbled towards Jay's Grave. The lapwings were on the wing again, crying their sad double notes – *pee-wit, pee-wit.* Rolling and kicking on the turf the pony foals enjoyed the sun and the smell and feel of the moor, which was like a big animal to them. They were leggy and awkward and their mothers watched them from under long lashes.

About mid-morning, Lucy crept away from the sleeping kitten and pursued the smell of water until she came to a floodpool at the roadside, where she drank. Then she stalked a baby rabbit but was troubled by an aggressive doe and ran off, pretending it was what she had expected. By chance a car was parked tight to the verge and a man and woman were sitting in deckchairs by a small hawthorn tree. Lucy came belling towards them, tail and ears up, certain of her charm and how to use it. Normally she would have flattened out and crawled forward ready to flee at the first sign of danger, but she could not afford to be away from Skip for long.

A lone tabby cat calling for attention in the wilds of

142

Dartmoor was irresistible, and Lucy was fed and returned swiftly to her kitten to present him with a chunk of ham. The ponies had gone but the lapwings were still at their aerial dance and in the evening when she left the down, their cries followed her.

She trotted past the turning for Bonehill Rocks and on to the hawthorn tree, against which a Gallaway cow was rubbing. The car and the people had gone but other cars cruised by until she met a fairly steady traffic flow on the Widecombe-Bovey Tracey Road at Harefoot Cross. The pony path at the roadside offered safe walking and the heather and deer grass carried interesting smells. But nowhere since Easdon had she put nose to the scent of cat.

At Hemsworthy Gate she danced over the cattle grid and walked the sheep-nibbled turf on the left of the road with Seven Lords Lands and Houndtor Valley sweeping north, and Saddle Tor on the rise ahead. The swish of cars hardly ruffled her consciousness now but the crocodile of ramblers beyond Saddle Tor carpark sent her over the road above Bagtor Down and a far-off glimpse of the sea. A car horn sounded but failed to shift the sheep which were lying on the warm tarmac and half-blocking the road. Few drivers or their passengers caught sight of the tabby and her black and white kitten as she dodged in and out of the heather and whortleberry bushes. But she made a cow jump and startled a few larks and pipits.

After Saddle Tor, the road descended to a dip with the great granite crag of Hay Tor's Low Man in the north east and Bagtor Down running to the edge of the plateau in the south. Then Lucy was climbing the hill, somewhat wearily, Skip asleep in her jaws. A coach had pulled up on the brow and behind it was a large carpark, a few cars and a hot dog van. Students from the St Hilary's School of English in Paignton were queuing at the hot dog van for Coca Cola and ices after climbing to the top of Hay Tor. Lucy trotted up to them, laid down her kitten and mewed. At once mother and son were surrounded by French boys and girls and food from the van was lavished on them. Refusing milk, Lucy lapped up a bowl of water and grabbed Skip and carried him to the turf of the east-facing slope beside the carpark, where she was eventually left alone.

The nearby road snaked down towards Haytor Vale and on into the woods above Bovey Tracey. The valley of the lower Teign was further to the south east and the panorama of South Devon lay between Lucy and the flashing lighthouse of Berry Head.

'The light,' she breathed.

Now Home was not just the tug of some mysterious force on her being. She was on the frontiers of the reality of the Home Place and the light set her heart thumping. Perhaps Ben was in the garden staring across the rooftops towards it, thinking of her. But more likely he had taken up with another she. How could he know she hadn't gone forever? Dusk gathered on the landscape and small lights showed where villages, towns and busy roads lay. Lucy sighed and Skip wriggled into her soft warmth. She licked him and Berry Head lighthouse continued to wink in the gloom.

Then she cleaned herself thoroughly and sicked up a fur-ball.

22

Peace Council?

He waited for Berry Head light to flash again in the star-freckled darkness. The shouts and cries of people leaving the nightclubs down in the town ended. There was the sound of smashing glass and a little later a police siren wailed. Then silence closed. The lighthouse flashed once, twice before another pause. The lights on the seafront were green; those in the streets were orange. Ben yawned and glanced around the garden, which his night vision presented curiously pale with deep shadows. He had returned from searching the streets and the churchyard. Sitting on the terrace he wondered how he could fight the emptiness that kept hollowing his stomach. A barn owl sailed across the garden and was gone. The ghost moths fluttered in the blueish white light outside the french windows. The lady had fallen asleep in front of the television.

'You tired, Ben?' Silver said.

The night was still and warm. Clouds drifted over the stars. In the summerhouse Jessie was talking to the kittens and Rainbow and Pepper were laughing. A slowworm slithered through the grass on the edge of the lawn.

'She's out there,' Ben said, nodding at sleeping Paignton. 'Maybe she's hurt.'

'Maybe you should go and look for her again like you do every night,' Silver said kindly.

'I can't help it.'

'And my words won't help. So go and find her.'

Ben visited their old haunts – the back of the Golden Lily, Slaughterhouse Lane, the churchyard. Then he went further into town, along Palace Avenue and over Torquay Road by Tesco's and down Victoria Street to Station

145

Square, loosing his misery in an occasional cry. Pet toms avoided him and a stray dog resting in the doorway of a shoe shop did not challenge him.

In Station Square he found grey squirrels from Victoria Park and Queens Park going over the litter before the gulls, pigeons and starlings did their dawn scavenge. There were fried chicken scraps and bits of fish in batter among the greasy cartons and wrapping paper, but there was no Lucy and no end to the heartache.

Presently he returned to Winner Street and sat for a while in the doorway of the Pocket Book Shop. Then he called her again and again, before running up Winner Hill with the peculiar rolling gait of a healthy young tom.

Scarnose was cleaning himself on the bench outside the house called 'Jocyn'. 'I just saw that Dancer,' he told Ben, raising his head from his lower parts. 'Skeets wants "to meet Silver".'

'What for? There's nothing to talk about. The Crazies have to go. That's all. They've got to go. They finished Button and they've made Lucy disappear. So why a meeting?'

'I know how you feel,' Scarnose sniffed, jumping off the bench and pacing up to him. 'But if Silver can sort somethin' out I for one will feel safer when I walk the streets.'

'They met the other night and what happened?' Ben growled. 'Nothing. They just eyeballed each other and strutted their thing. Listen, Skeets wouldn't know what the truth was even if it fell on him and ripped off his ears. Everything's a game to that headcase.'

'OK, but Silver's still gonna meet him.'

'Where?'

'At first light on the shed roof at Barnie's house. Barnie says the dog who helped you will be around in case of a double-cross.'

'Do you think it'll solve anything?'

'No, but I ain't Silver. He wants you with him, Ben. Maybe it's a war council.'

146

'Bloody words,' Ben said in a voice so full of venom, Scarnose looked at him in alarm.

Dawn broke and the last of the fledgling crows in the firtop nest was being encouraged to fly by its parents. One adult sat on the roof of Huccaby calling to it, while the other swayed in the top of Maylands' walnut tree. After an agonising hesitation the youngster flew to the chimney pots of Fairview and rasped out its joy at the achievement. Ben and Scarnose laid back their ears and ran up the alley between Fairview and Bayview at the back of Monastery Road. Barnie sat on the wall behind Fairview and the Maylands' toms soon joined him.

'You get trouble,' said the old tom, 'and you make for the yard. The terrier won't let you down.'

'You're a good cat, Barnie,' said Silver. 'Is the Crazy here?'

'He's probably waiting for you to get on the roof before he shows himself. I caught a whiff of him earlier on.'

Ben and Silver came and sat among the ivy and brambles that had crept from the hedge over the roof, and almost immediately Skeets and Smiley appeared from the other side of Huccaby's garage. The Maylands' cats and the Shadows sat a couple of yards apart.

'So what lies have you dreamt up this time?' Ben opened.

Skeets grinned. 'Does he do the talking for you, Silver?'

'Sometimes. What you got to say?'

'You know I don't make deals. You know I'm backed by a lot of hook. You've seen what my toms can do.'

'Yeah yeah,' Ben growled. 'And I saw Silver blow on you in the garden and put you to sleep.'

'Oh dear,' Skeets sighed. 'I hope we're not just going to sit here slagging each other. I mean, I'm here to talk about sharing.'

'How can you share what you haven't got?' Ben said.

'Ben,' Silver said, and Ben turned away in disgust.

'We're neighbours,' Skeets went on. 'All I'm askin' is for you to let us come down through your home patch to the streets for a bit of scrounge. No hassle, no aggro. We

147

can't come as a mob because mobs don't pick up scrounge. It's gotta be ones or twos.'

'Tough,' Ben said. 'There's just enough scrounge for us.'

'Please,' Skeets said. 'Let Silver speak unless you've taken over from him. This is a peace council. Why louse it up because you got a big mouth?'

Smiley chuckled.

'Ben's right,' Silver said. 'It's his territory you're talking about and you're squatting on part of his hunting ground.'

'We gotta live,' Skeets smiled.

'Not on our patch,' said Ben.

Silver's tail beat on the ivy. 'Leave it to me, Ben.'

'Yeah, OK. This is a joke, so none of it matters.'

'You're the joke,' Smiley said.

'No trouble, Smiley,' said Skeets. 'Silver has got status. You give him respect, hey.'

'If you don't want aggravation you move on,' Ben said.

'But we like it here,' Skeets boomed. 'And we don't beg for anything. Look. We're up there. You're down there. In between there's ground where we can sort this out.'

'It's sorted out,' said Silver. 'You come uninvited. Go while you still got tails.'

'You think we can't take you?' Skeets cried. 'You think that, dog muck?'

'I think you're playin' games,' said Ben. 'Your words are just blowfly buzz, vole farts.'

Skeets backed off. 'I tried. I tried,' he crooned. 'You let them off the hooks and they spit in your face. Is that gratitude? Is it? Is that wise? Is it? Is it?'

His voice rose to a screech and the back bedroom window of Fairview opened and a man shouted and waved a fist. The cats separated and Ben and Silver trotted down the lane.

'I told you,' Ben said. 'Word games.'

'But I make up my own mind,' Silver said. Ben's behaviour had annoyed him. 'Go and find Lucy. You're trying my patience. Maybe I could have sorted out something

148

with Skeets if you hadn't rubbed him up the wrong way. We owe it to the old ones like Jessie and Sam. A concession by the Crazies would make it a safer patch.'

Ben didn't voice his thoughts. He ran by himself past the silver gates and on into Winner Hill Road. Lucy was eclipsing everything. Perhaps when he no longer felt so desolate he could give the problem of the Crazies his complete attention.

23
Night Roads

The light was flashing in the distance when Lucy fed her kitten and set off. Had she not been carrying Skip, she might have crossed the moor and the fields in a direct line for Berry Head, but she was also a street feral and was happy on tarmac and asphalt. So she walked down the hill with a purposeful tread, never questioning her instincts or the force which tugged at her innards. Again the air was dense with the smell of sheep and the animals themselves were lying at the roadside all the way to the telephone box and the turning to Haytor Vale.

Her lower jaw was used to the weight now but she constantly changed her grip on Skip for fear of opening his hide. Yet despite her toughness and determination she was feeling the strain. Her pads were a little sore and the threat of traffic had left her raw-nerved. Then there was the worry of looking after Skip. All her fears, real and imagined, were centred on the tiny creature.

She was now off the open moor and descending the long lane through the in-country of small fields and hamlets. Beyond Haytor Vale with its pub and bungalows the landscape was friendlier. At Smokey Cross she bore left and took a vole from the verge. The morning was warm and grooming left her thirsty. Sunrise revealed a cloudless day and the lane winding on and on through tree-filled coombes. Near Lewthorn Cross there was another encounter with badgers, but the sow and cubs were surprised by Lucy's ferocity and followed their own path up and over the hedge.

Sitting at the wayside she watched the coming and going of bees in the white 'bugles' of bindweed and her paws curled and uncurled with pleasure as Skip drew the milk from her body. Rests were more frequent now. The sun shone from a clear blue sky and heat was flickering on the road. The gleam of greenness was all about her and the flies had an unpleasant talent for getting in her eyes. Every once in a while the green at either hand was broken by a field of ripening corn but the bigness of the place was still intimidating. The world of streets, gardens and houses was small and in it a cat knew where she was.

Lucy's pupils narrowed, for she was walking not only into Ilsington but into the sun. Then the road looped down Old Town Hill away from the village and ran on through the trees of Silver Wood and Ilsington Wood. At the brook in the coombe she could slake her thirst and keep an eye on Skip, who was tottering about in the long grass trying to focus properly on butterflies. He resented being carried everywhere and made his feelings known when Lucy swung him off the ground and lugged him off on another dizzy stage of her journey.

From Willis' Cross the narrow country road ran parallel to the long coombe until it crossed Liverton Brook and came past the ripening apples into the village of Liverton. Here Lucy met a friendly old domestic she who led her to the council house where she lived and shared her food.

The long straight road carried her past the garage and the Star Inn to the Bickington Road and the ominous roar of not too distant traffic. Here at the junction Lucy didn't hesitate. She trotted left to the roundabout and her first experience of heavy traffic in a dangerous situation. Instinct caused her to run towards the oncoming vehicles, keeping close to the crash barrier on the right hand side. Cars swerved to give her safe passage but at the slip road leading to the Plymouth section of the dual carriageway she and Skip were nearly killed. The cattle lorry actually passed over her when she froze in front of it but she ran on dirty, shaken and unscathed after it had gone.

Her exit from the roundabout was prompted by a gut reaction. It sent her trotting down onto the A382 Newton Abbot Road. Often the draught of a heavy vehicle hurtling by rocked her off-balance, and once she was bowled over into the wayside grass. But even when she was clear of the roundabout confusion, her route remained perilous. She hurried along the right-hand side and managed to avoid the Trago Mills traffic, dodged the cars entering and leaving Stover Golf Club and almost caused an accident at the little bridge. A Fiat 132 swerved to avoid her and sent an overtaking motorbike wobbling towards the oncoming traffic. Fortunately the incident ended with a lot of shouting and threats but no crash.

Ears tight to the skull, head high and tail in the pump handle position Lucy ran up the road to the entrance of Stover Girls' School and the chance to clean and feed Skip. Her heart was beating fiercely and she was panting. The sun blazed through the trees and exhaust fumes washed over her. But the urge to be on the move was compelling and the protesting kitten was reduced to a dangling lump and carried into the traffic roar again.

All went well until she was scurrying up the narrow stretch to Forges Cross. Two dustcarts racing past forced her to dive into the hedge but Skip dropped from her jaws and landed in the road. Lucy's speed prevented a tragedy and the kitten was snatched to safety from under the wheels of a brewer's dray.

The tabby was coated with dust and grime but she battled on, limping slightly for there was a small abrasion on the pad of her left forepaw. Being narrow, the way was hazardous for all small creatures. Every so often she came upon the remains of rabbits, hedgehogs, grey squirrels and birds. Then there was a dead fox cub and the still-warm body of a black she cat.

'No light in your eyes, little sister,' Lucy breathed. 'But there is in mine and in the eyes of this kitten. Live on in us.'

The noise and awful speed of the traffic and the pathos of the dead cat had got to her. She walked slowly, feeling crushed of spirit, hot, footsore and depressed. Eventually a meadow proved irresistible and soon she had made a nest in the grass and suckled Skip. The nest was fifty yards from the road and this was a wise decision, for Skip was more active now and although he could not walk properly she had no intention of allowing him to stray to his death after carrying him down from Cloud Country.

At Maylands, Rainbow and Pepper were playing with Louise's kittens and the sound of their laughter brought a smile to Ben's face despite his depression. He sat on the summerhouse roof watching the steady build-up of cumulo nimbus. The huge clouds were rolling out of the bay. The sea darkened and flared to brilliance again. Each gust of the south-west wind made the grass quake and whiten before it settled again beneath its purple sheen. Ben sniffed the air. It smelt of rain and sure enough, the zoo peacocks were calling. Then the pressure dropped and the fall of winged insects brought the swifts down with them. The low-flying birds skimmed Maylands' trees and their screams cut through Ben's thoughts. Behind the approaching thunderstorm he sensed something else that left him dry-mouthed and restless. He paced back and forth, dredging up the odd garaow of bewilderment. The young crow in the chestnut tree regarded him suspiciously through the shift of leaves, while his parents agitated from the nearby hawthorns and flung themselves at Ben in squawking swoops.

'Mad birds,' Ben growled, showing his displeasure in a series of staccato complaints.

At first slowly, the rain began to fall and thunder rumbled over the Three Towns. The Maylands gang retreated to the summerhouse and listened to the drumming intensify on the roof. Thunder cracked and boomed and lightning brought the cats' bellies close to the ground.

'To be out in this,' Sam said, shaking his head.

Throughout the afternoon the rain beat down and thunderstorms rolled across south Devon. Then, in the evening, the downpour became a drizzle and fog added to the gloom which by dusk was gothic. But Lucy had found shelter in a hedge and spent the last hours of daylight watching raindrops slide down the bramble leaves. Skip slept, with an occasional shuddering sigh and stiffening of the legs. His mother was waiting for the traffic din to end. She catnapped until sleep took her by surprise and when she woke there was no noise except the patter of raindrops on leaves and Skip's cries in the immediate darkness.

On the road again, covered in grime and grass seeds she met few cars and trotted into the outskirts of Newton Abbot where there were pavements and gardens. It was comforting to be among the hard friendliness of brick and concrete lit by street lights.

She came past St Leonard's Tower into East Street and walked the pavement, pausing with a little cry of delight to place Skip gently at her feet and sniff a takeaway carton. The doorway of the Cider Bar also provided smells that reminded her of Church Street and the Labour Club. At the top of the street she crossed over and trotted through the rain mist down to the Penn Inn Roundabout to bear right with the A380 Torquay Road. Some holiday traffic passed her, heading for Torbay; but the occasional car and caravan or car with cases on the roof were on the opposite side of the road and she had the pavement to herself. The railway line was on her right, below the embankment; and houses were over the way. Although her jaws were stiff and her left forepaw hurt every time she set it down Lucy felt at ease. A young rabbit killed by a car provided a meal and there was a quiet place at hand to feed a little red meat to Skip and lick her injured paw.

In Kingskerswell, just beyond the Black Swan pub, she had a scare coming under the bridge. There was no pavement here and the police car was travelling fast in response to an alarm call. Lucy crouched with her body pressed to the stonework but dashing on she was relieved to find the pavement again. The rain had stopped and the sky was clearing. Big clouds hurried across the stars and Lucy trotted despite the pain in her foot. Once past the Hare and Hounds and the garage she was beside a hedge of tall, ancient hawthorns which rustled and dripped in the breeze that had risen behind the rain. On the verge she killed a starling fledgling. The bird had been struck by a car the evening before and was close to death when the cat put it out of its misery. She preferred the taste of bird to rabbit.

Then she was at the Kerswell Gardens roundabout in Torbay and the tug of home drew her up the A3022 ring road and the dual carriage of Hamelin Way. Changing her grip on Skip, she ran close to the crash barrier until she was able to hug the bottom of the steep grassy banks. A car roaring by would hold the gleam of her eyes and other eyes in its headlights. Foxes were quartering the banks for voles but Lucy went unnoticed, and after half a dozen rests she reached the end of the carriageway. She cut directly across the roundabout and ran along the left-hand verge of the A3022 beside the field where the Monday Market was held. And when she dropped Skip in the grass and licked her sore paw she smelt the sea. The scent was wafting over the wet fields of Cockington and gripping Skip once more she climbed the bank, laid him down and jumped on top of the fence. Not too far off in the darkness Berry Head lighthouse flashed, and Lucy closed her eyes on a sigh.

24

Lights in the Chip Shop

Wearily, she turned her back on the ring road and came in search of warmth and shelter away from the headlight glare. Skip was asleep in her jaws and she walked carefully down Stantor Lane, past the cottages to the farm outbuildings of Stantor Barton. The big modern barn was full of hay, and the farmcats did not object to a wandering she and her kitten bedding down for the night. The half-wild shes, who had known the joys and heartache of raising kittens, brought her token gifts of mice and sparrows and Lucy was soon stoking up the purrs on the edge of a long, deep sleep.

The following day, she examined her injured pad and decided it would be best to lie-up till dusk and let the healing qualities of her tongue work on the wound. One of the farm shes called Nell became friendly with her and would climb up onto the bales for a chat.

'Watch out for the dogs,' she said as Lucy groomed Skip. 'They doan mean no harm but they'm a bit rough. I'll tell 'ee when to leave and I'll take 'ee over the fields to the place where the roads meet.'

Farm noises and smells didn't suit Lucy but she took the opportunity to sleep, tend her wound and groom some of the grime out of her coat. Dust and grit had got into her eyes, under the third eyelid, and she carefully dragged a wet paw over them until the irritation ceased. Then she examined Skip's neck to see if there was any damage. Satisfied, she slept again and dreamt of blackbird song and hawthorn blossom drifting down through sunlight into Maylands' garden.

Showers fell, cattle called and a tractor rattled along the

lane. The sun set and daylight faded quicker than usual, with clouds driving in from the west.

'Ready?' Nell called. 'The dogs are in the kitchen gettin' fed. Follow me – and look sharpish.'

At the top of the farmyard a narrow flight of steps ascended the bank to a gap in the hedge and a wheatfield. The cats ran between the stalks and the hedge to a stone stile and on over pasture among grazing heifers. Another stile saw them into a bigger field and the final stone stile, with the ring road beyond.

'Keep to the grass and you'll be OK.' Nell raised her voice against the traffic noise. 'There idn too many cars about. Go safely, lil sister. May life smile on you.'

'And you, Nell.'

The trail on the verge was no wider than a cat. It ran between tall grass, nettles and hogweed until a tarmac footpath at Five Lanes provided easier walking. The late hour had cut down the traffic but the pavement alongside Vicarage Road vanished just before the Olde Smokey House Inn and good fortune alone saw Lucy safely through the narrow section to Marldon Road.

Now the pavement was wide but the rain was falling heavily, and every now and then she was covered in the spray thrown up by passing vehicles. At the top of the slope where the fields gave way to houses she stopped under some trees and gave Skip a thorough cleaning. Rain slanted through the lamplight. Then, at the corner of Southfield Avenue, a couple of girls tried to catch her out of pity but she leapt into a garden where she stayed until it was safe. On the wall she looked about her and saw something which made her cry out with joy. Over the rooftops and sea to the south, Berry Head light was flashing.

'There, my little lovely,' she purred to Skip. 'Over there – the light. Our light. We're nearly home.'

The rain beat into her face and it was necessary to stop several times to groom the kitten. But she had passed the shops on the corner of Hoyles Road and Ramshill Road, and broke into a limping trot which became a sprint whenever she was forced to swerve around people's legs. Presently the descent steepened and as she splashed through the downpour towards the lights of the Dolphin Fish and Chip Shop on the other side of the roundabout, she heard the Parish Church clock chime the hour. She was only a couple of streets from the garden.

At the roundabout, she would have gone straight up Colley End Park to Monastery Road but a mongrel, let out for exercise by uncaring people, attacked her and she dashed down the upper part of Cecil Road to fling herself onto the wall of a vacant lot at the end of Winner Street. Skip was badly shaken and began to mewl. So Lucy scrambled down among the building material and sheltered under a sheet of polythene and soothed the kitten until the road was hers again.

Instead of coming up Winner Street to the bottleneck and Winner Hill Road, she ran along Well Street and came into Church Street by the Victoria Hotel. And here, in home territory at last, she was overcome by emotion and fatigue. Her foot was swollen and throbbing and happiness and relief turned to sorrow. She was tired and Skip was heavy and both cat and kitten were soaked. But the Central Fish Bar's lights were on and the aroma of frying food brought Ben poignantly to mind. A woman emerged from the door of the newsagents and bent to stroke her but Lucy hobbled on. The rain had spiked her fur and beaded her whiskers. It was a bitter-sweet moment. She should have been overjoyed but she did not know what home held for her any more. She had walked nearly fifty miles and now she was here she felt broken.

'Maraow.' Her cry carried up the empty rain-washed street and got a querulous, bell-like response.

Ben pushed his head between the Labour Club railings. Rain dripped from the eaves of the houses and he stared through his disbelief at the small, bedraggled she cat who was limping along the pavement with what looked like a drowned rat in her mouth.

'Is it really you?' he said softly.

And she nodded, unable to speak.

He squeezed through the bars and bounded up to her and pressed his nose to her nose. Then he smelt the kitten and licked it before walking with her back onto the Labour Club terrace where they were out of the worst of the rain.

The soaking had done nothing to dull the beauty of her autumn colours. There wasn't a detail of her appearance he had forgotten, but the reality took him by surprise.

'My lovely Lucy,' he murmured.

'There were three kittens,' she said as they lay together in the corner by the metal beer kegs, Skip sleeping between their warmth. 'Two are dead.'

She went on to tell him about her ordeal and Cloud Country, and how the feeling inside her had guided her home. He groomed her throughout her tale and licked the cut and blister on her pad. A group of men came out of the club laughing and when they had crossed the street to the chip shop, Ben decided it was time to get Lucy and Skip back to Maylands.

'Has Skeets gone?' she asked, putting Skip down at the bottom of Winner Hill Road and licking her bad foot. It was a question from a creature recalling a nightmare.

Ben explained what had happened.

'The Crazies don't come it so strong any more,' he added. The kitten swinging from her jaws fascinated him. 'But I can't work out what Skeets is up to and there's something about Silver that worries me. It's like he thinks the same as Skeets, you know – like he's got a kind of quiet thunderstorm going on inside him. His eyes tell me nothing.'

Lucy stopped and looked at him. 'But Silver isn't cruel, Ben. He isn't a Crazy on a weird sort of violence high. I don't understand you.'

'I mean this is a game between them,' Ben said. 'One of them is going to get wiped out and so maybe the game is enough. There can only be one winner at the end of the game, so why end it? It didn't start out that way. Skeets has made it happen. Everything's changed since he came. You have to watch where you go and what you do, and you keep thinking there's a Shadow in the shadows. Maybe I've got it all wrong but it's the way I feel.'

'There are other gardens, Ben, in other places.'

'I've thought of going. But I couldn't leave old Jessie and Sam and Louise's kittens.'

'I'd forgotten about her kittens.'

'Four – but a couple of other shes and Jessie are looking after them. Louise isn't interested.'

Lucy nodded. It often turned out that way.

'So I'm stuck,' Ben said. 'I follow Silver because this is my family.'

She rubbed against him and they plodded on to be met halfway up Monastery Road by Scarnose and Parson.

'Lucy,' Scarnose cried. 'Goodta see yuh. Where you been? Hey, is that thing in your mouth yours?'

'We missed you, Lucy,' said Parson. 'I've got to tell the others.'

'I'd like to go straight to the shelter,' Lucy said. 'I'm dead tired and me and the little one just want to sleep.'

She nuzzled the kitten who stood wobbling between her front legs.

'What's his name?' Scarnose asked.

'Skip.'

'Great,' and the ginger tom looked at Ben and added – 'Any sign of Crazies?'

'No. It's never too bad down the bottom by the fish scrounge.'

'Scrumpy got done.'

'Where?'

'In the big garden behind Barnie's house.'

'Badly?'

'Yeah. Skeets himself did it. He tried to kill Scrumpy. Got his killing teeth into his neck and if Scrumpy hadn't rolled over that would have been it. He's got a bad wound.'

Ben nodded and watched Lucy glide between the ornamental ironwork at the bottom of the silver gates into

160

Maylands. Relief flooded his being when he escorted her over the lawn.

'Somethin' else, Ben,' Scarnose said. 'Someone shot at Mellow earlier on. The slug just missed him.'

'Where was this?'

'Down the bottom of the lane by the red stone house you used to go past to stalk in the trees under the big house.'

'Right on the edge of Skeets' patch,' Ben said. 'It was stupid of Mellow to go there.'

'Yeah, but it's an interestin' development,' said Scarnose. 'The only time I can remember anyone shooting a cat was when old couldn't-give-a-sod-Billy caught it down by the pigeon house. But he asked for it. He was always tryin' to grab the birds.'

'It would be OK if a human did us a favour,' said Ben. 'I'd like to see Skeets get it between the eyes.'

'As if there ain't enough to worry about,' Parson said.

'It ain't all bad news,' Scarnose announced, romping ahead of them through the wet grass and sending raindrops flying. 'What about Lucy's kitten? Hey, everyone, Lucy's back and she's got company!'

All the gang save Pepper, Rainbow and Louise who were out stalking gathered round her and Jessie and Rita were soon pouring purrs onto Skip.

'Let them get inside,' Jessie cried, wriggling back into the summerhouse through the broken panel in the door. 'You want Skip to catch cold?'

Lucy discovered Louise's kittens with her nose and was soon welcoming them into her warmth.

'The purrrr-fect solution,' Sam chuckled.

'Every night we left a bowl of food untouched up by the house,' said Jessie. 'I knew you'd be back. You can't lose Lucy.'

The shes pressed around Lucy. They uttered little cries of pleasure and bunted her with their heads. In the corner, Skip and the other kittens were exchanging mews. Ben smiled and sought Lucy's company in the darkness which was alive with the smell of cat living.

161

'Tell us where you've been,' said Rita.

'How long did it take you to get home?' said another voice.

'Didja have any adventures?' Rita bawled.

'What happened to the other kits?'

'Howja get the bad foot?'

'What's it like in Cloud Country?'

'Later, later,' Jessie blared in her kazoo-like tones. 'Can't you tell she's worn out? She's been further even than Button went. Let her sleep.'

'I s'pose she'll take over all the kittens now,' Rita said jealously.

'No,' Lucy yawned. 'But I'd like to share them with you, Rita. Maybe you could help out a bit with Skip, too, if it's OK with you.'

'OK? Try and stop me! C'mon Luce – let me give him a cuddle while you take a stroll through dreamland.'

'Listen,' Parson cried. There was silence. Then the wind freshened and raindrops splattered on the roof as the chestnut tree rocked. Parson poked his head out of the hole in the door.

'Rain's stopped. Stars are shining and old City's singing up by the house.'

'I don't know that one,' Scarnose chuckled. '*Up By the House* – a new song for mooncrooners.'

'It would be good to welcome Lucy home in the traditional way,' said Silver, who had chosen to keep well in the background up till then.

'Usual place?' Scarnose said.

'Where else?'

Half a moon lit the bay and the roofs had that silver gleam which Ben liked. He was higher than he had ever been on a catmint trip and he no longer felt lost and empty. Bounding through the grass with the other toms, he was first up the rockery and onto the terrace. Then he sat and stared out over the bay to the place where the sea ended and the sky began before his head went back and he mooncrooned the wordless celebration of his kind. The rest of the toms pitched in.

'But this don't get rid of Skeets,' Scarnose observed after the performance. Ben gazed at him, his golden eyes thoughtful. For Skeets, he mused, getting here was the thing. He had to burrow into the dark and fill it with his violence. Ice gurgled in Ben's gut. Skeets didn't want it to end. Everything he had said to Lucy was true. But there was something beyond the obvious, something even more chilling that eluded him.

The young barn owls called to the parent birds and flapped onto the summerhouse roof. They were as white as Silver in the moonlight. Scarnose fidgeted into a comfortable crouch beside Ben, folding his paws under his chest and slowly narrowing his eyes. A ghost moth fluttered close to him and he swatted it and flicked it into his mouth.

'Take things as they come,' he said and Ben laughed.

It was the feral philosophy.

The owls were off, white whispers against the stars. The lady went to the lavatory and pulled the chain. The sound of flushing water set the cats' ears twitching.

25

Dreams

Shadow activity increased and there were skirmishes over the next four days. Lucy was with the kittens down by the summerhouse and Ben slept on the terrace. It was mid-afternoon and the heat was relentless on roads and roofs. Flies buzzed around the jungle of mallow, poppies and garden flowers at the bottom of the rockery, and the laughter and screams of children on the beach and green carried across the houses. It was Paignton Carnival but the herring gull chicks were interested only in the next meal, and the young crow perched on Maylands' TV aerial rasped out his demands to ever-attentive parents.

Ben slept curled on his side, muzzle between forepaws. Then his teeth chattered and he kicked out his legs with ears and tail twitching. In the dream he was running through the dark again, downhill this time, the stink of decay in his nostrils. The night was one long, nasty surprise of amorphous things. Ben wasn't a cat. He was merely a part of the darkness, as helpless as a kitten in a sack sinking in black water. Looking up from the suffocating depths he saw the moon wearing Skeets' death's head grin and woke with a cry, feeling sick. Where was Lucy? Then he heard her talking to the kittens and calmed down.

They met when the young were asleep and rolled in the catmint together until they sailed out of the moment. Then they gazed unseeing through half-closed eyes up at a sky haunted by swifts, whose cries were fainter than the sounds made by the children on the seafront.

Hidden in the shrubbery behind the bust of Sir Francis Drake, Smiley considered the situation. He was certain the Shadows could muscle in and claim the garden any time they chose. Why did things go wrong? It was the black and white tom they had to watch. Silver had yet to demonstrate why every cat in the neighbourhood respected him. Get rid of the black and white hardcase and resistance would crumble. The church clock struck four and Smiley transferred his attention to the shes and kittens. They were in their corner of the garden catching the best of the afternoon sun. A couple of toms were up on the terrace. Three Shadows, Smiley thought, could hit the kittens and be away before any of Silver's gang could retaliate. The smile which had earnt him his name broadened. Skeets would like it.

Smiley crept away and came down onto the pavement. He was hot, hungry and irritable. Trotting to the part of Winner Hill Road that narrowed in its descent to Clifton Road he stopped, slumped back against the wall and began to groom the moistness from his coat. If the bee had not chosen that moment to settle on his nose and cause him to lose his balance in his efforts to dislodge it the airgun pellet would have hit him between the eyes. Instead it ricocheted off the wall and hummed away, louder than the bee. Ears flat and tail low, Smiley sprinted back up the hill and another shot whined past him. But a nearby garden provided refuge and he lay under the hedge and waited for nightfall.

The bang woke Smiley and he dashed across the flower bed and crouched quivering on the lawn. Bright lights climbed the sky and there were three more muffled bangs followed by cascades of gold and silver stars. The Quaywest Beach Resort firework display had begun and the explosions brought most of the Maylands toms to the terrace to gaze fearfully at the sky. But a pulverising burst of noise sent them running for the summerhouse. Before long all the gang were there, shes and toms huddled together in a shivering heap. Jessie's deafness left her unmoved and she was purring and licking the kittens, ignorant of her companions' suppressed hysteria.

Smiley ran up through the back gardens. Skeets sat alone on the roof of the yellow van gazing in rapture at the sky. A rocket whistled up higher than the small popping lights and exploded with a crump and a shower of brightness. It was a dream, Skeets decided. He had come to rainbow's end and was passing through a series of dreams. One minute he was there in the boring, old Now of everything, smelling the same old smells, feeling the same boring old sun on his coat, doing the same boring things; then he was in a dream place. This one was really good. The sky was falling to bits, all noise and light. But he was certain there was a sensational dream above it waiting to receive him and hold him forever. All he had to do was knock the white cat off the roof. That was the catch. If he failed he would never get into the big dream. He had to wait for the sign. He had to be sure when the time came. He grinned and said: 'Why are you scared, Smiley?'

'All that banging, and I was shot at earlier on.'

'Were you hit?'

'No, I was lucky.'

'Good. You're a good cat, a good friend. Come up here. There's nothing to be afraid of. Lights and noises won't hurt you.'

Smiley settled uneasily beside him.

'How did you get into my dream?' Skeets said in his low, dangerous voice that dismayed Smiley.

'You invited me in.'

'Are you sure?'

'Yeah. You called and I came running like I always do.'

'Of course! You're a good cat, Smiley. Howja like this dream?'

'It's one of the best. You done me a real favour lettin' me share it with you.'

Skeets nodded graciously, and the sky blazed and another rocket ascended to explode with a detonation that shook Smiley.

'Stay cool,' Skeets murmured and dizziness claimed him and he blacked-out.

Smiley stared down at the twitching, writhing body

166

and licked his lips. 'That was close,' he murmured. 'Too close.'

A series of detonations crackled over the bay and gulls began to cry from the roofs. In the summerhouse, Lucy's kitten was grooming his mother and adding his purrs to the chorus rising from the other young ones and shes. Jessie wheezed in her sleep and Sam groaned. Normally Lucy would have been out taking exercise but the fireworks were too disturbing for her to abandon the cat warmth. Ben was absent but not far off. In the strange silence between explosions she could hear him sharpening his claws on the chestnut tree. She knew it was him because he kept growling, 'Crazy noise. Crazy noise,' after each loud bang.

The following morning the wind carried an acrid smell and the ferals walked around the garden crinkling their noses and frowning, but it was another warm day and there were no blackbird hysterics to set them on edge. Jessie hoisted herself up the rockery and flopped down on the terrace.

'Are you OK, Mother?' Ben said.

'I'm too old, too tired. I'll be glad when the light has gone out in my eyes.'

'Don't say that,' Lucy shuddered.

'I spend so much time asleep I might as well do it permanently,' the old cat smiled. 'I hurt all over, inside and out. It's no fun. Soon you'll be talking about me like we talk about Button.'

'That's too sad,' Lucy said, thinking of Skip.

They had a nap and watched the birds flying in and out of the trees and the butterflies fluttering over the rockery. The sun was high and the day cloudless. Ben gazed at Lucy, recalling Jessie's words. No one would care if the moon never shone again but when the light vanished from the eyes of a creature you loved, it left your heart empty.

'Is it all right to join you?' said a voice.

Barnie, the old black tom from Fairview stood at the end of the terrace with his friend the Jack Russell.

'The dog will be OK?' Ben asked. 'We got kittens runnin' around.'

'You know he's fine. Didn't he help you that time you got in our house?'

'Yeah. Come on over. Anythin' wrong?'

'No,' Barnie grinned, approaching the ferals and seating himself nearby. The terrier joined him and loosed a stream of whining barks.

'You understand dog, Barnie?' Lucy said.

Barnie nodded. 'I've lived with him for more summers than I got claws on my front feet. He's more than a friend. The people at our house left the front door open so I sneaked him out for a stroll.'

'What's he saying?' asked Ben.

'He wants you to know he's your friend. Any time he can help you fight this Skeets animal you give him the wink.'

'If I say thanks he'll understand?'

'Yes,' Barnie said. 'He understands me, don't you, Jamie?'

The dog wagged his little stump of a tail and uttered a string of gruff barks.

'He wonders why,' Barnie continued in an embarrassed voice, 'you and the other toms don't band up on Skeets and take him, mob-hooked.'

Lucy stared in disbelief at the terrier.

'I know,' Barnie sighed. 'It's not our way but it's what his kind would do. He's only trying to help.'

'But what is the answer?' Ben said. 'Now Skeets is a thing that creeps in and out of the dark givin' everyone nightmares. No one's prepared to risk what he can dish out. Still,' he added in a brisker tone, 'I'm grateful for Jamie's offer. Thanks, Jamie.'

A man was calling the terrier and Jamie's ears perked up and he ran off. Barnie followed.

'That sums up pethood,' Ben said sadly. 'You belong to people.'

'And you know,' said City's voice, 'it don't seem that bad when you're old. They call you and give you food

168

and shelter and make you feel wanted.' The old cat was lying in the mallow. 'Maybe it would be better for Jessie if she were a pet,' he concluded.

'No way,' said Ben. 'She lives free, she dies free.'

'That's OK when you're young,' City said. 'And it's OK in the summer but it ain't so hot when you're stiff in all your joints and can't pee properly and can't catch anything except a cold and the snow's up round your ass.'

Ben's heart melted. 'I didn't mean to sound – to sound – '

'Here, I hope I'm not out of line grabbin' you like this, Ben,' City said.

'Don't worry, it's our garden here. We're free to do what we want and say what we want.'

Old Jessie lay dead to the world and might have slept for much longer if it hadn't been for the ants. They were black and had wings. Throwing themselves into the air from the lawn, they pursued the queens in the nuptial flight, swarming over the garden until Ben and Lucy could stand it no longer and ran for the summerhouse.

Halfway across the grass Lucy stopped and cried, 'We can't leave Jessie to cope with this.'

'You go on and I'll go back for her,' Ben said, spitting ants off his lips.

The air was dark with them. They swirled around like drizzle and the swifts and other small birds swept through the swarm to feed on the wing.

'Jessie,' Ben called from the foot of the rockery. 'Jessie.'

There was no answer, and fearing the worst he came up the rockery in leaps and bounds.

'Jessie!'

The old she stirred. Flying ants covered her face but she made no effort to wipe them away with a paw. Ben licked her muzzle and sent his tongue skating over her head, dislodging the insects.

'You OK?' he smiled.

'They little black things don't worry me, Ben. I've seen 'em before, summer after summer. They idn a lot of bother. But you're a beautiful tom.'

'Let's go back to the shelter.'

'I was enjoying that nap,' she said.

The ants were a crazy irritation. They danced well into the evening and the insect-eating birds took their toll. Up at the monastery the air was dense with them. They clogged Skeets' nostrils and burrowed into the corners of his eyes but he bellowed out the purrs.

'First the night sky falls apart with bangs and flashes and all sorts of pretty popping lights,' he crooned. 'Now it's a new dream of raindrops with wings. The sky is dancing for Skeets.'

He rolled his eyes.

'Who's providing these dreams? Who? Skeets is The Cat but surely no cat has ever been blessed with such dreams. Maybe,' and his eyes rounded, 'maybe I'm more than cat. Maybe everything wants to keep Skeets happy like the Shadows keep me happy and do what I tell them.'

Smiley and Dancer sat under the holm oaks and marvelled at the sandy tom's behaviour.

'That Skeets,' Dancer breathed.

But Smiley detected behind the words a desire to question Skeets' status.

'He offers the chance for you to do anything you bloody well like, when you like, to whoever or whatever you dislike. That's it, ain't it, Dancer?'

'What else is there?' Dancer said. 'You gotta look after number one. Skeets knows. Number one looks after number one and the rest of us.'

Smiley nodded and spat ants, but he wasn't convinced Dancer understood or cared. Skeets occupied a lofty place far above the limitations of restraint which kin groups valued. He was the quintessence of what night meant in cat terms – a kind of living darkness with hooks that could sink into the instincts and drag an animal off to Nirvana where all was possible.

26

Stalking

There was only the here and now of life. It varied with the seasons and the weather and as a creature aged, but the living of it was attended by moments of intense happiness which made everything seem worthwhile.

Ben and Lucy lay on the summerhouse roof and watched the kittens romping around Jessie in the grass below. The day was windless. Sunlight flooded the garden and the cats were serene. Their purring mingled with the drone of bees.

Scarnose, Sam and City sat on the terrace gazing absently about or sending their teeth chattering like clippers through the fur of a leg or tail.

'Ben is a different tom since the Skeets trouble began,' Scarnose said.

'He don't mess about,' City nodded.

'There's more to him than meets the eye,' Scarnose said. 'I reckon he's deeper than Silver. I've felt it for a long time. When Lucy was missing he was all hooks and aggro.'

'And he's the kindest tom I've ever met,' said City.

'Ben is different,' Sam said. 'He's more determined than Silver. He wants to get on with things. And he cares.'

'When he's my age,' City smiled, 'he'll have a lot of scar tissue on his heart.'

'Is that good?' said Sam.

'It probably will be for Lucy and you and the rest of the gang,' City said.

'You got a lot of sense, City,' Scarnose said respectfully. 'Some of the old toms I know tend to come the Wise Pussy guff.'

He winked and grinned at Sam.

'There's common sense and there's wisdom,' Sam remarked coolly.

Parson sauntered up to them and acknowledged Scarnose as the top cat present by lowering his head and eyes before him.

'We're gettin' an earful of Sam's wisdom,' Scarnose chuckled and Parson smiled. The gang knew most of Sam's daft aphorisms by heart but a new one had them rolling with laughter.

' "Because the crow takes a bath in the pond",' Scarnose choked, ' "it don't make him a duck".'

Sam's tail swished but Scarnose pressed on.

'It really kills me when you go all mysterious, Sam. All them fancy words, you know – "Watch out for the wind with the hooks of ice on the night of the full moon". I mean, come on.'

'You were born thick,' Sam said. 'Your brains are swinging under your tail.'

City and Parson laughed but Scarnose continued undeterred.

' "A cat may bark but that don't make him a bulldog".'

Parson and City were spluttering and rolling about, their legs kicking.

' "A rat with no teeth will run from a vole". Yeah? Wow! – who would've guessed it? And what about "Promised scrounge won't feed a hungry tom"? Ain't that smart? Ain't that amazing?'

'Thick,' Sam growled, and haunches swinging and tail lashing he descended the rockery. But the seagull swooping to land on the roof of Maylands spoilt his dignified withdrawal. The yellowish-white dollop of her mutes hit Sam on the side of the head and he took off in a vertical leap which reduced his audience to a yarooling tangle of helplessness.

'The bird was only passing a comment, Sam,' Parson croaked, but Sam was pawing at his ear and rubbing his head in the grass.

'I swear I'll die laughin' if I hang around with him,' Scarnose hiccupped.

172

'You'd just die if you hung around with Skeets,' City said. 'And it wouldn't be a laugh. That tom ain't no joke.'

'Then why take up with him in the first place?' Scarnose said.

'I was alone. I was old. I was a bad ass and he was good to me at first. Then he got worse and I began to wonder when I'd get the chop. When, not if.'

'He's something else,' Parson murmured.

'Yeah. He's the sort of Crazy you don't want to meet in a dark alley on a dark night,' Scarnose said.

Their mood had changed and they went their separate ways feeling down and insecure. Apart from Skeets a new peril had surfaced. Sam called it the presence beneath the presence, but the youth with the airgun was very real. For him it had become a challenge and the summer holidays allowed him to concentrate on the council estate ferals and strays. He wasn't patient enough to lie in wait for wandering animals or he would have been more successful. Yet before long he had replaced Skeets as the thing the cats feared most, stalking the monastery garden and the quieter streets near the Lions' Club. Now the Shadows experienced some of the terror they had been dispensing since their arrival, but for Skeets it was a new spice. He had met the giant figure on two occasions, both at dusk, but had escaped unharmed. Nothing could hurt him. He was The Cat and he was beaming with self-satisfaction when Smiley ran out from under the oaks and took his place among the toms lazing in the carpark sun.

'I was shot at,' he panted. 'Down by the high wall.'

'Garrg,' Skeets said at the end of a chuckle. 'Garrg, Smiley.'

Dancer and Squib glanced at each other.

'Garrg,' Skeets growled at the Shadows.

'Garrg,' they chorused dutifully.

'It wasn't no joke,' Smiley said. 'It wasn't funny.'

'Of course it wasn't,' Skeets purred. 'But you have to get it in perspective, Smiley. You're unharmed and I daresay you learnt from the experience.'

'True,' Smiley admitted.

To have disagreed with Skeets would have been foolish and moments later he was proved right. The pale-eyed tom flew into one of his poisonous rages and leapt at Skiffle.

'Why?' Skiffle cried. 'What did I do?'

'You shook your head when Smiley confessed he had learnt from the shooting incident.'

'So what did he learn?'

'To agree with me, you fool. I'm the one with the vision. I'm the one who can slip in and out of dreams and bring you with me when I choose.'

The hooks of both front paws opened Skiffle's face.

'There,' Skeets grunted. 'Point made?'

'Point made.'

'Point taken?'

And Skiffle nodded vigorously.

'I beat you up, Skiffle, and I bet it's suddenly as clear as day.'

'That's true, that's true.'

'Smiley's words,' Skeets smiled. 'In future, think of the trouble you can avoid by seeing things from my point of view.'

'We try to all the time, Skeetsie,' said Slippery Jim. 'But not havin' your vision makes it difficult.'

'Skeetsie?' Skeets boomed. 'Skeetsie! You got the front to call me that? I'm Skeets, Skeets. Go on, say it.'

'Skeets.' Slippery Jim's voice shook. 'I didn mean no offence. You got more status than any cat I've ever known. There are hardcase toms who would queue to kiss what you got under your tail. Yeah – out of affection and respect.'

'Affection,' Skeets sighed. 'I like that. Loved and honoured. How touching! I'm warm inside and I feel so . . . humble.'

'Humble,' Dancer snorted when he and Squib loped off together for the stalking. 'Him, humble! Look,' he added quickly, 'I admire what he's done and what he's doing. With him there ain't no rules. We just take over and take. What I can't swallow is the way he keeps

174

roughin' us up. We're his toms but he's got to go over the top like he did with Skiffle.'

'We lost City through it,' Squib said. 'And one day you and I will cop one of his moods. I don't want an eye hooked out just because Skeets is pissed off.'

'Who does?' Dancer said. 'We could've taken the garden and dropped Silver. So what's happening? I tell you the lame brain has really flipped.'

'He's got a gut full of wasps,' Squib growled.

'And a maggotty ass,' Dancer said, and they chuckled.

The patter of light, swift footsteps behind them brought them up sharply. Reekin was preceded by a body stink pungent with fear.

'You saw what he did to Skiffle?' he panted. 'He could've blinded him. Why did he do it? We're Shadows, ain't we? We got status. We ain't mice.'

'So what do you suggest, Brains?' Dancer asked.

Reekin stared blankly at him.

'OK, Dancer,' Squib said. 'Reekin's with us. Ease up on him.'

'And Smiley's with Skeets,' Dancer said. 'And Scrag, Boomer, Bang, Slippery Jim – '

'But for how long?' said Squib. 'All we gotta do is be smart and wait.'

Dancer's nose clenched and he sniffed and said, 'You got a point. So we wait and don't say nothing to upset him. Understand, Reekin? Just play along and you won't lose an eye. Got it?'

'Got it. I ain't too bright, Dancer, but I'm with you and Squib. The garden's down there and we're up here. We came a long way to find the end of Skeets' rainbow but Silver's mob've still got the best scrounge and the best shelter. I don't get it.'

'Why does it rain? Why does it get dark? Where do the stars come from?' Dancer said.

'I should know?' Reekin growled.

'And I should know what makes Skeets tick?' Dancer said.

'Let's find a quiet spot and get our heads down,' Squib

said placatingly. 'Life tends to sort itself out. Silver's gang have got it coming to them. We're still the Shadows.'

Reekin's eyes brightened. 'And we can still do the Shadows stuff. Hey! Yeah. Don't forget the shes.'

'Shadows,' Dancer grinned.

'You wait,' said Squib. 'It'll be OK. We're gonna have fun.'

Reekin rose and stood on his hindlegs, yarooling and pirouetting, his eyes closed.

'Bumhead,' Dancer said through his teeth.

27

A Little Street Fighting (i)

Jessie was ill. Her wheezing became worse and she could not keep down her food. She was weak, yet remarkably cheerful and pure inspiration to the shes that loved her. When she was forced to rise and leave the summerhouse to relieve herself she would collapse in the grass, her sides heaving, until she had enough strength to return to her nest among the sacks. Trying to lick her shoulder she fell and began laughing.

'You take it easy, Mother,' Ben said.

'I am taking it easy,' she wheezed. 'You think I fall over or wobble about for fun?'

'Come and lie with the kits,' Lucy said.

'What?' But she had heard and came to blast the young ones with purrs which made Sam grimace.

It was stuffy in the summerhouse. Flies buzzed around the little wet patches the kittens had left on the floor. Ben jumped off the settee and stretched. Lucy caught his eye and they smiled before he glided out of the hole in the door and paced silkily around the building to his scratching place at the chestnut tree. Then he sprayed the bole and pushed cautiously through the hedge to check the air with his nose before dropping into Winner Hill Road.

Physically and mentally he had never felt better. Swaggering along beside the parked cars he knew he wanted action and he was galloping towards it before the pavement ended at the sharp descent to Clifton Road. The evening smelt of sun-drenched gardens and parched earth. The pigeons from the Winner Hill loft were spreading their wings and holding the last of the sunlight on their feathers as they circled the rooftops.

Ben changed sides to avoid a woman exercising a spaniel. Dog and cat looked at each other and Ben came swiftly down to Ivy Lodge and darted into the grounds of the monastery. A blackbird alarmed but the undergrowth was thick and he was sure of himself on the old hunting trails. Hunting Shadows, he thought with a smile that revealed his canine teeth. He thought, too, of Jessie and the kittens and how Skeets had clouded their lives.

'Where are you?' he whispered, and the mouse scuttled from under the oak leaves to die on his claws.

The taste of blood heightened his aggressiveness.

'Skeets.' The challenge echoed among the trees. 'I want you, Skeets. Skeets. *Skee-ee-ee-ee-ee-ee-ee-eetssssss.*'

A twig snapped under a heavy foot and Ben stopped and laid his belly to the ground. There was another crackle of vegetation and the rasp of a match being struck followed by the smell of cigarette smoke. Then a human voice called, 'Pussy, Puss Puss Puss.'

Ben turned and retraced his steps but between the ash tree and the back of Ivy Lodge the path was open. Children had flattened the grass and nettles each side of it, to clear a way to the sandstone wall and a lamp-post descent into Winner Hill Road. Ben paused to remove a bramble feeler from his chest fur and the heavy airgun pellet ploughed a shallow furrow in the crown of his head. The weapon's dull crack sounded too far off to be real. There was no pain and Ben was gone in a mad dash that saw him through Ivy Lodge garden and into the road. Evening was darkening to dusk and the street lamps were on. Ben wiped his wound, sniffed the blood on his forepaw and trotted up the hill.

The youth positioned himself on the monastery wall and took careful aim, but a moving target is difficult to hit and the slug went wide. Holding himself low, Ben sprinted for cover and narrowly avoided crashing into the policeman's legs. The policeman was tall and bearded and his dog was on a short leash. Ben was around him and gone as the second airgun pellet hummed off the surface of the road. A brief glimpse of the youth slipping back

178

into the garden was enough to send the policeman running for Ivy Lodge.

'You'll live,' Lucy announced. She licked the wound and Ben's muzzle. 'It's just a scratch.'

'I went looking for Skeets,' Ben said, and he looked directly at Silver in the failing light on the terrace. 'Anyone any objections? Skeets, Smiley – I don't care so long as I can use my hooks.'

He began grooming Lucy's head and the tip of her tongue showed pink between her teeth. Silver watched them silently then he stretched and ambled off.

'How's Jessie?' Ben asked.

'Unwell but bearing up,' Sam said.

'She is a remarkable old cat,' Lucy said. 'She's with the kittens now.'

Bats swooped into the dance of the moths and Scarnose sat on the edge of the pond mesmerised by the carp. Parson was asleep on the birdtable and Rita and Scrumpy were rolling in the grass. Distances were blue and calm. Lights on the sea moved slowly and Berry Head lighthouse was flashing. In the drawing room the lady was singing and the television was on too loud, but despite the din City lay asleep against the french windows.

When the rest of the gang slept Ben prowled around Maylands, marking and spraying and inspecting dark corners where tomcat stink demanded his close attention. Under the Monastery Road hedge a familiar voice called to him.

'Shadows have hooks, Frog-gob.'

'Shadows are nothin' – you're nothing, Dancer. Nothing.'

'Hey,' Dancer laughed. 'Ain't you got a mouth? Ain't he got one, Squib?'

'It's big and it's on legs,' said Squib.

Ben climbed one of the cat runs into the hedge. The two Shadows sat on the wall opposite, by the fig tree.

'Try me,' Ben said. 'I'll take both of you, one at a time or together. A couple of Shadows just about make one real tom.'

179

The laughter vanished from Dancer's voice. 'Any time, any time.'

'Like now?' And Ben loped across the road and ran to the gateway below the fig tree and up the steps into the garden. Smiley was bristling on the path by the porch. Dancer and Squib walked along the wall and sat at the bottom of the steps.

'This suits me,' Ben grinned, fluffing out his fur and lifting his back.

'Who wants it first?'

'There's only you and me,' said Smiley.

'And what about the two bad smells behind me?' Ben said.

'They won't interfere.'

The eyeballing failed to lead into banter and bluff. Then the fur flew and hooks and teeth scored from the frenzy of blows. Ben flung himself backwards and clawed Smiley's face. The black tom retreated, snorting blood, and Ben hit him again but he curled and rolled to savage Ben's hindquarters. Another double contortion clamped them once more in the eyeballing and growling before they met broadside with a blur of hooks.

'You had enough?' Smiley gasped, staggering clear, and Ben's hindfeet slammed the breath out of his body. He fell on his side and tried to protect his stomach and Ben cuffed him about the face and muzzle. Pain spread from his lacerated eye to his cheeks and nose.

'That's it,' he grunted, but Ben was on a plateau of violence way beyond reason. His hooks tore into Smiley's head and shoulders.

Unable to stand back and watch the annihilation any longer, Dancer leapt in and barged Ben clear of his victim, giving Smiley the chance to take refuge between his friends.

'All of you, then,' Ben hissed.

A swerving charge deceived the Shadows. More cuts appeared on Smiley's muzzle. Squib's ears were ripped and Dancer's upper lip was badly bruised by a hindfoot.

'We're going,' Dancer cried. 'Ease up, we're through.'

They tried to cover Smiley's retreat but Ben kept coming.

'C'mon,' he growled. 'Give me a real fight. Give it to me.'

Dodging the feeble side swipes of cats on the run he buried his claws in Squibs' back near the tail.

'For Lucy and Jessie and the kittens. For Button. For me. For all the cats you trampled on and roughed up.'

But he was tiring and when the Shadows ran hard up Monastery Road he sat and watched them go. City joined him.

'I saw it,' the old tom whispered. 'I heard the commotion and saw it all. Silver stopped Scarnose coming to help you.'

'What d'you mean?'

'Silver was right, Ben,' City said. 'We thought it was a trick to get us away from Lucy and the other shes and the kittens. But I saw you in action. You are among the best street fighters I've ever seen. Maybe the best.'

'I don't care,' Ben said. 'It doesn't matter.'

'It will to Skeets – and Silver.'

Ben looked up at the stars.

28

A Little Street Fighting (ii)

The good weather held and the days passed with the Maylands toms prowling restlessly around the home patch. Ben's victory kept him buoyant and City was required to retell the story of Smiley's humiliation. But Ben was content to accept Silver's leadership and it amused him to find Scarnose hanging on his every word. When he wanted to, Scarnose could look like a crumpled marmalade scarf dropped by a down-and-out, but his eyes twinkled like a kitten's in his moments of joy or excitement.

It was late evening. Mars showed red in the south-east of the sky and stars shone from a haze. Ben had made a foray in search of scrounge and street fights. Lucy had found him at the back of the chip shop and for a while life was untroubled. They had sat at the gate and waited to be called and had jumped onto the tea chest to gobble the fish pieces. Lucy's endearing ways worked at his senses like the catmint high. He escorted her back to the summerhouse and the kittens and stuck his head through the hole in the door.

'Is Jessie OK?' he said.

'No,' said Rita. 'She's a scrap of wind that won't eat and falls over every time she gets up.'

'Can I help?'

'You can disappear. She needs peace and quiet.'

The shes were grooming Jessie's long wispy fur.

'Tell her I love her,' Ben said.

'I'll have to shout,' Rita said. 'She's deafer than ever.'

Darkness was a playground for the lights. They were in the sky and the sea and all around the edge of the bay. Ben chose a spot on the south end of the terrace and slowly entered the stark lunar landscape of night vision. Silver appeared more ghostlike than ever, dancing on the summerhouse roof. The white tom was up on his back legs after the moths but Ben did not know this. He saw him as a pale silver flame, an image that was disturbing and charismatic. The white tom was lost in his dream world and this comforted Ben. Beyond everything there had to be the love of life. The rest was verbal vomit and Skeets. He was as life-denying as the cat flu they all feared.

Ben dozed and woke beneath a big, naked morning sky. City lay close to him, scratching at his fleas and groaning because his hip-joints hurt. Down under the conifer hedge Scarnose and Scrumpy were teasing a slow worm. Lucy and her friends were amusing the kittens by the summerhouse.

Seeing the smile on Ben's face City said, 'Those little tikes.'

The kittens were romping on the flattened grass. They wrestled and struck out with their back feet, holding a brother or sister in their forepaws. Then they parted, retreated and advanced, side-on, to pounce. They swatted at flies and inched forward on their bellies, rumps swaying, before hitting an imaginary prey.

'Little tikes,' City grinned.

The sparrowhawk cut into the buddleia below the bamboo and snatched a greenfinch. The ragwort swayed and the young crow called from his firtop nest. Ben sprang down the rockery in two leaps and crept up on Lucy.

'Oh!' she gasped as he appeared at her side. 'You startled me.'

'I want you to come with me to the green scent,' he said when their noses had logged each other's smell.

'OK,' she smiled.

The Parish Church bells rang out.

'Not our green scent,' Ben said. 'There are better leaves in the garden at the front of Barnie's house.'

He went through the silver gates first and made sure it was safe. Saturday night's drunks had left the debris of their takeaway suppers all over the road and on the steps of the alley leading to Fairview. Pancake rolls and fried chicken scraps provided scrounge and the cats fed despite the complaint of gulls, magpies and crows.

Afterwards they came to Fairview's garden and the catmint and presently they were rolling and treading to the green scent high.

'What happens when you breathe it?' Ben asked.

'I'm not here. I'm part of something else that has nothing to do with gardens and streets. It's . . . different. It's like coming out of your body and being the sunlight.'

'Am I with you?'

'You're part of it.'

'Yeah, it's something else,' Ben grinned.

The mint smell clung to their coats and they were constantly sniffing each other on the return to Maylands. A cloud covered the sun and was followed by another. Ben glanced up and the coldness touched his heart. He half-heard Lucy say goodbye and dreamily watched her running for the summerhouse and the kittens. Then, as he entered Maylands he was suddenly in the long dark running towards a sky full of stars. The little snowdrift waited for him.

'Why?' Ben shivered.

Scarnose was at the walnut tree, drawing his claws down the frayed bark.

'You OK, Ben?' he called.

The sun went out and the swifts were flying low. Big cauliflower-shaped clouds sailed in from the Atlantic and thunder followed them. The storm brought cooler weather that lasted for nearly a week and Maylands became a drenched, dripping jungle of summer in disarray. But whenever the sky cleared at night the stars shone with a brilliance that pleased the cats.

'What makes it all happen, Skeets?' Reekin whispered.

'It's there to make us feel good,' said Skeets. 'Like the green scent high and the sunrise and the street fight.'

'How come you know everything?' Squib said.

'Because he's Skeets,' Reekin said. 'He gets the dreams, don't he? And he finds out things in the dreams.'

184

'But I still get shot at,' Skeets said icily as if it were Reekin's fault.

'Yesterday evening I was down in the trees and bang! Let me tell you it was a close thing, too close.'

'That's a pity,' Dancer said and Skeets' dead, yellow eyes fixed on him.

'When a cat can't take a walk on his own patch without that sort of hassle,' Dancer gabbled on. 'It makes you think.'

'It makes you think what?' said Skeets, softly.

'Well, you know, Skeets. I mean, it just makes you think,' was Dancer's pitifully inadequate reply.

'Come here, Dancer. Come on, don't be shy.'

'But I – '

'Come . . . here . . . Dancer,' Skeets growled through clenched teeth and he broke into song as Dancer slowly advanced.

'When the red, red robin . . . comes bob, bob – ' The words gurgled in Skeets' throat and he fell over, kicking feebly.

'Haul your tail out of here,' Smiley rapped. He glared at Dancer. 'Go – you *and* your mouth.'

The Shadows were dismayed by Smiley's zestful self-deception.

Dancer and Squib trotted down Berry Road to stalk in the cemetery.

'And where will it end?' Dancer said.

'I didn't come along for this sort of trip,' Squib growled. Then he laughed. 'We all know what you meant when you said that's a pity. You got away with it by sheer luck, friend. He would have had your eyes.'

'Don't I know it!'

They crossed Colley End Road and strolled through the cemetery gates. Squib squatted behind a headstone and said, 'We gotta do something, Dancer.'

'Yeah. We gotta hope Skeets cops one in the head next time we hear a bang,' and Dancer aimed his hindquarters and sprayed his signature on the headstone.

★

The greenfly were blown over the terrace and City sneezed insects. The sun beat down from an interlude between the sort of Atlantic depressions which reduce British seaside towns to corners of hell. The kittens were playing in the drive watched by Rita and Belle.

'Jessie rambled on again last night,' Rita said. 'We had everything from Button's death to Lucy's big walk. Poor old love.'

'She drags about with those dead back legs of hers,' Belle said.

'I never want to get old,' said Rita.

And delivering his manic laugh, Slippery Jim cleared the fence to land among the kittens and select a victim.

'Na-owwoww,' Rita cried and was on his face before he could bare his fangs.

He shook his head and beat at her but Belle came to her aid and two enraged shes are a match for any tom. He turned and slammed into the fence. Clawing up the woodwork he passed Parson, who was on the way down. To complete his discomfort he fell onto a parked car and ricocheted off into the road and an undignified retreat.

'Are the kittens OK?' Ben cried from the top of the drive.

'Yeah,' Rita yelled. 'It was the one with the weird laugh.'

'Which way did he go?'

'Up the hill.'

Slippery Jim sat on the wall on the right-hand side of Monastery Road halfway between Huccaby and the entrance to the council estate. He was licking his wounds, but caught sight of Ben when the black and white tom crept along the top of the wall to within five yards of him.

'Try something bigger than a kitten,' Ben whispered, and Slippery Jim laughed to cover his panic.

'I'm gonna take you apart,' Ben continued, pacing slowly through the valerian. 'You lot want aggro so this is it. Only, what I got to offer is bad news.'

Racing over the shed roof Skeets hit him solidly with head and shoulders and knocked him off the wall. Like all healthy cats, Ben knew where he was when he was upside down and was able to land on all fours. But Skeets pinned him to the asphalt and left him counting stars and nursing a gashed ear. It might have been ugly for Ben if the milk float had not rattled up Monastery Road and sent Skeets scampering ahead of it. Pursued by Slippery Jim's laughter Ben took his wounds back to Maylands.

'See?' Skeets purred. He swaggered across the Lions' Club carpark. 'See what I mean, Jim?' Reekin and Squib fell in behind the sandy tom. 'The black and white one is nothing.'

'Not against you he ain't,' said Slippery Jim, and Smiley, who had been dozing against the tyre of a Peugeot, looked up.

'You were great,' Slippery Jim continued, sensing Skeets' delight in the flattery.

'Honest animal,' Skeets said. 'One day the white tom and I will meet and I'll step over him into my new dream.'

'But the black and white tom is dangerous,' Smiley said and Squib had to agree.

In spite of being contradicted Skeets stayed calm and the eruption of malice which the Shadows expected didn't occur.

'Dangerous for you and the rest, Smiley, but not for me.'

'You were eye to eye with Silver once,' Smiley said. 'Is he nothing?'

'I was never eye to eye with Silver,' Skeets said in a voice full of good humour. 'You are mistaken, Smiley.'

'But the garden, you and Silver – ' Squib began, and Smiley shook his head.

'Smiley is mistaken,' Skeets grinned.

'I'm sorry. Sometimes I get confused,' Squib said.

'Dream more and think less,' Skeets chuckled and he hooked a red admiral butterfly out of the sunlight and settled on his haunches to tease it with an extended paw.

'Everything is possible,' he murmured. 'Everything is possible – for Skeets.'

187

29

The Cricket's Song

The lady brought water to the summerhouse for the kittens. She pushed three plastic bowls through the door and filled them from her watering can. So Jessie was able to drink without making the long trip to the terrace. Wet days and nights passed and there were no serious encounters to disturb Maylands. The elderberries were purple and the apples on the Fairview trees were big enough to attract the children who ran up the alley after school.

The airgun menace affected the council estate cats more than Silver's family. Apart from Ben's occasional sorties the Maylands toms kept away from the monastery. Sometimes a dull report was followed by the buzz of the slug passing close to an ear. This happened mainly at the Clifton Road end of Winner Hill, under the monastery wall. But the bearded policeman who lived in Clifton Road was vigilant and the youth's pot-shots in the open were less frequent. If anything, the boy became more cunning.

Late one evening, Ben lay under a parked car in Church Street waiting for the pigeons to come and glean grain litter outside the Animal Magic pet shop. Rain had fallen and the street smelt clean and stony. It was Sunday and the chip shop was closed. The street lights had just come on when he heard a cat crying softly in pain. Trixy, the Winner Hill Siamese, was beneath a van parked opposite the Labour Club and he was cut terribly about the head.

'Crazies?' Ben said.

'The one with the mad laugh. He wasn't like a cat, Ben. It went beyond the street fighting you lot are good at.'

Ben accompanied his friend through the bottleneck and up Winner Hill Road to his home.

'Where did it happen, Trixy?'

'On Dolly's patch. Two Crazies chased me down the hill and I ended up there. One watched while – while – '

He gulped.

'It'll be OK,' Ben said. 'Get some sleep.'

'What's Silver going to do?'

'He'll sort it out. Those Crazies can be beaten. They're not that hard. Rita and Louise saw one off the other day.'

Trixy smiled.

Ben's resentment deepened. The streets were his. He had been born to them. So why did he have to creep around and walk wide of the Shadows?

'Skeets,' he hissed.

A couple of boys came rattling down Monastery Road on skateboards. Another shower of fine rain drifted through the lamplight. He walked past the silver gates and on up to the entrance to the council estate, inviting a confrontation; but if there were Shadows about they lived up to their name despite his yarooled taunts.

He returned to the summerhouse and did not disturb Lucy, who was sleeping in a circle of kittens among the other shes. He lay beside Jessie and gently licked her ears and knobbly spine. She was so light and frail and grateful for any show of kindness. Burrowing into his warmth she began to roar out the purrs until the young shes were awake and laughing in the darkness. Looking up through the window Ben could see one very bright star and hear the high-pitched squeaking of bats.

Outside the Lions' Club, Skeets was also listening to the bats. To him they were birds that flew by night and his cries of frustrated bloodlust broke from the chatter of his teeth.

'When the red, red robin . . .'

Squib and Dancer raised their eyes to the sky then stared down at the ground, aware that Smiley was watching them.

'There'll be no more sobbin' . . .'

They waited for Skeets to grind out the final refrain but there was just the leaf-rustled hush, the patter of raindrops from the trees and the squeaking of the bats.

189

'Squib, old chum,' Skeets chortled. 'You look like the sort of street fighter who's dying for a scrap. So here's what you do.'

Squib stared at him and licked his lips.

'You attack Silver's garden.'

'Just me?'

'Just you, my fine young friend.'

'But why? It's crazy. I'll get slaughtered.'

'Oh dear,' Skeets sighed, ' – doubts. Now that is unfortunate. A doubting tom has no corner in my dreams. The garden, Squib. I wanna see your tail vanishing down the road. Go and do the hook stuff in the garden.'

'No,' Squib growled.

'From doubt to disobedience,' Skeets smiled. 'It's bad for gang morale, Squib. I give you an order and you spit on it so what am I to do?'

'But it's crazy, Skeets,' Dancer said. 'What'll we gain by Squib goin' down there and gettin' crippled?'

'Only I can tell,' Skeets said and he rose and stretched. 'So off you go, Squib. Bring me the black and white tom's tail between your teeth.'

'I ain't moving,' said Squib.

'But you are.' Skeets' voice climbed to a screech of madness and he took Squib at the end of a rush. The other Shadows noted the way Squib fought back hard, preventing Skeets from really working him over. But the end was inevitable and Squib limped off under the oaks to lick his wounds. Dancer followed him.

'Do it for me,' Skeets called. 'Anything I ask you to do, you do it. I brought you to the end of the rainbow and if you want everything this is the way you'll get it.'

'Yeah,' Smiley echoed and Reekin and Slippery Jim added their assent, more dutifully than willingly.

'Bloody headcase,' Dancer growled, sitting beside Squib. 'You hurt bad?'

'No, a few scratches and bruises from his big back feet. Nut'n much. But you could get the hook outa my head.'

Dancer located it with his teeth and extracted it.

190

'That's it, Dancer,' Squib said. 'And I ain't talkin' about the hook.'

'You're leavin'?'

'Yeah. You comin'?'

'Yeah. I got my eye on a little patch down past Silver's place.'

'What about Silver's mob?'

'All the aggro's gotta end. I've had enough, you've had enough. A bit of street fightin', yeah, fine – but we were nuts to go along with Skeets. It was fun once but it ain't no more. Skeets is over the top and if he's in the end of the rainbow I don't wanna be there with him.'

'So we make peace with Silver's mob?'

'If they let us. If not, we just take off. Anyway, it ain't Silver we talk to. It's Ben. He's the real tom in that mob and he's got more heart than any cat I've met.'

'What are you two talking about?' Skeets cried.

'I told him he's got to do what you say, Skeets,' Dancer said.

'Good. Walk him down the road and remember this, Squib. If you don't come back with the black and white tom's tail I'm goin' to have yours. Got it?'

'Got it,' Squib grunted and then he whispered, 'Goodbye, Maggot-mouth.'

'Keep cool,' Dancer said as they left the estate and walked down Monastery Road. 'We don't want him on our asses.'

'Where we goin'?'

'To the garden. We gotta speak to Ben. We can't have him and Skeets after our tails.'

'They won't trust us.'

'No, but we ain't got no choice. Still, this Ben is different. He helped me once when I was down on my luck. Then I went and bit his ass.'

They sat outside the silver gates and called until Scarnose came and peered through the wrought ironwork.

'Yeah?' he growled.

'We wanna speak to Ben.'

'You mean Silver.'

'No, I mean Ben,' Dancer said. 'Will you get him?'

'If this is a trap remember we're mob-hooked. We can put ten heavies on the street, no trouble. Hurt Ben and I'll gut you.'

Luckily, Silver was stalking down on the Winner Hill building site so an embarrassment of status was avoided.

Ben sauntered to the gates and confronted the Shadows.

'Talk,' he said.

'We're finished with Skeets,' said Dancer.

'Uh-huh. And my mother can fly.'

'OK, I know what you're thinking. We asked for this and we don't expect you to trust us. But you don't know what it's like up there. Skeets is so far over the top he's out of sight. Look what he's just done to Squib. All the time he turns on us and works us over like we're just things. He is totally nuts.'

'So what do you want me to do – kiss it better? Ask you into the garden where you can kill a kitten or finish old Jessie? You think I got the brains of a mouse?'

'No. Don't trust us. Maybe that'll come later. All we want is a small patch down over,' and he nodded towards Winner Hill Road.

'Then we'll have Skeets up there and you down there,' said Scarnose.

'Yeah. It sounds bad but we wanna play this straight, Ben.'

'You've never played it straight.'

'This time it's different. Look. We could've just cleared off and you wouldn have known. We didn't have to tell you nothin'. All we want is to be out of the Shadows. There's more like us. They'll see us livin' peacefully next to your patch and they'll take off. Skeets ain't popular.'

A shower fell but the cats sat through it while Ben deliberated. Then the airgun cracked and Squib screeched. All the cats came in panic to Maylands terrace.

'You OK, Squib?' Dancer asked.

'I got a hole in my ear that shouldn't be there,' Squib grinned wryly.

City ambled up to them.

'Would you trust this pair?' Ben said.

'Last spring, no. Now I'm not so sure. I walked with Skeets once. Dancer's sly as they come but Squib is usually on the level.'

'Thanks,' Dancer rasped.

'They legged it,' Scarnose said.

'I ain't surprised. Enough is enough.'

'I'm goin' to give you a chance,' said Ben. 'You cross our hunting ground and you show respect. Keep to your home patch and things may work out. If this is a trick kiss your eyes and tails goodbye.'

'Look,' Dancer said eagerly. 'There's an old shelter above the wasteland down below,' and again he nodded in the direction of Winner Hill Road and Dan y Craig. 'We'll be there. If any of your shes fancy a good time they'll know where to find us.'

'Step out of line and I'll come lookin' for you,' Ben said.

'You're a tom who deserves a lot of respect,' said Squib.

When they had departed Scarnose said, 'You know them Crazies, Ben. This has gotta be a trick.'

'I don't think so,' said City. 'Them two are running scared. You can smell it. You can't pretend that stink.'

'In any case,' Ben said, 'I'd rather have the Crazies divided. It makes it easier for us. Sam can watch from the hedge down there and we can take them any time we want.'

'But Skeets can hit us from two sides now,' said Scarnose.

'He always could. What was to stop them creepin' around and coming in from all sides? We've split the gang. Skeets'll have no direct contact with those two.'

'It's smart thinking,' said City.

'Let's hope Silver goes along with it,' said Scarnose.

Silver returned from hunting, listened to Ben and went off to think about it. His eventual approval was met by Ben's brief explanation.

'You were absent. I had to make a decision without consulting you. I'm glad you think it's OK.'

'If the others desert Skeets he's finished,' Silver said. 'Then maybe he'll go.'

'He won't go, Silver,' City said. 'This is the end of his rainbow and he wants you.'

'Why? *Why?*'

Ben was surprised at the edge of desperation to Silver's question.

'Because he's nuts,' said Scarnose. 'You fight him and win and that's it.'

'No,' said City. 'Skeets has gotta win before it ends. Silver can't win unless he kills him.'

Silver sighed and padded off to lie-up under the conifer hedge.

'Why don't he just go and give hook to Skeets?' Scarnose was genuinely puzzled.

'Because he knows that if he loses, the Crazies will take over the garden and give us a bad time,' City said. 'This is one of those problems you can't solve while Skeets is alive. You wanna fight him, Scarnose?'

'I have kittens thinking about what it would be like to tangle seriously with that headcase,' Scarnose shuddered.

'He's hard,' Ben said. 'He gave me a rough time.'

'Because he surprised you,' Scarnose said.

'Maybe. But he's quick and heavy.'

'And mad,' City added.

But things did not go entirely Maylands' way. Mellow was caught at the junction of Colley End Park and Monastery Road and beaten up by Smiley. The Rut quarrels, when toms competed for shes, were comprehensible to strays like Mellow and the handful of domestic toms who hadn't been neutered but the ceaseless war waged by the Shadows bewildered the fraternity. Mellow simply wandered from under a parked car into a whirlwind of hooks and flashing fangs. One gouging rake opened a gash in his belly. He crept into Maylands seeking sanctuary although he was a loner who went where he pleased and did what he liked.

Later, Scarnose and Ben met at the walnut tree and

194

clawed it with enthusiasm fired by hatred. Silver sat and watched them.

'There will be more deserters like Dancer,' he said. 'We just have to play Skeets at his own game.'

The use of the word 'game' brought a grimace to Ben's face.

Then the swifts were gone and so were nearly two weeks of August. One evening the sky was loud with their screaming and the next morning it was silent. But the crickets sang in the Maylands' shrubberies and gulls cackled from the roofs. The kittens watched the gulls and Jessie watched the kittens.

The old cat appeared to have made a recovery. She tottered out onto the lawn and lay down for the young to roll over her. They nipped her grey muzzle and bit her ears but she loved it. They were the life she felt ebbing in her blood. Well, she thought, it would be good to go to sleep never to wake again. She was perpetually tired but the kittens filled her with joy. The light that went out in Button's eyes shone so brightly now in Skip's.

To be in the grass in the garden, the sun warm and the scent of the kittens in her nostrils, made everything worthwhile. She had seen many sunrises and had walked through almost as many summers as she had toes. She had given birth to a whole tribe of kittens, little toms and shes who had walked out of her life to make their own. She had known sickness and pain, joy and sorrow and grief. She had shivered in the cold and panted in the heat. She had leapt to catch the falling leaves and had risen on her haunches to sniff the spring blossom. Rain, snow, sunlight, frost and grass seeds had been carried on her coat. She had run and walked and jumped and climbed. She had lain still under starlit skies and the sounds, sights and scents of the world had become one with her being. She had mated by starlight and called to the moon, and she had known hunger and plenty. Always she had lived according to her instincts and kept her bargain with birth.

Now she was half-asleep in a daze of happiness among

195

animals that loved her. I'm lucky, Jessie thought; and the crickets sang from the deepening night.

30

Games in the Rain

The lawn was littered with cats, all of whom wore smiles of sun-drugged contentment. Trees rustled and shook their shadows across grass that was stiff, pale yellow and dry. A small flock of starlings landed on the summerhouse roof and kicked up a din. Water gushed down a pipe, a gull cackled and the fire engine leaving the station in Cecil Road sent the sound of its siren undulating through the morning.

Scarnose stopped scratching and ran around the side of the house to the kitchen. The smell of frying bacon was almost as intoxicating as the scent of catmint or valerian. But the lady did not see him outside the window and his vigil was fruitless. When he returned to the terrace he was in a bad mood.

Most of the cats were restless. The sultry weather held something ominous, although the smell of rain did not become apparent until evening. By then all the Maylands' toms had gathered above the rockery to watch the massing of big anvil-headed clouds on the horizon. The far-off rumbling of thunder set them licking their lips. But for Silver, the darkness racing towards him held all the fascination of impending oblivion and he wondered if Skeets shared that strange sensation which was distilled from terror and excitement.

A clap of thunder brought the toms' ears and bellies down. Only Silver sat upright, ears erect, breathing calmly. The darkness with its great boiling clouds was over the town now and rain hit the garden.

'This is the moment,' he announced through the hiss of the downpour.

The others looked at him.

'I'm going to the big house to call out Skeets.'

Ben nodded. Silver was his old self. He exuded the confidence and toughness that had made him the top feral. Lightning flashed and the white tom was bathed in a phosphorescent glow as he loped away.

Scarnose gave Sam an enquiring glance.

'He's seen something we haven't seen,' Sam said, backing against the french windows as the rain blurred to a deluge. Lights came on in the houses and the thunder brought the toms together in a trembling scrum. But Silver walked purposefully through the rain that was streaming off Monastery Road to find Skeets sitting unconcerned on top of the yellow van. A flash of lightning revealed his face and the closed eyes and the blissful smile. At any other time, Silver would have been unnerved. The old chapel looked grim and stark in the lightning brightness and trees kept appearing and vanishing like uncertain carnivores.

Silver sat in front of the van and gazed up at Skeets. The rain stung his ears. Then it eased and Skeets' eyes opened.

'The dream has come to me,' he said, lifting his head in a pose that left his jaw jutting seawards.

Smiley and the rest of the Shadows stayed under the oaks.

'What's goin' on?' Scrag whispered.

'We're in one of Skeets' dreams,' Chips said and Smiley looked at him.

'There's goin' to be a scrap you won't forget,' said Slippery Jim.

'That Silver looks pretty cool,' said Reekin.

'He's got to be nuts,' said Skiffle. 'No tom in his right mind squares up to Skeets on Skeets' patch.'

Thunder cracked and a great detonation was followed by a rumble that carried across Devon. Skeets jumped off the van and the rain fell hard again. Sheet lightning lit the carpark as the two cats strutted up to each other and entered the eyeballing ritual. Whenever lightning struck, Silver glimpsed in Skeets' eyes the evidence of mental disorder. One pupil was large, the other small; but the storm had flushed away Silver's fear. To him, the big sandy tom looked like a creature approaching the end of a descent into darkness more dense than the storm darkness. He heard himself yarooling in reply to the taunting maraow. Rain-spiked, the cats were more ridiculous than frightening and Reekin couldn't suppress a giggle despite Smiley's glare.

The encounter had become a slow motion dance with the fighters adopting a series of poses according to a choreography rooted in feral instinct. There was the arching of backs and the tails lashing and the broadside approach and retreat, and there were the cries. Then Silver drifted in, swung at Skeets' head, missed, recovered and backed off to parry the equally sedate counter attack.

'What is this?' Scrag muttered. 'They're playing, not fighting.'

'Maybe if you shut your mouth and watched you'd see some real action,' Smiley said.

But he knew the preliminary posturing was going on too long and it puzzled him. Paws were swung, hooks flashed but no contact was made.

'I've seen more action from blind kittens,' said Chips.

'Maybe I ought to pass on that comment to Skeets,' Smiley said.

'It's a joke,' Chips said.

'Like the fight,' Scrag growled, ignoring Smiley.

And the ballet continued. Skeets and Silver rose on their hindlegs, made threatening gestures, dropped onto all fours again, advanced, retreated and maraowed.

'Very pretty,' Scrag sneered.

The rain stopped and the storm rumbled inland. The sky began to clear and raindrops ticked on the leaf litter. The evening brightened and the first stars were visible above the bay. Skiffle yawned and a minibus came round the corner of the Lions' Club honking its horn at Skeets and Silver. There was an immediate separation that was by no means reluctant. Both toms strode off in opposite directions as though each was claiming a moral victory.

But Silver was shivering on the descent of Monastery Road although it wasn't cold. Early in the fight he had felt his confidence and courage drain away. Skeets had toyed with him, and in one awful moment of revelation he had become aware of his opponent's complete lack of fear. It had left him like a vole with crushed back legs crawling about in front of the watchful, purring executioner.

At the entrance to Huccaby he paused and groomed himself while his composure returned. The evening calm was startling after the thunder, lightning and mental stress. Behind him the familiar caterwauling rose from the council estate and he licked his lips.

'That was fun,' Skeets said at the end of his cry.

'You played with him?' said Smiley.

'Of course. What else? I told you – it's a game. When it's time for the white one to go I'll remove him. I'll go into the dream and remove him.'

Reekin fidgeted and yawned.

'But you weren't impressed, were you, Reekin?' Skeets grinned.

The enlarged pupil of his right eye fascinated Reekin and he shook his head instead of nodding.

'Such candour,' Skeets continued. 'I wish I didn't have to keep explaining to bird brains like you. It really is boring.'

He walked up to Reekin and stood facing him. The church clock struck the hour and as he began to savage Reekin, Skeets wondered why there was no screaming in the sky.

'See?' he panted when it was all over and Reekin lay before him with blood on his face. 'See what I can do? Do you see? Do you? Do you, Reekin?'

'Why juh do this to me and let him walk away?' Reekin groaned.

'Because I wanted to. Because *garrg*.'

And he turned gleefully to the others and let another 'garrg' slip from between his teeth.

Scrag and Skiffle would not meet his gaze and nor

would they join in the imitation of the dying Wayne. They showed him their tails and walked away.

'Sulky, sulky,' Skeets purred, smiling at Reekin who was applying a wet paw to his face. 'What a sulky pair. But I'm sure they'll get over it. In fact I shall persuade them to get over it.'

'They just wanted to see you in action, Skeets,' Smiley said. 'You're the best.'

'And I disappointed them. Yes, perhaps I should have damaged Silver a little.'

'They expected it,' said Smiley.

'We sure did,' Reekin added, getting the message. He had escaped lightly and had no intention of finishing up on the end of one of Skeets' rages again.

'I see, I see,' Skeets sighed. 'You wanted Skeets to put on a show. I am sorry, Reekin. If only I'd known. I'm selfish. I should share myself with you all more often.'

'Yeah. You got your dreams but we've only got you,' Reekin said.

Skeets' enlarged pupil became even bigger and he nodded sadly. 'That's true. I'm touched, Reekin. Deep down I'm touched. You know what an old softy I am inside.'

'An old softy,' Reekin choked.

Early next day Reekin searched out Skiffle at his couch among the roots of an oak.

'You take care of yourself, huh,' he said and Skiffle blinked sleepily up at him.

'Don't let old Softy get his hooks in your face,' Reekin continued.

Skiffle sneezed. He had a cold and saliva was strung vertically across his gape when he yawned.

'I've had enough,' Reekin said. 'You and Scrag and the others can have Skeets all to yourselves. I hope you live to enjoy whatever there is at the end of his bloody rainbow.'

'Where you going?'

'Anywhere, so long as it's away from here and Raving Rat Breath.'

Skiffle grinned.

'I'll probably make for the woods on the hill over there where Jake's toms hang out. This ain't fun no more.'

'You watch out for yourself,' Skiffle said, sneezing and drooling mucus.

'And why don't you do yourself a favour and get out while you still got eyes?' Reekin called over his shoulder as he trotted off.

'Maybe I will. Skeets is out of sight and I'm beginning to think I can't handle this.'

It was a sentiment the other Shadows shared but this did not prevent Boomer reverting to type and roughing up Barnie that evening. It happened on Huccaby's garage roof. The old black tom was watching the birds at the bird table of No. 23 Monastery Road when Boomer appeared and gave him the choice of jumping to the ground or showing his hooks. Barnie was brave and put up the sort of resistance that surprised Boomer, but eventually he weakened and scrambled onto the roof of his own shed, only to be knocked off it into the yard with Boomer in close attendance. The kitchen door was open and Jamie the Jack Russell was on Boomer before the cat realised he had blundered. Avoiding his claws, the terrier gripped him by the neck and shook him, and if the lady of the house hadn't intervened Boomer would have died a rat's death. Hardly believing his luck, he ran up the back gate onto the wall and left Jamie leaping about and barking.

'You done well, Boomer,' Skeets said and he lidded his blank yellow eyes. 'We've got to take the war to them.'

It was a good time for Skeets to be told about Reekin's departure.

'Don't fret,' Skeets smiled. 'There's only room for a few good toms in my rainbow dream.'

'Am I there?' Scrag said.

Skeets laughed. 'Wait and see.'

But Boomer had not done well. His attack on Barnie prompted the people at Fairview to phone the RSPCA about 'aggressive strays'. Theirs was one of several complaints received by the Animal Centre in Torquay, and the inspector was alerted. He visited Maylands after learning Silver's gang were in residence but the lady claimed they were her cats and threatened legal action if they were touched. Another lead brought him to the council estate on the very morning Smiley beat up a pet tom and Skeets was shot. The marmalade and white tom needed veterinary attention but Skeets' good fortune prevailed. The airgun pellet hit his right forepaw and passed between two toes, leaving the skin unbroken. The inspector heard the shot and gave the information to the police; the bearded constable was again involved but his enquiries came to nothing.

31

Goodbye to the Seasons

A gang of teenagers went down Winner Hill Road, their ghetto blaster pounding out pop music. Lucy shrank from the noise and returned to the examination of Skip's head. Her smile of pleasure was gilded with sunshine. The weather was warm again and winged insects massed around the shrubs and flowers. Louise had vanished and Rainbow, Pepper and Belle had given themselves to Dancer and Squib and were sharing the patch below Dan y Craig. The Shadows still went about Skeets' business but if they had hooks those hooks were blunted. Scrag and Chips ran off to join Reekin in Primley Wood after one of Skeets' outbursts had left Scrag with a permanent limp. Half a dozen Shadows found it difficult to terrorise the neighbourhood and for a while they concentrated their attacks on pets. Ebony, Trixy and Simon from No. 15 Monastery Road all suffered and the little she, Smokey, needed stitches in her muzzle; but Barnie fought back and Ben, Scarnose and Scrumpy raided the council estate to scar Bang and Skiffle.

On the edge of the casual street violence Jessie became worse. Her physical frailty was pitiful, but her good humour continued to astonish the family. She would demand to be shown the kittens and they would be brought to her and engulfed in purrs. Her body was one great ache of arthritis and she was totally deaf, but her mind was clear and her speech lucid whenever she freed herself from dreams of the past that set her rambling on with episodes leaping up to blur into others. She spoke of Button and kittens whose names meant nothing to the shes around her, and she recalled her own mother. A night had passed and the sun had risen in a cloudless sky.

The mechanical road sweeper was rumbling along Winner Street and gulls were cackling from chimney pots. Jessie slept on the floor beside the settee but her twitching eyes and limbs told the others she was dreaming.

In Jessie's dream it was autumn and she was a kitten. The sun was shining and the wind blowing and she lay with her brother and sister under the sycamore tree. The monastery garden was sheltered by high walls. The soil was warm in the strawberry beds and a few apples still hung on the trees. There were no council houses, just the gardens and the field where the novice priests played football. This garden was Jessie's birthplace and the priest in charge of the seminary put out food for her mother and the three kittens. Now Jessie was there again, breathing its scents and smells, watching the light break into the shadows as the treetops danced in the wind. Then the sycamore spinners came whirling down and she and her brother and sister were leaping to catch the propeller blade seeds. The kittens were laughing and tumbling over each other and the spinners fell through shafts of sunlight and were swatted and hooked. She could smell little Susie and Peter and hear their mother calling to them as she returned from scrounge.

'Come on, Jessie,' the warm voice said. 'Come outside. Come and play with the spinners.'

Jessie staggered to her feet and dragged her body through the hole in the door. The shes followed and watched her take half a dozen drunken steps across the lawn. Then she stopped, and stood swaying with her muzzle raised to take in the smell of the sea for the last time. Where were the spinners? Where was her mother and her brother and sister? Her gaze was sorrowful but she was ready to say goodbye to all that the seasons held.

She did not fall over. She lay down and gave a cry and the light went out in her eyes. Released from the Winner Hill loft, the pigeons circled Maylands on a rush of wings holding the gleam of morning on their feathers.

'We love you, Jessie,' Lucy sobbed, licking the grey face.

There was nothing more to be said. Each member of the family walked up to Jessie and placed a nose briefly to her muzzle before departing. In this manner Ben paid his respects to the old she.

'She was content at the end,' said Lucy.

'She will be missed,' he said.

Bringing water to the summerhouse, the lady found Jessie's body and buried it beneath some roses. Silver, Ben and Sam sat with City on the terrace and considered the gap Jessie's death had left in their lives.

'But soon it'll be like last winter,' Sam said.

'What was last winter like, apart from cold and wet?' said Ben.

'Exactly,' Sam smiled. 'Soon we'll speak of Jessie without pain. Things fade.'

'We won't forget her,' Silver said.

'Of course not,' said Sam. 'But her name won't make your heart ache. Things come and go. So do cats.'

'I want to think about her with heartache,' Ben said and City chuckled, but Silver narrowed his eyes remembering how the life had left his legs during the clash with Skeets. Perhaps it would be better for them all if Ben took control. He swallowed miserably, thinking of the pleasant days he had spent dreaming on the sunroof when life in the garden was perfect. Everything had changed. Ben had changed. The black and white tom had eclipsed Scarnose and proved himself to be a street fighter no cat could ignore. But would Silver be permitted to sit on the roof letting his thoughts loose like butterflies? Would he have respect and status? It would be hard to step aside and let some other tom run the family. Things were changing. They expected summer to last forever but it didn't. Suddenly nights were longer and the leaves were falling. But maybe this would be the endless summer. Maybe the bang which threatened them all would snuff out Skeets and things would return to normal.

He watched Ben rise and stretch, quivering in every muscle. Not so long ago he had mistrusted Scarnose, recognising in the stray's contempt for any sort of order a threat to his position as top tom. Ben was always the quiet, loyal, caring ally, good in a scrap but never brilliant or forceful. Skeets had changed that. 'Skeets . . .' the name escaped quietly in a hiss.

Up the road, the object of his hatred was mauling a dolly dropped by a child in the Lions' Club carpark. He pounced on it, gripped it in his forepaws and raked it with hindfeet, again and again. Boomer and Slippery Jim regarded him in alarm.

'When he done it to that puppy on our way here,' Smiley said, 'you weren't upset.'

'It ain't a creature,' Boomer said. 'What's the point?' He had a septic right eye and it was hurting him.

'Skeets don't need a point, OK? Get that into your thick head.'

'Things were different when Skeets did the puppy,' said Boomer.

'Nothing's changed,' said Smiley.

They gazed steadily at him and he turned away.

'Smiley,' Skeets crooned. 'Is anything wrong?'

'No. We were just plannin' some action with Silver's mob.'

'That's good. How does this strike you? I want you to take out this Ben – permanently. Do it in your own time, only – get it done. Silver ain't no problem.'

'True,' Boomer said, grinning at Smiley.

'You'll do it, hey?' Skeets beamed.

Smiley nodded and the blank yellow eyes glazed over.

'In your own sweet time, Smiley. You will do it, won't you?'

'Yes.'

'See?' Skeets shrieked without warning, as he turned on Boomer and Slippery Jim. 'See? Do you see? Smiley is in the end of the rainbow with me. So, do you still wanna come? You do? OK, you follow Smiley. Do as he tells you. He's a good cat.'

And all of a sudden his voice dropped to a whisper.

'I need some . . . amusement. I need a she.'

'One of Silver's shes is sleeping on the wall down by

the garden,' Slippery Jim said. 'She was there when we came up the road.'

'Let's pay the little pet a visit – a surprise visit. Smiley has work to do.'

The small black she had curled herself into a ball among the valerian on the wall opposite Huccaby but she was woken by the stink of tomcat and opened her eyes to stare into Skeets' leer.

'Hello, Pretty,' he purred. 'What blue eyes you have. Let's go down in the garden and play.'

Boomer was in the road below and Slippery Jim was on the wall behind her. Rainbow licked her lips and tried to keep cool. Skeets dropped onto the vegetable patch at the back of a shed and called to her. She made the descent without comment and Slippery Jim landed heavily beside her. Moments later they were joined by Boomer.

The three toms strolled around her in a purring circle and Rainbow crouched, waiting for the inevitable. The explosion in her head and the pain occurred marginally before the bang scattered the Shadows.

Barnie found her. She was stretched out lifeless on a sheet of old corrugated iron beside the shed. The airgun pellet had entered an ear, killing her instantly; but Barnie didn't know this. Apart from the dribbles of blood at her nose, ears and mouth she was unmarked.

He fetched Silver and Ben and they walked over the garden gathering the smell of Skeets and his companions.

'But how did they kill her and why?' Ben asked.

'Skeets don't need reasons,' Barnie said sadly.

'Maybe she died of fear,' Lucy said when she was told. 'I have nightmares about Skeets. Remember what Rita and Lucky were like when they went over to the Crazies?'

The shadows were once again full of menace and the Maylands cats walked cautiously at night. Skeets' presence hung over the slow decay of summer.

'He's here for good,' Sam said gloomily. 'We can't win.'

Silver, Ben, Sam, City and Scarnose sat together on the terrace watching the moonrise. Crickets sang from every corner of Maylands. Occasionally a paw was lifted and swung at a moth but the toms were reluctant to do anything really energetic. They had believed Skeets was finished and it would be just a matter of time before his capers came to an end. Now it was obvious he was as dangerous as ever, as dangerous as the threat of the gun and the silent stalker.

'Jessie's lucky to be out of it,' Sam said, and Ben looked at him in anger and amazement. To be nothing on such a night was too awful to contemplate. The stars were bright and the scents rising off the garden were dark and tempting. Down at the pond Lucy was watching the carp and Rita was pacing lazily across the lawn. A shooting star fell and vanished. Ben shivered. He was keenly aware of the way things just went on happening when the light went out in an animal's eyes. Yet that was also comforting. Jessie was dead but cats like her still watched the moon come up and the play of the stars. He made no effort to puzzle it out. Some things were made to understand; others could never be known with nose, ears, eyes, tongue or mind. One day the light would go out in his own eyes. Then the kittens would walk his trails and different voices would be raised in the mooncrooning.

He came to the pond and laid his nose to Lucy's and groomed her ears. She was night-scented and her fur carried the moonlight.

'I'm hungry,' she confessed, and he led her through the hedge into the road and down the hill to Church Street.

Settling on the Labour Club terrace they gazed between the railings at the lights of the Central Fish Bar. People came and went but few noticed the ferals sitting beside the beer kegs.

'Jess was beautiful,' Lucy said, as though she could read his mind.

'I miss her terribly,' he said.

'So do I. She was like a mother to me.'

'To us all.'

The aroma of fish and chips was strong but they had no heart to go on the scrounge. Trailing up Winner Hill Road they cried outside No. 5 and were rewarded with a

209

bowl of cat food out of the tin. By the dustbins a little later they heard Dancer screeching at Parson in Orchard Patch. Then a police car siren wailed and Ben recalled how things were before Skeets arrived. Jessie had paraded Belle's three kittens on the terrace until the lady caught sight of Maylands' new residents. Then it was extra scrounge to meet the demands of the little newcomers. Those kittens had died of the cat flu that had carried off two old toms and a she. It happened long ago when Ben was a yearling but it seemed like yesterday.

Lucy returned to Maylands and sat by the Lawson's cypress hedge waiting for small creatures. He walked his hunting trail and Dancer fell in silently beside him.

'Rainbow's dead,' Ben said.

'Skeets?'

'Maybe. It looks like it. Three of them had her.'

'Skeets is really out of sight now.'

'Look, I want to be alone,' Ben said.

'I understand,' and Dancer turned and leapt a garden wall.

Anger was rumbling in Ben's gut when he strode through the monastery garden, looking for trouble. He yarooled his challenges but received no replies. Even his strut across the Lions' Club carpark failed to raise the Shadows and he departed bawling insults.

Skeets had broken into a hen-house on the other side of the estate and was killing his third fowl. The birds' panic-stricken commotion excited him but he was lucky to escape the wrath of the people woken by his raid.

'Another of those bloody monastery strays,' someone said. There was a brief glimpse of Skeets fleeing in the torchlight.

He was ecstatic. Blood and feathers clung to his muzzle, the moon was up and the stars shining. Then Bang told him about Ben's visit.

'But I don't understand,' Skeets murmured, his eyes lifeless. 'You, Slippery Jim and Skiffle were here but did not lay a hook on him.'

'You said he was Smiley's,' Bang gabbled.

'We wanted to take him,' Skiffle added. 'I could have taken him and Slippery was begging to have a go but you said he was – '

'Smiley's,' Skeets agreed. 'Where is Smiley?'

'Stalkin',' Slippery Jim said gratefully. 'He goes up the road to some gardens.'

'So, this Ben was here, strutting his thing on my patch,' Skeets said.

'Yeah. He's blamin' you for the death of that black she.'

'With the lovely blue eyes,' Skeets sighed. 'What fun she would have provided.' Then he growled. 'I must have a word with Smiley. We can't have little toms calling me out.'

'I'm sure Smiley will do him,' said Slippery Jim. 'But you said he could do it in his own sweet time.'

'I did, I did. But I think that sweet time oughta be soon. Very soon.'

Eager to change the subject Skiffle said, 'Them kittens down at Silver's garden are gettin' out and about now, Skeets.'

'Let them know the Shadows are also out and about. Speak to them with your hooks.'

Skiffle grinned.

32

Welcome to my Dream

Lucy slept on her side, body curled and a forepaw slung across hindlegs which were extended to her chin. City marvelled at her repose and the kittens' explosive energy. Like Sam, he spent most of his time asleep but he could only envy Lucy's peacefulness. Her body gently rose and fell as she breathed.

The afternoon was almost spent and the crickets were singing. Every now and then a kitten caught a cricket but the hover flies were elusive. Tacker was more active than Skip and both little toms were more competitive than Jill, Scruff or Nicky. They threw themselves about, rolling and growling and pretending to bite any loose skin. Mistiming a leap, Tacker landed in Skip's embrace and received several hindfoot kicks. The she kittens pranced around them until Nicky put Jill to flight, gave close chase and hauled her down. Then all five scattered and hid to begin stalking each other.

City chuckled at the sight of their tails swishing and their rumps wriggling in rumbas of concentration. The wrestling and pouncing continued until the youngsters were tired and fell asleep. Forgetting himself, Ebony from Colley End Park stepped out of the conifer hedge onto the terrace.

'Why do cats with collars go around with stupid smiles on their stupid faces?' Scarnose growled as he sat down beside City.

'They got nothing to worry about,' City said. 'Everything's provided.'

Ebony was allowed to pass because he wasn't a challenge and Ben wanted all the neighbourhood cats on their side.

'You wanna walk with me?' Scarnose yawned. 'I'm

212

goin' down around the bit of open ground at the bottom of the hill.'

'OK,' City grinned. 'If any of them nasty Shadows hit you I'll take care of 'em.'

'You couldn't take care of a legless mouse,' Scarnose said amiably, patting the old tom on the head with a forepaw.

'I could once. I haven't been old all my life.'

'Life's what we're doin' now.'

'That's smart,' said City. 'Maybe you oughta feed that to Sam. It's genuine Wise Pussy guff.'

'You wanna set of genuine Wise Pussy hooks in your old Wise Pussy head?' Scarnose grinned.

And they wandered off with night closing around them.

Ben watched their departure from the summerhouse roof. Stars gleamed in the bay and the lights along Paignton seafront were bright in the clear cool air. Silver sat at the other end of the roof. Both animals had known loneliness so their silence was meaningful. The chirring of crickets was a gentle background music to their thoughts.

Ben slept and when he woke, Silver was gone. The stars twinkled and the cold filmed his eyes and made him aware of his nostrils. He blinked and pawed at his eyes. The breeze passed over Maylands, rattling the bamboos and stirring the trees. Ben stretched and yawned on his descent to the lawn. Then he walked to the rockery and searched for woodmice. Dew beaded the begonias which had managed to survive among the wild flowers and weeds. But he did not catch any mice and slouched grumpily along the terrace to the overgrown bed of red hot pokers by the front door of Maylands. Outside the gates, a bottle was smashed and young men shouted and laughed on their way up the hill. The silence closing behind the din had a tingle to it and Ben paced cautiously into the road. The street lamp at the corner was on and the metal of parked cars creaked as it contracted.

Barnie sat on the steps of the alley leading to Fairview. A discarded cigarette end smouldered close by.

'No Crazies about,' Barnie said. 'But I heard Slippery

Jim's woodpecker laugh early on. He's up to no good.'
The old black cat licked his lips.

'I dunno, Barnie. D'you ever get the feelin' this is one of those nightmares you're stuck in till the light goes out in your eyes?'

'No. Skeets is a cat. One day his luck'll run out.'

'But who's goin' to take him?'

'Silver?'

'Perhaps,' Ben said quietly. 'The white one goes deep. He's difficult to understand.'

Ben walked down the hill. If it was about strength then it was strength that did not trample on frailty or weakness. Status and respect were important. Jessie and Lucy, City and Barnie – they had gentle qualities he respected. Maybe there were strengths Silver, Scarnose and Skeets would never recognise.

He ran through the Winner Street narrows into Church Street and stumbled on a dead pigeon in the gutter. After it was eaten he wandered on as far as the church and called Dolly, but received no reply. Fearing the worst he hurried to her shelter and called again in an urgent tone.

'Leave me alone, buyh,' said Dolly's tired voice. 'I idn well and they Crazies gave me a rough time the other night.'

'Are you hurt?'

'No, just weary. My bones ache. Let me sleep.'

'Sorry I disturbed you, Mother.'

'Yes. Tread carefully, my handsome.'

Returning to Maylands, Ben slept until mid-morning when Lucy's distant maraow of anguish brought him to his feet. Scarnose was also alert on the gates end of the terrace.

'Skip's gone missing,' Parson said, dashing out of the bamboo.

'What you mean, "missing"?' Coldness flooded Ben's gut.

'He ain't here. He just went off. Lucy's gone lookin' for him.'

'Watch the garden, Scarnose,' Ben growled and he

214

pushed through the gate into the road. Lucy's cries were coming from one of the big gardens at the back of the houses in the top half of Monastery Road.

Ben raced along Huccaby's drive and went through the privet into the neighbouring garden. He crossed the lawn, took the wall in a leap and streaked over the next garden, lifting the birds from the bird-table. Balanced on the top of the fence he saw Slippery Jim stalking something small and black and white that crouched under the apple tree. Lucy was a couple of yards away, throwing herself at Smiley.

The chill in Ben's entrails turned to fire and he sprang into the grass. Hearing his father's cry, Skip lifted his head and mewed. Slippery Jim saw in the feral bearing down on him a madness he had thought to be the monopoly of Skeets. Without hesitation he shot across the lawn and was gone before Ben's hooks could lacerate his departing hindquarters.

But Smiley wasn't so lucky. Forced to confront Lucy, he was taken on the surge of Ben's fury, slammed against the wall and made to fight with all his guile and speed to ward off the hissing, growling hook machine.

Despite his strength and experience he was taking a thrashing when people ran from the house to end the fight. Clawing up the fence in a daze he was bitten on the hindleg by Lucy.

Skeets was unhappy. His yellow gaze fell on Smiley while the black tom attended to his wounds.

'I send you to hook a kit and what happens? You get hooked by kitty's she and kitty's tom. It's a mean scene. Tell me, Skiffle, am I wise to place my trust in street fighters like these? Toms who cannot see off a kit?'

Skiffle slowly shook his head and hoped the others would appreciate his dilemma.

'Smiley's hurt,' said Slippery Jim.

'It's part of the game, stupid,' Skeets purred. 'You think you can just walk into the end of the rainbow without blood and guts? You wanna be like them fat house toms with fancy collars and people callin' you to the food

215

bowl? You wanna surrender what you got hanging under your tail?'

Skiffle and Slippery Jim shook their heads vigorously.

'OK,' Skeets said in a velvet whisper. 'Silver's mob will crack. They'll come apart and I'll be sittin' on the roof. All you gotta do is what I tell you to do. Got it?' The pair nodded with an eagerness that made Skeets chuckle.

'Mind your heads don't drop off,' he said. Then he groomed himself with savage haste as if his coat were infested with fleas.

The airgun attacks became more alarming and the bearded policeman was often on the estate in his off-duty hours. But living dangerously was a catmint high to the Shadows, who found it harder to come to terms with Skeets' wildly erratic behaviour. He oscillated between moods yet his toms got a buzz creeping into gardens to steal petfood from bowls on doorsteps. These raids attracted attention but the situation was aggravated by Skeets' compulsion to spray the washing piled on benches or seats, fresh from the clothes line.

Three occasions in different back gardens were enough. The big, battle-scarred toms with their bullet heads and small, ragged ears were seen and the RSPCA Animal Centre in Torquay received angry phone calls. The inspector came and set a humane trap under the holm oaks and caught Boomer. His cries of rage and fear brought the other Shadows running.

'What are you doing?' Skeets chuckled.

'Get me outa here,' Boomer wailed and Skiffle and Slippery Jim did their best. They clawed at the metal bars while Boomer beat away from the inside until he gave up.

'Garrg,' Skeets chuckled. 'Ohhh Garrrrg, Boomer, you lovely bloody comedian.'

'Save me,' Boomer pleaded in a small voice.

'But we can't, Volebrain,' Skeets said. 'Only a cat with a head full of mousebits would fall for that one.'

'Just get me outa here,' Boomer mewled and Smiley

was reminded of the Maylands' kitten he had terrorised under the apple tree.

'Can't be done,' Skeets crooned. 'All we can do is – ' and he turned, beaming at the rest of the gang. 'All together now, on the count of three. One, two, three – *garrrrg.*'

'*Garrrrrrg,*' Smiley, Skiffle and Slippery Jim chorused.

'Yeah, that's it, Skeets,' Boomer hissed. He was angry now. 'You're a head case. You're so far over the top you're outa sight. OK, I ain't no good. I'm a bad ass like the others so maybe I'm gettin' what I deserve. But you are somethin' else. You're the stink of a long-dead rat. You're one of your worst bad dreams and you'll end up like a pile of dog muck that every cat walks around.'

'You're sulking,' Skeets said. The words were squeezed out of a dead smile. 'You're upset. You're a . . . garrrg, a yesterday cat, Boomer. I shall miss you and your ready wit. Give us one last joke before they take you away. Please. Do it for Skeets.'

'Kiss my ass.'

'Garrrg,' Skeets chortled. 'Garrrrg.'

'You sick old she,' Boomer said, and Skeets would have sprayed him if they had not seen the RSPCA inspector approaching.

So Boomer was taken to the Animal Centre and housed with other strays and unfortunates. The trap was re-set but avoided by the surviving Shadows. When it was sprung by a small dog it was removed.

'Boomer was right,' said Skiffle. 'Skeets is a sick old she. OK,' he added from a growl, seeing Smiley's hackles rise, 'you're his tom and as far as you're concerned the sun shines from under his tail. OK, OK, but you show me your hooks and I'll give you aggro you'll never forget.'

'And where did you get your new guts from?' Smiley sneered.

'He shouldna gone on like that to Boomer no more than he should've done what he did to Reekin and Squib. No way.'

'So what's your move, All-Mouth?'

217

'My move is out. I'm moving out and no one stops me. I'm takin' off – understand? That leaves just you, Slippery Jim and Lame Brain.'

'We're enough.'

'Enough to do what?' Skiffle said scornfully. 'It's all over except in Sick She's head.'

And he walked off.

'It don't matter,' Skeets purred when he was given the news. 'I have my faithful Smiley and Jim and their hooks. I don't need no more. This is all ours now. There's only room for three in my dream. It's always been like that. Believe me, when we get the garden we'll recruit a new gang, new Shadows for new aggro trips. We are going on a violence high that will take us to the stars. Welcome to my dream.'

Smiley closed his eyes, but there was only darkness.

33

Nightwatch

A man was playing the organ in the garage of the house called Jocyn at the junction of Winner Hill Road and Monastery Road. The misty September morning was glazed with sunlight warm enough to bring people to the beach. Berries were ripening and birds were flocking and the hedges of Maylands were patched with cobwebs.

As the mist cleared, the coterie of toms took their place on the terrace and turned to the sun. Sam put his nose to a dew-drenched leaf. A little yellow had crept into the foliage of the chestnut tree behind the summerhouse. And Skeets was part of the actual decline of summer, a sensation of decay and corruption which all the cats experienced.

A car passed. A Flymo snarled.

Around Maylands, nature had been trimmed to suburban respectability by shears, secateurs and mowers. The dustmen called and banged about and departed. A milk float hummed by, gulls sent their calls floating across the rooftops.

Scarnose deserted the pond and the carp cabaret and stepped quickly through the grass which sun and rain had reduced to a kind of string full of flies and moths. He scuttled up the rockery and a complete spider's web wrapped itself around his muzzle. His spluttering and feverish attempts to dislodge it had the terrace audience yarooling.

The day was so still they could hear the snuffle of hedgehogs in the shrubbery and the fall of individual leaves. Now and then a conker bounced off the roof of the summerhouse and Lucky pushed her head out of the window to complain. This led to more laughter on the

219

terrace but elsewhere Smiley had nothing to laugh about. Striding across the Lions' Club carpark to find a place in the sun, he was stopped by a command from Skeets.

'Go and remove the white tom from my dream. Do it now. I'm too comfortable to budge.' The voice came from under the yellow van.

'I'm goin', Skeets.'

'In *my* own sweet time,' the voice chuckled.

Smiley sat down and lifted a hindfoot to scratch his ear. Skeets was singing now.

'When the red red robin . . .'

'*Smiley.*' It was Slippery Jim calling to him in a whisper from behind a holm oak.

'Whatja gonna do, Smiley?'

'Show him my ass for good.'

'Can I come with you?'

'No. Go look for Reekin and Skiffle up in the woods.'

'No hard feelings?'

'Don't be bloody daft. Just get outa here.'

Slippery Jim's feet scuffed through the leaf litter.

'Goodbye, Skeets,' Smiley said.

'See you in my dreams,' Skeets crooned.

A little later, Smiley eased through the ornamental iron-work of the silver gates and paced fearlessly onto the terrace.

'Well, well, well,' Scarnose declared. His ears folded back at the tips and his whiskers bristled. 'We got company, Silver.'

But Silver's nose had detected Smiley and he did not bother to spare the black heavy a glance.

'I want you to know,' Smiley said, 'I'm goin'.'

'And we're supposed to believe you?' Scarnose scoffed.

'Everyone's deserted him – Dancer, Squib, Reekin, Slippery Jim – everyone,' Smiley went on, ignoring Scarnose.

'Yeah yeah,' said Scarnose.

'I believe him,' said City.

'Whether you do or don't don't matter,' Smiley said. 'It's how things are.'

'And now you're going too?' Ben said. 'How far? Down the road to meet some new Crazies?' He laughed. 'Have I a hole in my head? Do I look brainless?'

'I'll walk for a day and a night,' Smiley continued, addressing no one in particular. 'You didn't beat me.'

'There was no need to, All-Mouth,' Silver said. 'Skeets did it for us.'

The Maylands toms chuckled.

'But you are the worst of that bunch,' Ben said. 'Skeets is nuts. You know what you're doing.'

'So get out while you're still wearing a tail,' Scarnose said.

'Yeah. You get my back up,' said Scrumpy.

'Mind I don't break it,' Smiley grinned.

Haunches rolling and tail erect he swaggered back the way he had come.

'Give him something he'll remember,' Silver said to Scarnose. 'Hit him as he leaves the garden.'

'You mean do the dirty?'

'It's the best way,' said City, and Scarnose departed and the toms smiled at the caterwauling that came from the road.

In human terms the clash lasted less than five minutes, but for Scarnose it was a major ordeal. Smiley caught him by Barnie's steps and drove him along the alley in a running fight. Why does it happen to me, he thought, trying to stand his ground. Obviously Skeets hadn't undermined Smiley's self-confidence and Scarnose was hard pressed to defend himself. The noise of the Flymo cutting Fairview's lawn drowned the screeching and growling. The Flymo lead ran from the point in the hall out through the open front door and the Jack Russell came with it. The sight of the cats locked together raised his hackles and he tore into a rump which unfortunately belonged to Scarnose. The cats and dog became a rolling, squirming ball of busy legs, hooks and teeth. But swift action by the woman saved Scarnose from harm and gave Smiley the chance to flee up the alley, over the wall and away from Monastery Road in the pursuit of his own destiny.

'I really saw off Rat-Breath,' Scarnose crowed. 'He won't forget that goin' over in a hurry.'

His ears were laid back, his muzzle was bleeding and he walked with a limp.

'You mean, he looks worse than you?' Sam said.

'Smiley ain't no pushover,' Scarnose growled. 'I'd rather have been bitin' your ass but at least I gave him somethin' he'll remember.'

'Yeah, a laugh,' Sam grinned and Ben's voice cut through the chuckling.

'But Skeets has got to be shown some real aggro,' Ben said. 'He's been relying on other cats' hooks. It's time the grin was ripped off his face. I want that Shadow out of the shadows.'

Silver nodded and licked his lips. His tranquil blue eyes carried no clues to the disturbance in his heart.

'The game's over,' Ben continued. 'That thing up there in the trees has to go or be dropped.'

'Yeah yeah,' Parson cried.

'And who's gonna do it?' Scarnose asked. 'You, Parson?'

The meeting on the terrace had turned into a war council and the toms were getting high on an adrenalin overload.

'I will,' Ben said bluntly.

'No,' Sam said. 'If Silver is The Cat he must do it.'

'What d'you mean – *if* Silver is The Cat?' Silver demanded in a voice close to a growl and Sam got the message.

'Sorry. You know what I meant.'

'Do I? You just stay the harmless Wise Pussy and leave hookwork to those who have proved themselves.'

'Fine,' said Ben. 'But let's have more hook and less mouth. I want it safe for Lucy to walk anywhere she likes, any evening without fear of that Crazy chopping her.'

Again Scarnose gazed at the black and white tom and wondered what had happened to the easy going, warm-hearted cat of early summer. Silver also flashed Ben a look of bewilderment and anxiety. His leadership was being

222

eroded and he was in no mood to call Ben out. Further-more, he was no longer certain he could take the new Ben in the sort of fight the family expected.

'Skeets will get his,' he muttered.

'When?' Scarnose asked.

'Soon, OK? Soon. I gotta think this out. Right?'

He made his way to the summerhouse roof to sit and brood. A chestnut fell near him and bounced over his head but he did not flinch. Parson and Scrumpy sniggered and Ben glared at them. He sensed what was going on in Silver. For the white tom everything was at stake – his reputation, status, respect. Maybe he was also dwelling on Skeets' capacity for stoking up aggression into moments of breathtaking violence. Maybe he could not cope with the prospect of the physical consequences of a fight with Skeets and what it meant in flesh and blood terms.

Throughout the night Silver sat on the roof staring at the starry horizon, and the Maylands' cats crouched or lay on the terrace wondering when he would make a move towards the monastery. A big, yellow moon shone on the bay and barn owls came and went noiselessly over the garden.

'Believe me,' City whispered. 'Your Silver is like Skeets in many ways.'

'Who says so?' Scarnose exclaimed. 'You put that about and I'll rip off your ears.'

'He's another of those dangerous dreamers,' City said.

'Out of dreams come schemes,' said Sam in the meas-ured tone he saved for Wise Pussy deliveries.

'Yeah,' Scarnose chuckled. 'And the bird with no head can't sing.'

'Knock it off,' said Ben, but he couldn't help smiling.

At dawn he met Lucy at the walnut tree and was stand-ing up on his hindlegs to sharpen his claws when Trixy came through the silver gates.

'Dolly isn't very well,' he said.

'Crazies?' Ben asked. He and Lucy pushed through the ironwork to Trixy's side.

'No. She's just sick.'

223

'And old,' said Lucy, recalling poignantly the death of Jessie.

'She's not dying,' Trixy said. 'At least, I don't think she is. She's got a cold and a cough, and the Crazies have left her too frightened to leave her patch. I tried to get her to eat but she won't take any notice of me. She needs her own kind.'

They ran down the hill.

'Is it true about the Crazies?' Trixy added. 'Is there really only one left?'

'Yeah – Skeets,' said Ben. 'And he's meaner than a mad dog.'

'This won't help me sleep.'

The ferals laughed. Trixy was popular. He often shared his food with Ben and kept an eye on the edge of the territory.

'Don't worry,' Ben said. 'One way or another Skeets will be taken care of.'

In the churchyard he left the talking to Lucy and cleaned the dew off his coat while she questioned Dolly and coaxed her from her lair.

'Why bother with me, m'dears?' she sniffled. Her eyes were running and she was drooling. Her coat was matted and greasy and she looked ready to drop.

At first, Lucy thought the old grey had the dreaded flu but Dolly didn't show any of the pronounced symptoms.

'We want you to come and live in our garden,' Lucy said.

'But this is my hoam and in any case, I'd just be another mouth for you to feed.'

'Don't be silly,' Ben said. 'We lost Jessie not so long ago and no family is complete without an old she.'

Dolly sneezed a couple of times then crouched, neck and head extended, to cough. Each spasm convulsed her.

'You need peace and warmth and regular food,' Lucy said. 'No more argument. You're coming with us.'

They returned to Maylands at her uncertain pace, stopping every so often to let her catch her breath. During one of these pauses she gasped: 'I got soaked so often

224

back along I never recovered propper. Then they Crazies put the wind up me and I stopped goin' out fer scrounge.'

'It's all over now,' Ben said. 'You can have Jessie's place in the shelter.'

'And you really get the best in your garden?'

'Every day. Then there's the street scrounge and the odd bird, vole or mouse.'

'Purrr-fect,' she smiled, wiping a paw over her eyes. 'Tez more'n I could hope for at my age, and to be honest, m'dears, I was gettin' lonely in the old place.'

The final stretch to the gates exhausted her and she had to take a long rest outside. Ben crouched and closed his eyes. The church clock struck six and he sailed out of himself into the long dark. There was the familiar street lamp at the end of the featureless, shadowy road and the little drift of snow at the wayside. Ben could hear himself groaning. Then the light went out and darkness was total. Fearfully he opened his eyes and breathed a sigh of relief. The sun was on the sea and flocks of birds were on the wing. The dream had not trapped him and he uttered a mew of joy.

'What is it?' Lucy enquired. She pressed her nose to his then proceeded to lick his muzzle.

'The funny gut-ache of a dream. Remember how I felt when I saw Dancer for the first time and there was all that talk about Shadows?'

'Get some sleep,' she said. 'Go to the shelter and sleep.'

'I can't. I've got to find out if Silver's made up his mind.'

'What if he hasn't?'

'I'll give him till dark. Then if he can't do it I'll provide the aggravation Skeets seems to want.'

34

The Fight

But Silver was in no hurry to commit himself to the most unpleasant duel of his life. The evening was calm without a breath of wind and the white tom was central to the stillness in Maylands. He continued to sit on the summer-house roof and Scarnose and Parson couldn't take their eyes off him.

'What is it about Silver that grips you?' City asked.

'Silver? Who cares about him?' Parson said. 'We're waiting to see if one of them nuts drops off the tree onto his head.'

Scarnose snorted and City smiled, but he was finding it hard to look beyond the good things of life to the sort of weird street brawls Skeets had stirred up. What had happened to the bluff, banter and bash of his early days? The mooncrooning knockabouts never harmed anyone. But he had shared Skeets' madness not so long ago. He had been a Crazy.

The old tom swallowed. The stillness had an unpleasant edge to it. Birds passed silently overhead and silently a leaf fell.

All the gang congregated in the garden, toms and shes together on the terrace. Dusk brought the lights on in the Three Towns, but Silver remained on the roof until the moon rose. Then he came to the terrace and addressed the toms.

'Ben and Scarnose can come with me,' he said. 'I don't want this fight forgotten.'

It was the time of day Ben loved. Moths fluttered around the street lamps and dew strengthened the scents the cats passed through on their march up Monastery

Road to Berry Drive and the Lions' Club. The gleam of Skeets' eyes could be seen under the big yellow van.

'This is it!' Silver cried. 'C'mon, c'mon – show me your hooks or your tail. Fight or get lost.'

Skeets trotted up to them with the eager bouncing gait of a kitten.

'But you were on the roof in my dream,' he grinned. 'You were sitting there looking at the moon and every time I come out of that dream my head hurts. Look,' and he walked quietly round Silver. 'Why don't you keep out of the dream, then we wouldn't have to quarrel. Leave the dream to me and go away. If you don't, I'll have to spill your guts all over the place.'

'You wanna dream? OK, so I'll give you a nightmare.' And Silver unsheathed his claws and brandished a forepaw.

'I'm not alone,' Skeets announced, glancing at Ben and Scarnose. 'I have my Shadows. They're all around you, watching, waiting. Shadows have hooks – big hooks. *Garrg.*'

Ben and Scarnose glanced over their shoulders but Silver smiled and shook his head.

'There's just you and me, Skeets,' he crooned.

'And that's enough,' Skeets replied, unsheathing his hooks and taking a couple of swipes at the moonlight. 'But you'll want to begin, won't you-ooo-oo-ooaow?'

His voice lifted in a staccato maraow which Silver took up and returned with equal venom. The white tail scythed in a low arc. His ears were erect and his pupils tiny and he bared his teeth in a growl which brought a similar response from Skeets. The great sandy tom inched sideways, hissing, and Silver trod slowly forward to meet him in the eyeballing. The watching cats had never seen the ritual enacted with such flamboyance. The street fighters arched their backs and fluffed out their fur and growled into each other's faces. Neither would retreat, although Silver found the gaze of those malignant, unblinking yellow eyes nerve-racking.

Skeets' hot breath was on his muzzle and Silver turned

and edged away, his ears pressed tight to his head now. If Skeets had been fighting by the rules he would have granted the white feral the pause he needed for self-examination but he merely chuckled and pounced. Up he flew to dive down and pin Silver beneath powerful front paws. Like a tom taking a vole, Ben thought. He was forced to admire Skeets' awesome strength and nimbleness.

Silver rolled over and tried to shake off his assailant, but Skeets used the opportunity to go for his throat and savage the underparts with teeth and claws. Then instead of finishing Silver, he stopped and danced around him on hindlegs, dropping to the ground every so often before regaining his balance and caterwauling joyfully. If his tail lashed from side to side it was with a kind of vicious rapture.

Shaken and out-manoeuvred, Silver screeched when his tail was bitten at the base.

'Garrg,' Skeets cried in a fit of laughter, and his hooks rasped on the tarmac.

Silver sprang up but was bowled over and smothered by Skeets' bulk. Once more the teeth and claws got to work until Skeets was out of breath and had to rest. Seeing the state of Silver's face Ben stepped between them.

'Hah ha,' Skeets nodded. 'So it's gonna be like this.' And his teeth gleamed.

'No,' Silver cried. 'Get back, Ben! This is my fight.'

'But Ben will get his chance when I've finished with you.'

Silver's yarool became a screech and he flung himself at Skeets, who scampered playfully out of reach under the van.

'I see you, Whitey,' he crooned. 'Come and get me. Don't be afraid. I'm only gonna cripple you.'

Silver chased him round the van three or four times then up over it and in and out of the trees before Skeets allowed himself to be caught in the carpark again. A forepaw struck and narrowly missed Silver's left eye. Three dark lines on his muzzle began to leak blood. He sneezed and his fur spiked in blind fury. His own hooks opened one of Skeets' ears but nothing could dim the lunacy in the yellow eyes.

The sandy tom's bloodlust peaked to exultation. He drove Silver before him out of the carpark in a running brawl, punctuated with clashes which were a series of destructive embraces in a trance of violence.

Rolling, kicking, growling and screeching they came down Berry Drive into Monastery Road where Silver tried to make a stand. But Skeets' ferocity was matched by his stamina and apparent immunity to pain.

'What sort of animal is he?' Scarnose whispered.

Ben couldn't reply and in any case it was a rhetorical question.

The stink of the fighting toms hung on the darkening air. They separated and arched their backs and met eye to eye on quivering legs until Skeets lifted a hideous cry out of his blood and unleashed another attack.

'He'll kill Silver, Ben,' Scarnose said.

But Silver somehow managed to break free to stand swaying against the wall in front of Huccaby's drive. His growl became a hiss of defiance which seemed to take even Skeets by surprise. The white tom whisked around with flailing paws to slash at Skeets' head before he was sent reeling by a counter attack.

They fought among the parked cars on the Colley End Park flat and the Maylands gang came and sat on the nearby walls to watch. Dizzy from the blows he had taken, Silver lurched from under a parked Cortina and was clipped on the head by a passing motorbike. He tottered away, fell and got up to stagger down the road past Maylands' gates until he collapsed at the wayside. Then all the lights went out in a power failure and Ben's dream of the long dark became reality. The moon shone in a stillness that was ghostly after all the din, and beside the wall Silver lay like a little pile of snow. In ones and twos the gang gathered around him in a protective half-circle. Some of the shes were crying their distress.

'He isn't dead,' Lucy said. 'He's breathing.' And she

began to lick Silver's face until he opened his eyes and smiled at her.

For a while Skeets was forgotten. His taunts went unheard and as he padded up Monastery Road, he was slotting himself smugly into the dream Silver had vacated. There was the summerhouse and the chestnut tree, the rooftops, sea and sky. It only needed himself to complete the scene. He was the great unbeatable tom, The Cat.

Smiling, he paused to wipe a wet paw over his muzzle and the youth with the airgun stepped out of the shadows and took aim. At that moment, a car swung into Monastery Road and caught both the boy and his target in the headlight beams. Skeets felt a burning pain in his right hindleg, heard the bang and flopped down in one of his blackouts. The youth ran, but the couple in the hatchback had recognised him.

The man braked and he and his wife got out and hurried over to Skeets, who was still unconscious.

'The little swine got him in the leg,' the man said. 'Let's get him in the car and home. Wrap him in my old mac.'

'It looks as if he's been in a fight,' the woman said. 'Poor old thing. It's that big, sandy stray – the one with the angelic face. He's like a teddy bear.'

The man laughed and turned the ignition key.

'He needs a vet,' he said. 'I'll phone as soon as we get in.'

'And let the police know about young Gillespie and his gun. He could have killed old Sandy.'

The bang of the airgun had sent the Maylands gang running for the garden, but Ben and Scarnose mastered their fear and returned to escort Silver, slowly and painfully, through the gates to safety.

'That was some fight,' Ben said, but Silver refused to meet his eyes. After licking his wounds he dragged himself off to the summerhouse and slept.

'Meanwhile, what do we do about Skeets?' Scarnose asked.

230

'I fight him, you fight him, one by one we all fight him until he gets sick of it.'

'I won't be fightin' him,' Parson said. 'I like my face the way it is. I don't want it ripped off.'

'Seriously, Ben,' Scarnose said. 'What we gonna do?'

'Seriously, I dunno. We'll just have to take things as they come, like you're always saying. Skeets can be beaten.'

'Yeah,' said Scarnose, heavy on the scepticism.

35

Teddy

Several days passed with Ben expecting Skeets to strike again, but nothing happened. The black and white feral roamed throughout the council estate and made a thorough search of Skeets' old haunts but there was neither sign nor smell of the murderous tom. None of the pets he met near the Lions' Club had seen him and the mystery left Ben baffled and worried. Maybe Skeets had gone off to recruit a new gang of Crazies. It had to be something like that, for Skeets had no reason to keep low after his defeat of Silver.

He puzzled over it in Maylands. The first frost since spring had spilled some gold into the garden trees. Leaves and horse chestnuts pattered down in the sea wind that came and went before a calm, sunny spell. Craneflies danced awkwardly across the french windows and Ben watched them, although his thoughts were elsewhere. The lady was singing while she fed the carp and Sam rubbed his body against her wellingtons. Dolly and Scarnose were close at hand, their attention riveted on the rising fish. Slowly, the rooftops of town emerged from the mist that was thinning and dispersing. Gulls wailed.

'What's Skeets playing at now?' City said.

'Hide and Seek,' said Parson and he shivered. 'It's weird – him around yet . . . invisible.'

'Like a cold wind,' City said.

Ben looked at them and nodded. This vanishing act had to be Skeets' last attempt to generate terror. It fed on the uncertainty of walking through a sea mist in which everything appeared larger than life – people, other animals, the light on top of a lamp-post. The evil presence might have been the mist itself. It left no pawmarks, no tomcat stink, no fresh fraying of the places where Skeets had once sharpened his claws.

Ben trod the stalking trails feeling sure of himself again, despite his doubts. The Crazies were finished and if Skeets was still around, one day he would make a mistake and be taken out. But it was marvellous to come down off the sandstone wall behind Ivy Lodge and walk unmolested up to the carpark and on into Monastery Road. It was like walking out of bad times into Lucy's smile.

One sunny morning when the airgun threat had been forgotten, Silver approached him on the terrace. Since the fight the white tom had kept to himself, choosing to sit on the summerhouse roof gazing out over the bay. The ordeal had left him even more withdrawn than usual. He desired only to stare through his dreams at the noiseless, far-off seabirds.

'You are The Cat, Ben,' he said. 'If you need me you know where to find me. I'm behind you all the way.'

'You're still the one and only Silver,' Ben said.

And Silver smiled and returned to his rooftop reverie.

'That was nice,' said City. 'He did it with dignity. Some worn-out toms try to hang on to their status even though they're jokes.'

'Silver ain't no joke,' said Scarnose. 'He gave everything when he took on Skeets.'

'Exactly,' said City. 'And he's wise enough to step down with his reputation and tail intact.'

'Yeah,' Scarnose sniffed. 'Yeah. That's what I meant. It ain't no Wise Pussy guff.'

He swung around and grinned at Ben. 'OK, so what's it like being Big Tom?'

'Boring,' Ben smiled. 'And dangerous. It means I'll have to mix it with Skeets when he decides to show himself again.'

'But you'll win,' Scarnose said emphatically.

'Yes,' Ben said, and the other cats knew it was a simple statement of fact, not bravado.

That evening the lady roasted a chicken for the gang and served the meat outside the french windows. Toms

233

and shes sat before their bowls tapping the hot portions with their paws, testing the temperature until they could put their noses to it and then their teeth.

'You get everything in the garden,' City told Dolly before going off to dig a hole, lower his rump to it and deposit his bits.

But if it was the cats' paradise then it was paradise flawed, for no matter how hard he tried Ben could not get Skeets off his mind. Lucy often found him brooding in some corner and sat beside him until he was ready to speak.

During these periods of depression he rummaged through the past, hoping he would find a clue which would lead him to Skeets or, at least, to understanding what Skeets was up to. He pictured Jessie playing with the kittens or trying to groom her long grey fur and falling over in the process. Lucy watched him smile until he recalled Dancer's voice in the wild part of the monastery: 'Shadows have hooks.' Button's death, Rainbow's death, the light going out in Jessie's eyes, the long dark and the little pile of snow. Yes, they had come through some bad times.

Lifting his head he cried a waowl of misery and Lucy licked his face.

'Dolly isn't here to take Jessie's place,' he said. 'Jessie was . . . Jessie. Dolly is old and beautiful in her own way.'

'I know,' Lucy said. 'Look, don't keep worrying about Skeets. Isn't it possible he's just had enough and cleared off like the others?'

'No. He gets his kicks out of making cats afraid. This is his big trip.'

'But he's crazy, so how can you be so sure?'

'I feel it. He's still here, somewhere.'

Skip and Tacker ran up to them and insisted Lucy come and inspect a strange bird they had discovered lying dead in the Monastery Road hedge. A halo had appeared around the sun and the peacocks of Paignton Zoo were calling; but Ben had smelt rain some time before the first

234

drops fell and the sky darkened west of Torbay. The sadness of the peacock cries heightened his own melancholy and he prowled about Maylands in the downpour until the shower passed.

Swallows were flocking and many fork-tailed birds were on the telephone wires of Winner Hill Road. Ben sprayed the hydrangeas by the pond and sniffed at the toadstools growing on the lawn. The sun blazed down, its rays angled and intensified by the next huge cloud. A wasp landed on Ben's head and he swatted it off, but Rita was slower when one perched on her nose. Her wavering screech informed the gang that she had been stung and Scarnose and Parson were quick to cash in on her misfortune.

'Well, if it isn't old Swollen Gob,' Scarnose grinned, waltzing up to her.

'That's a cat?' Parson exclaimed. 'I've seen more attractive sights under dogs' tails.'

'I hope the blowflies breed in the gap where your brain used to be,' Rita growled.

'Temper, temper,' said Parson. 'You don't wanna upset your old buddy, Scarnose, do yuh?'

'Kiss my ass,' Rita cried.

'Wow,' said Scarnose. 'That's some invitation.'

Wasps swarmed to the blackberries in the hedges and birds descended to eat the elderberries. It was a time of plenty, but behind the commonplace Ben occasionally found elements of his dream world, of fear made tangible. Stalking the margins of the lawn one night he was startled by the cry of an owl. The white bird was perched on the head of Sir Francis Drake, gazing down at Ben like a threat. Its strangled screech lifted the hair in a ridge on his back.

'Only a bird,' said Silver's voice.

Ben jumped but Silver was there, at his shoulder.

'Is this what being The Cat is all about?' Ben asked.

'It's part of it,' came the reply. 'You are perpetually mixing it with your own fears and doubts. But you'll be OK, Ben. You get down to it. You act. I think about acting and end up just thinking.'

The following evening, Ben and Lucy sat together on the Labour Club terrace and took in the aroma of fish and chips. The Central Fish Bar was doing a good trade and every time the door opened, the ferals got a whiff of the food they loved. On the scrounge trail a little later they trotted down Slaughter House Lane and waited outside the chip shop gates. But no one called them and they ambled morosely up Church Street and saw Dancer sitting in the doorway of the Pocket Book Shop.

'Hey, Ben,' the black tom drawled. 'Whatja think about Skeets?'

'Not a lot,' Ben said.

'I mean, him doin' a bunk after messin' up Silver.'

Ben disliked the gloating tone.

'Dancer,' he growled. 'Don't make a habit of walking my paths and,' he added as Dancer's ears flattened, 'don't even think of crossing me. Do not take liberties.'

'Would I do that? Come on now, Ben – would I? Would I?'

'Skeets isn't holed up on your patch, is he, Dancer?'

'Ben! I am offended, shocked even. Skeets is really bad news. Believe me, I would rather let rats sleep in my ass than have him paddin' round my patch.'

'For once I believe you,' Ben said and he smiled at Lucy.

Walking the Winner Street bottleneck they were startled by the honking of domestic geese at the back of the corner house.

'What was that?' Ben said, scampering up Winner Hill Road behind Lucy; but she was laughing so much she couldn't speak. Before long she had to stop to pull herself together and seeing her trying to suppress the giggles Ben started chuckling. This set Lucy going again and lolloping round the corner by Winner Hill Garage Scarnose nearly tripped over the helpless pair.

'Skeets is back,' he said, and his words hit Ben like a bucket of cold water.

'You saw him?'

'I couldn't believe it, Ben. He was sittin' in the road just up from our place and he scared the life out of me.'

'What did he do?'

'Nothing. He just smiled and started groomin' himself like nothin' has happened.'

Ben felt Lucy's breath on his ear and her nervousness crackled between them.

'Don't worry,' he whispered. 'I'm gonna take him out.'

'How?' said Scarnose.

'I'm gonna do what Silver should have done – have his eyes.'

'Yeah yeah,' Scarnose grinned. 'A big blind tom wouldn't be no problem. Why didn't we think of it before?'

Lucy was left at Maylands and the two toms trotted up Monastery Road as far as the house called Dunroamin. Lights were on in the downstairs window but the garden behind the car bay was empty. The faint stink of Skeets was enough to rekindle old anxieties in the pit of Ben's stomach. He and Scarnose ranged through the streets and gardens, questioning any cat that crossed their path. Nothing came of it and finally they returned to sleep at Maylands.

The next morning was cloudless and the gang collected outside the french windows for breakfast. Most were unwilling to accept Scarnose's news, but Ben issued a warning in terms none of them could ignore and loped off to continue the search.

Among the chrysanthemums Skeets' smell was stronger. He had also sprayed a rear wheel of the car. Ben sniffed at the offensive odour and obliterated it with his own pungency. Then, on an icy ripple, the hair stiffened along his spine as he felt the presence. He looked up. Staring down from a bedroom window was Skeets himself. The big sandy tom beamed at him, turned and was gone.

'It can't be,' Ben whispered. Maybe Silver was right about perpetually mixing it with his own fears. Maybe it had pushed him over the top. Maybe he was out of control and lost in a nightmare.

He fetched Scarnose and the pair of them walked up Monastery Road.

'Things can get at you,' Scarnose said. 'When I used to spend half my time watching the fish down at our place I saw things that weren't there. They were in my head but they looked as if they was in the water. You know what I mean?'

'Yeah. You think I'm nuts.'

'I'm sorry, Ben.'

'Don't be. It can happen to anyone so why not me?'

'In a house,' Scarnose said incredulously. 'Him, in a house!'

But Skeets was waiting. He was crouched on the gravel of the parking bay and the Maylands toms stopped and gazed at him in bristling astonishment.

'Hullo,' Skeets purred. His voice was soft and friendly, although the yellow eyes were as blank as ever. Yet Ben failed to detect any malice in his demeanour.

'It's a trick,' Scarnose murmured. 'It's gotta be some sort of sick trick.'

Ben went over to Skeets in a stiff-legged strut but he remained seated, rattling out the purrs. Scarnose's gasp was confirmation of what Ben saw but refused at first to believe.

Skeets was wearing a collar and a name disc.

'OK,' Ben growled. 'You're playing a new game. So here I am.'

Skeets' smile became broader and his eyes narrowed and his tongue appeared between his teeth. Ben licked his lips and was considering his next move when a woman's voice called, 'Teddy! Teddy! Here Ted.'

'That'll be the food bowl,' Skeets crooned, and tail upright and curled at the tip he swung round and strolled off to the back door.

'Hey,' Scarnose cried. 'Look under his tail. *There's nothing swinging!*'

'Nothing to swing,' Ben crowed. 'Nothing. Nothing.'

And his voice soared to a yarool of triumph while Scarnose danced around him in a circle of maraows.

'He's a no-tom pet. Him – the Big Bad cat, a nothing on legs, a fireside fleabag. All collar and nothing dangling under his tail.'

'It couldn't have happened to a more deserving animal,' Ben laughed.

Skeets, alias Teddy, had entered a permanent dream shortly after the vet's knife had separated him from his cathood. Confined to the house to get accustomed to his new surroundings and recover from the operation, he had found everything satisfactory. There was the fireside, human love, an armchair to sleep in and blackouts that contained tolerable nothingness. For a companion, the woman had given him a teddy bear as big as himself and sometimes when he was alone he sang to it.

'When the red, red robin . . . comes bob, bob bobbin' along . . .'

Then he would grin and embrace it and attack it with teeth and flailing hindfeet. His weight often made the teddy bear squeak and so it became the perfect victim, a thing that did not run or fight but simply acquiesced to Skeets' insatiable love of violence. He would creep up on it and pounce and slash it, or just roll around with it in his front paws, licking the torn face.

'Teddy's playing with teddy,' the woman would say, and Skeets would pour out the purrs for the rewards which came in tins and packets. The only reminder of the past was the scar on his hindleg where the pellet had been removed.

36

The Good Place

Autumn closed around Maylands and the neighbourhood maples were turning from yellow to crimson. Dead leaves made a slow descent through the stillness. The swallows had gone and the ferals were quiet and thoughtful. But although Ben knew he had come through the darkness, there were occasions when he was compelled to walk up to Dunroamin for a glimpse of Skeets, the spent nightmare, just to put his mind at rest.

Leaves continued to fall and drift against walls and hedges. Mist lay low on Paignton, with the top of the Parish Church tower poking out of it. Ben joined Silver on the summerhouse roof to study the scene and they watched the flocks of greenfinches and starlings whirr by. Maylands' chestnut tree was one of the local assembly points for starlings. Many flocks gathered there to chatter and scream after leaving their roosts. It was the same late in the afternoon – birds crowding the top branches and the clamour flattening the cats' ears.

Ben glanced at Silver. The white tom sat, eyes closed, body gently swaying, moisture beading his whiskers. Ben smiled and a blackbird landed in the hedge nearby to set his teeth clicking. Lucy was on the lawn with Dolly, and the kittens were chasing each other round the sundial.

Ben yawned, stretched and came down to join the shes, lifting his paws high out of the wet grass and spiderspin. The black and white kitten ran after his father and pretended to attack him.

'You lil toad,' Dolly chuckled. 'You'm a prancy lil mite. Yes, you are.'

And Skip came belling in to receive her licks and purrs as the other dew-soaked kittens raced over the lawn.

240

'Hey, Ben,' Scarnose called from the terrace. 'I'm starvin'. Catch me one of them tomcat's snacks.'

'Which one?' Ben grinned.

'A tasty little she.'

'Watch your tongues,' Lucy laughed, gathering the kittens around her. 'You frightened them.'

'There, there,' Dolly breathed, darting angry looks at Scarnose before crouching to comfort the brood.

'Old Ginger Ugly Gob wadn so cocky when Skeets ruled the roost – no my! He was Pussy Jump-Quickly, ma lil boodies. A sparrow only had to twit in 'is ear and he'd take off.'

The kittens laughed and Scarnose smiled. A matriarch like Dolly could get away with anything.

Ben padded up the rockery and sat beside his ginger friend. The mist had thinned to a haze and the sun was touching rooftops and gleaming on TV aerials.

'Things are good, huh?' Scarnose murmured.

'Couldn't be better,' Ben nodded.

'But, you know, every time I bump into Skeets,' Scarnose added pensively, 'I'm on edge, waitn for him to turn nasty. I keep thinkin' Smiley and the rest of them will be back one day and Skeets will become, like, Skeets again.'

'With nothin' swinging under his tail? Him and his collar? Big Teddy No-Tom? C'mon, could it happen, Scarnose? Could it? Skeets was a bad dream and it's morning now, OK?'

'Yeah, OK, you're right,' Scarnose said, narrowing his eyes to follow the dance of a butterfly. 'Only, just once in a while I get a chill in the guts and have to go and check out the situation.'

'Me too,' Ben said.

'You?' Scarnose said in open surprise.

'Yeah. Sometimes it hits me like it hits you.'

'That's good to know.'

Strolling around Maylands, Ben enjoyed all the things the Shadows had eclipsed. He looked up at the bust of Sir Francis Drake. Sunlight was picking out the snail trails on the bronze and he rose on his hindlegs and sniffed the rich nuances of decay that wafted from the shrubbery; but the bamboos by the pond smelt of cats. Scarnose, Parson and Sam had sprayed the bottom of the poles and he put his nose to their signatures.

Now Ben was full of the mysterious happiness that can rise from a calm, cloudless autumn day to become part of a creature. A robin sang and the crows called to each other in the top of the fir. Goldfish breaking the surface of the pond and the patter of leaves failed to disturb the hush, and he had never felt so peaceful and contented.

He rolled in the grass before completing his prowl and returning to Lucy.

'You're restless?' she said.

'No – I feel great,' he grinned, and she groomed his head with a gentleness normally reserved for the kittens. Gazing at her he could only marvel at the brightness in her eyes. Small, ordinary events lapped around them. Silver remained in his daydream on the summerhouse roof and Rita was nagging the other shes from her couch on the rockery. Snug against the french windows, old City coughed and sneezed, and suddenly the firs released a great flock of starlings to fill the sky with their din. Then silence returned and Ben and Lucy lay close together, milling the sunlight into purrs.

Dusk thickened. For the cats of Maylands, there was the slow fadeaway of light and the deepening of silence without the passing of time. More leaves fell and over the rooftops the clock face in the tower of the Parish Church was lit up, but the full moon above Tor Bay was enormous and the stars brilliant.

Most of the adult ferals and strays had congregated on the terrace to stare at the sky, when across the constellations came flock after flock of winter thrushes. The fieldfares and redwings called to each other as they arrived to complete their migration flight from north of the Baltic.

The cats lifted their heads and watched them. Where had the birds come from? Where were they going? Ben sighed. Where was he going? What had he gained?

Respect? Status? Yes, but what was it all about – Skeets, the summer troubles, the dream of the long dark, the birth and death of animals . . . Silver seemed happier now that Ben was top cat. He had his roof and dreams. So what was it really all about – the waking and living and sleeping, the terror and joy and pain of life . . .

Smoke climbed from the chimneys of houses in Winner Hill Road and Winner Street; fallen leaves rustled beneath the feet of mice and voles. Then City sneezed, three times, and shook his head until his ears clacked and the toms each side of him yarooled their laughter.

'I god a code,' he said.

'OK, den keeb id do yerself,' Scarnose replied, and Sam sniggered behind the general guffawing.

'Scarnose is all heart,' Ben smiled.

'I know, I know,' said the ginger tom. 'And it makes me feel kinda . . . humble.'

A little later the lady called them to the food bowls and the gang collected before the french windows.

Cleaning himself after the meal, Ben considered how he would spend the night. Maybe he would take the stalking trail to the monastery or wander the streets below for scrounge. Raising his muzzle he read the faint breeze that was blowing off the bay. Beneath the garden scents was the aroma of frying fish and chips and exotic smells from the Golden Lily.

One by one the cats dispersed to go their own ways. Dolly and Rita led the kittens to the summerhouse and City curled up against the french windows, but Ben and Lucy sat side by side, facing the sea, open to everything the night held. Berry Head lighthouse flashed in the bottom of the sky and owls called as they sailed over Maylands.

Then, from somewhere close by, the mooncrooning began.